An American Baroness

Also by Jane Shoup

Down in the Valley

Spirit of the Valley

Will of the Valley

Knightfall

The Restoration

Zan, Birth of a Legend

The Key

A Choice of Captors

Ammey McKeaf, Book One in The Chronicles of Azulland

Heirs to the Throne, Book Two in The Chronicles of Azulland

Into Shadow, Book Three in The Chronicles of Azulland

Charity Cases

Santa:2020 The Final Ride

The Time Tunnel of August Kaplan

To Scott, the best partner in the world.

Chapter One

London, England
April 14, 1820

Mrs. Eliza Weatherly rode in the hired carriage next to her husband and across from the youngest two of their four grown daughters, Alice and Jocelyn. It was the girls' first trip to their father's native London, and their excitement was palpable. It was gratifying to witness, although Eliza had found the journey tiresome. She had kept a good face on for everyone's sake, but it had occurred to her on more than one occasion that perhaps she was getting too old and set in her ways to enjoy travel. Certainly, she could still endure it, but enjoy it?

Alice, their third-born, was twenty years of age with fair hair, delicate bone structure and eyes of two different colors, one blue and one green, a curious birth defect of some sort. Alice was clever, but Eliza feared the girl had more imagination than good sense. She fancied herself a writer and was forever scribbling down stories, weaving tales and delving into research. Her mother did not exactly object to it, so long as it was kept as a diversion, but too often it was a preoccupation.

Jocelyn was just over a year younger than Alice with darker hair than her sister. She possessed a simple, wholesome handsomeness, as she favored her father. The youngest of their brood was a sweet, thoughtful young woman.

"Did you know," Alice spoke up, "that in Roman times, London was a walled city of only a square mile? They called it Londinium."

"Londinium," Jocelyn repeated. "I wonder if any of it is still standing."

"Not much, I would think," Alice mused. "The great fire of sixteen sixty-six destroyed nearly everything. That was the year following the black plague that killed most Londoners."

Jocelyn shuddered at the thought. "How terrible. But how do you remember that date?"

"Because it's sixteen sixty-six! Who could forget it?"

"The great fire didn't destroy everything, dear," her father corrected. "Think of the great buildings that have stood for five or six centuries."

"Of course, you're right," Alice relented. "Westminster Abbey was built in the twelve hundreds, wasn't it? I cannot wait to see it."

"Girls," Eliza said. "Your father and I have a gift for you." She reached into her traveling bag for cloth wrapped packages and handed them over. Jocelyn's had a blue ribbon tied in a pretty bow and Alice's had a yellow ribbon. Each was an identical size, an inch thick and six inches wide by eight inches tall.

"It's a book," Alice said with delight.

"No," Mr. Weatherly teased. "We thought you might think so, but it's actually a new hat for each of you."

The girls laughed as they quickly unwrapped journals embossed with the word London, the date 1820, and their names. "How lovely," Jocelyn said. "Thank you."

"Yes, thank you," Alice said to her mother. She looked at her father. "We shall wear them on our heads with pride."

"We can tie them on with the ribbon," Jocelyn played along.

"Indeed," their father replied. "Everyone will ponder what mode of fashion American ladies have taken to."

"Wouldn't it be amusing if we started a trend?" Alice said as she thumbed through the pages. Each page had a place for the date and the day's agenda, morning, midday and evening.

"Our monogram is on every page," Jocelyn remarked as she traced her J W E with her finger. "It looks to me as if your stay," she said, bumping her sister's shoulder playfully, "will be particularly exciting since each page begins with AWE."

"And in capital letters, too," Alice replied. Alice's full name was Alice Emmanuel Weatherly.

"It's for writing your plans and thoughts," their mother said. "Perhaps your memories of the day. Alice, it is not for one of your stories."

"I understand," Alice replied with a hint of strained patience.

"I'll start on it later with my memories of today," Jocelyn said, perceiving the tone in her sister's voice and wanting to keep the mood cheerful. "Coming into port, the sights we've seen so far."

Richard nodded out the window. "This is Bryanston Square we're coming to. Ours is number fourteen."

"I cannot wait to see Granny and Aunt Julia," Jocelyn said. "I only hope we won't be upsetting to Jeremy."

"He'll adjust, I dare say," their father said. "He's practically a man now. Besides, it's a comfortable home with enough room. The top floor that isn't attic space is Jeremy's province, part bedroom and part *studio*. He fancies himself an artist these days," he said. "A painter."

"Ah," Alice murmured.

"Another artist in the family," Jocelyn said. "I wish I had artistic talent."

"Just to remind you," Eliza spoke up, "Rose Fisher is the housekeeper, Mrs. Halley is the cook, and Fisher's niece and nephew joined the household a few months ago when they were orphaned."

The girls nodded. They had read their aunt's last letter explaining that Dinah, who was thirteen, and Ethan who was a few years younger, had lost their fisherman father in a squall.

"Julia says they're adjusting," Eliza concluded.

Richard grunted. "They're lucky to have their aunt and to have a roof over their heads."

Alice huffed at him. "Where is your empathy?"

"I have empathy," he replied defensively. "I feel for them. I only meant that there are those who are far less fortunate."

Alice's eyes flashed. "They apparently did not have a mother and then they lost their father and home."

"Yes, but they had somewhere to go, didn't they?"

"No arguing, you two," Eliza insisted. "Look, this is it."

The girls leaned closer to the window on Jocelyn's side to see the home as the carriage stopped. "Oh," they both said at the same moment and then laughed. The stately red brick home was pleasingly symmetrical with long windows, and the front door had a pretty fanlight above. "It's so charming," Jocelyn exulted. "It's just as I imagined."

"Indeed," Richard Weatherly said. "Now let us get out. I am weary of sitting."

The door opened, the steps were put down and the driver offered assistance from the vehicle beginning with Jocelyn. The front door was flung open and Julia, Richard's sister, emerged with her arms flung wide open. "You're here," she cried exuberantly.

"Aunt Julia," Jocelyn said as she hurried forward to embrace her.

"Jocelyn! All grown up. You look so like your father and Clara."

"Yes," Jocelyn laughed. "I do."

"And a bit like me," Julia added happily.

"Thank you," Jocelyn said, beaming a great smile.

"And Alice," Julia said as she reached her. She hugged her and then studied her a moment, her gaze going back and forth between Alice's eyes. "You are so lovely." She reached for Jocelyn with her other arm. "Both of you. I have longed for this day."

"So have we," Alice said. "It's wonderful to see you."

"And to be here," Jocelyn added. "Seeing the house. Seeing everything! I can still hardly believe we're here."

"Julia," Eliza said wistfully, having reached them.

Julia hugged her sister-in-law and they exchanged heartfelt compliments about how well the other looked. "Richard," Julia said fondly to her brother as he reached her.

He kissed her cheek, and then pulled back to arm's length to assess her. "You have not aged a day since we were last here. How have you managed that?"

"Sleeping well, rising early and a brisk walk each day."

He wrinkled his nose with affected distaste. "I would prefer you to say glasses of whiskey starting about three o'clock in the afternoon."

She laughed. "It's good to see you."

"It's good to see you," Richard returned. "How is Mamma?"

"She's well," Julia replied guardedly. "She naps a good deal."

"And how is our cousin?" Alice asked.

"He's perfectly well," Julia assured her. "He'll show himself when he feels up to it. Now hurry inside and see your grandmother. She is as eager to see you as I was. It's just that she lacks the vigor to check the door every few minutes, much less run out and accost you the moment you arrive."

The girls started inside with smiles and light steps.

"The parlour is down the hall on the right." Julia said before turning back to Eliza. "How was the voyage?" she asked as they followed the girls.

"Long. Nearly seven weeks."

"Well, you're here now. We'll have a marvelous time."

"I'm certain of it," Eliza returned with a warm smile.

~~~

That night, dressed in a nightgown and wrapper, Jocelyn prepared to write in her journal for the first time. The light of the candle was the only illumination since Alice was already asleep. Alice frequently woke in the middle of the night and had trouble going back to sleep due to the activity of her mind. "If you could just stop thinking," Jocelyn frequently counseled. "Yes," Alice always agreed. "If only. Although some of my best ideas come to me at three a.m."

Now, as Jocelyn considered what to write, she absentmindedly traced her monogram with her finger. "I'm so thrilled to be here," she whispered and then she readied her pen and wrote the same words. It was true that Granny had aged more than she had prepared herself for, but she was as loving and kind as ever, and Aunt Julia felt like a kindred spirit.

Alice turned over in bed and muttered something, and Jocelyn looked over her shoulder to see her sister lying on her back with her arm flung over her face. Hopefully, she wouldn't start working on a scene in her mind. They needed to sleep well since they had a full day of sightseeing tomorrow.

Turning back to her task, Jocelyn dipped and tapped her pen again and began her first journal entry.

Friday, April 14

JWE

I am so thrilled to be here! We arrived this afternoon and Aunt Julia rushed out to greet us. She was as ecstatic as we were. Granny has aged considerably since we last saw her, but she seems in fine form for a lady past seventy. As Papa always says, old age may not be kind, but it is better than the alternative. Aunt Julia is wonderful, and I know that we will be the best of friends. We have all enjoyed getting reacquainted again, although our cousin, Jeremy, has hardly spoken. I was surprised by how exceptionally handsome he is. I hope he will allow us to know him.

Tomorrow, we will go sightseeing and we will make an appointment with a dressmaker named Madame Devy who has a shop on Grafton and Bond. We will all have new gowns made including Aunt Julia. (Papa insists.) I am so glad. What adventures await us, I have no idea, but I feel they will be momentous.

Chapter Two

Seated at the desk in the corner of the drawing room where she spent most late afternoons, Lydia Walston, widely known as Lady Merton, was attempting to write a letter, but she was too distracted to accomplish much. She glanced at the empty doorway and then the clock on the mantel with frustration. Her husband had promised to be back by four, and it was nearly five in the afternoon.

She took a breath and then slowly released it because in the presence of others, a lady remained calm, sagacious and placid, no matter what the aggravation, even if said aggravation happened to be caused by one's husband who could be maddening in his rash, irresponsible, foolish, selfish behavior. A lady could most certainly let her husband know her thoughts and know them well, but, in the presence of others, it was a different matter. Calm. Sagacious. Placid.

She looked over at her three grown children who were playing a board game, a silly thing called The Royal Game of Goose.

"No," Nigel complained as one of his pieces got bumped.

The girls laughed, and their mother could not help but grin at their antics.

Ada, her youngest, at eighteen, squealed with glee. "I won!"

"Barely," Nigel replied with a grin.

"She won," Lakely chimed in.

"Because of you," Nigel retorted. "If you hadn't held me back—"

Lakely shrugged. "Better her than you. Best of all would be me, of course."

"Of course," her siblings repeated sardonically.

Nigel was the eldest of the three and had never given his family cause to feel anything but pride. He was twenty-six and handsome with sandy brown hair, the same color as Ada's. In fact, the two of them resembled one another. Lakely, who was twenty-two, had very dark hair, much like Lady Merton's had been before the passage of time and her husband's reckless shenanigans began turning it a silvery gray. Lakely was an undeniable beauty. The exquisiteness of her looks had come from Lydia's lineage, although it had passed her over. In truth, Lakely resembled Lydia's youngest sister Rosemont.

There had been another Walston son, a first-born son, but he had been taken from them. Jamie had been gone now for longer than he had lived, but his mother never stopped remembering him, even advancing him in age in her mind. He had been her angel.

Nigel stood. "Well, that was amusing, but if you will excuse me—"

"Nigel," his mother spoke up. "Wait, please. Your father will be home soon, and we need to speak with you."

"I'm meeting my friends," he reminded her with a jab of his thumb toward the door. "We're having dinner. I told you."

"I know, dear, but we need a short discussion with you. Your father promised to be home."

"And so he is," came the voice of Lord Merton as he walked in with a brisk step. "Hello, all." His gaze swept over his wife briefly, but did not linger since her recent, icy demeanor was better avoided if possible. Not that it wasn't deserved. He knew that it was.

"Girls," their mother imperiously said as she rose.

"Mamma," Lakely returned.

"Give us the room," Lydia said with strained forbearance since Lakely was enough to try the patience of a saint. "And go upstairs to yours," she directed to her middle-born child with a lifted brow.

Ada rose at once, but Lakely resisted. "Can't we stay?" she wheedled. "Family should pull together in times of ... well, whatever this is a time of."

"Lakely," her father scolded. "Your mother has asked you—"

"Now," her mother interjected, brooking no further argument or discussion.

Ada left, sensible to the tension in the air, while Lakely shrugged, stood and started out at a below than acceptable rate of speed, pausing to pat her brother's arm on the way. "Good luck," she said.

Whereupon he gave her a sharp look of suspicion and then turned to look at his mother as she came closer. His father was also moving closer. "What is this about?" he asked.

"Shut the door," Lydia Walston said sternly to Lakely. When her eldest daughter glanced back over her shoulder, her mother's eyes narrowed. "Your turn will come soon enough." That warning drew a reaction of alarm and Lakely quickly closed the door.

Lord Merton sighed almost inaudibly. "Sit," he said to his son. "Please. Let's all sit."

They all took a seat around the table his sisters had just vacated. Nigel glanced down at the game board. "Do we really want a goose between us for this?"

"Nigel," his father said grimly. "I ... lost a bet."

The declaration caused a sticky moment of silence. "But you stopped," Nigel replied tightly. "Two years ago. You promised."

The shame on James Walston's face was heart-rending which took his wife by surprise. She had felt many things of late, mostly fury and betrayal. Empathy had not been in the mix.

"I know," her husband replied. "I am so sorry."

Nigel leaned back in his chair as if trying to prepare himself. "How much did you lose?"

"It is significant," his father uttered brokenly.

"Nigel," his mother said. "The estate is in peril."

"What do you mean?" he asked tonelessly.

"I mean that we now have more debt than assets."

Nigel looked accusingly at his father. "You never really did stop, did you?"

"I did! I swear it. But then—"

Nigel rose. He walked away from his parents and began pacing in an attempt to tamp down the panic and anger rapidly overtaking him.

Lydia also stood. "Darling, there is a simple solution."

Nigel turned to her with resentment etched on his features. "Let me guess. I should marry an heiress. Is that it? Is that the solution to *our* problem? *I* should marry money?"

Lydia glanced at her husband who was staring down at his tightly gripped hands looking as if he was in hell.

"How much?" Nigel demanded. "How much did you lose?"

"Thirty-four thousand pounds," his father replied.

The amount stole Nigel's breath. He went to the closest armchair and sat. "My God."

~~~

"Do you know what that's about?" Ada asked her sister when they reached the top of the staircase.

Lakely nodded. There was a regretful expression on her face.

"What?" Ada asked with wide eyes.

"It's not good."

"I assumed that much. What is it?"

Lakely motioned her younger sister onward so they would not be overheard. The two of them went into Ada's room where Lakely closed the door and leaned against it. "It's the gambling again."

"No!"

Lakely nodded. "The debt is worse than ever."

"How do you know?"

Lakely gave a one-shouldered shrug. "I just know."

Ada's eyes flashed. "Lakely!"

"Fine," Lakely relented. "I know because a letter came to the house and the man insisted on waiting for a reply. Fortunately,

Beatrice had opened the door because Crichton was somewhere else, so I took the letter from her and went to find Father." She paused and then sniffed lightly. "He wasn't in at the time."

"Which I imagine you knew before you took it. Am I right?"

"Do I keep track of everyone's schedule?" Lakely hedged.

"You read the letter?"

"The seal came loose," Lakely replied with a fluttering of her eyes. "The letter practically fell out."

"Oh, Lakely. What if Papa had caught you?"

"He didn't."

"Or Mamma? Even worse. Were you able to seal it again?"

"Of course. It's not that difficult. Just the right amount of heat," she said, whispering the last of it. "Anyway, the letter was a demand for payment."

"So he's gambling again," Ada said quietly. She sighed. "He promised."

"I know he did. And that's just the first thing."

Ada's eyes widened.

"Oh, the debt is considerable," Lakely amended. "Perhaps even enough to ruin us. So it's a rather large thing, I admit."

"What's the other thing?"

"They've found someone for Nigel to marry in order to wipe out the debt."

"How would that wipe out the debt?"

"She's wealthy, darling. Use your head. She has a hefty dowry."

"Who? Who is it?"

"We don't know her. She's an American."

"An American? How do you know this?"

Lakely hesitated. "I just do."

"Lakely!"

Lakely rolled her eyes. "I heard mother and father discussing it."

"You are incorrigible with your eavesdropping."

"How else would we know anything?"

"We would know eventually."

"I prefer to know sooner rather than later," Lakely retorted. She gave her sister a sour look. "Don't always be so good. It's boring."

"I have to be boring," Ada retorted. "Because you are audacious enough for both of us. What if we were both like you?"

"It's a valid point," Lakely conceded. "I'm not certain Mamma would have survived it."

"Neither am I. So how did they find this American?"

"Our father knew her father at school before he moved to America."

"Did he? How long has all this been going on?"

"The communication between them? A few months."

"A few months," Ada complained. "You should have told me."

"Why?" Lakely asked gently. "There is nothing we can do about it. Besides, I haven't known how things would unfold."

Ada walked over and sat on the bedside chair mulling everything over. "What if Nigel doesn't care for her?" she fretted.

"I imagine he'll do it anyway. He will be plenty put out, but in the end, he'll consent. Family honor and all that." She came and sat on the edge of bed next to her sister. "Are you going to scold me for sitting on the bed?"

"No, I am not. I have it on good authority that it's boring to always be good."

Lakely grinned. "You're not boring."

"This all makes me want to cry," Ada said. "Nigel deserves the chance to meet someone and fall in love just as it should be."

"You mean with violins playing and coy blushes and the young lady peeking over her fan as she makes eyes at him from across—"

"Spare me, if you please! You're not nearly as cynical as you pretend."

"Actually, I think I am."

"Be serious. I truly did think this would be the year. That's what they all keep saying. The season with the reason."

Lakely rolled her eyes. "They say it, but they don't mean it. They will marry whenever they damn well feel like it or when they have to. When their families insist or when it becomes necessary, as in this case."

Ada shook her head. "I didn't think Nigel would be the first of them."

"Nor did I. I would have thought Hugh would be the first," Lakely said as she ran through Nigel's group of friends in her mind. "He's the sweetest of the bunch."

"So polite and intelligent," Ada agreed. "It's a shame he has to wear those spectacles because he is rather handsome," she added as if the thought had just occurred to her.

"Yes, just not as handsome as the others. I can tell you who'll be the last of the five to marry. If it ever happens."

"Dab," Ada smirked. "I doubt it will ever happen. So when will we meet this American lady? Do you know her name?"

"Alice. She's twenty and from Boston. She's here with her parents and a younger sister visiting family."

"Oh, my! It's so sudden."

"I imagine Nigel is thinking the same thing."

"I feel so badly for him. Don't you?"

"Of course, I do."

"I hope she's nice. And pretty. Do you know if she is?"

"I don't know anything about her, really. I know some about her father, since he was the one corresponding with our father."

Ada's eyes bulged. "You read their letters?"

"He didn't exactly hide them," Lakely replied defensively.

"Tell me."

"On the condition you stop judging me for being inquisitive."

"Not to mention enterprising. All right, done. In many ways, I admire it."

Lakely nodded in acceptance. "Papa and Mr. Weatherly, their name is Weatherly, were at Eton. I don't think they were particularly good friends and I have no idea how they reconnected all these years later. The correspondence between them seems rather baldly to the point about a possible marriage connection. I've gathered that Weatherly is not titled, but he must be gentry."

"Is that what he wants for his daughter? A title?"

"It would seem so, and he is willing to pay handsomely for it."

"I wonder how she feels about it," Ada mused.

"I wonder if she has any more choice than Nigel does," Lakely said as she rose.

"It is so sad," Ada said.

Lakely started for the door. "Many things are sad, darling. There is poverty and hardship in the world. No one gives a tinker's damn what a woman thinks." She turned back from the door. "You and I can't promenade into White's and play cards and have a fine meal and brandy as Nigel is about to do."

"Nigel and the others can only get in because of JG," Ada replied in a conciliatory tone.

"You or I could marry JG and they wouldn't let us in."

Ada grinned. "Poor JG. Even as heir to a duke—"

"Oh, some lady will grab him up and be thrilled of it. You'll see. I wouldn't waste sympathy on JG."

~~~

Thirty-four thousand pounds! Nigel couldn't speak.

"There is a man," his father said, "who has made his interest in your sister known. He could help with part of it."

So he and Lakely were both to be sold off.

"Nigel," his mother said. "Your father knew someone at school who went to America and did well in business. He has a daughter, and her dowry would fix a great deal."

The bitterness Nigel felt was choking. "So," he said to his father. "There's a man you once knew who acquired a fortune and a daughter, and I should marry her and that is that."

"No, that is not that," his father replied. He stood and walked to the unlit hearth. Turning back around, he said, "I cannot be trusted. I have proven it time and again. I convince myself that I can control it, but then the desire, the *need* to play and to win

15

takes over and conquers all self-control. So, upon your marriage, everything will be handed to you." He paused. "I'm going to Reims. The vineyard is part mine."

Clearly, this was news to his wife. "What?" she exclaimed.

Nigel looked at her and then back at his father who met his gaze.

"Son, I loathe myself for this situation. I know that is no consolation, but it is true."

"I am not moving to France," Lydia stated before Nigel had a chance to speak.

James looked at her. "I understand, my dear. But I cannot stay."

"This is madness," she cried. "We discussed putting control of the estate solely in Nigel's hands. He can turn things around. We still have assets and interests that can prosper."

"Until I falter again. I still have my name and reputation. Even if I don't deserve it, I would prefer to keep them intact. Don't you see? Leaving the country is not madness. Destroying the estate and my children's legacy is madness. My compulsion to wager is madness. It overtakes my better judgement every time. *Every* time."

"But if you don't have the funds for it," she tried again. "You will live on an allowance. That's what we decided."

He shook his head. "If I didn't have a farthing and everyone knew it, others would back me out of friendship or their own gain. Honor means something to all of us, so the debt would have to be paid. I would like to believe I am strong enough to resist temptation, but how much evidence do we need that I am not?"

Nigel realized that the depth of his father's anguish had stolen his own fire of indignation. "Tell me about this man in America," he said in a flat voice. His parents' attention came back to him. He suspected, for a moment, he'd been forgotten in the exchange. The fallout from it still lingered in the air like a noxious smell.

"His name is Weatherly," his father replied. "Richard Weatherly. He's been in Boston these last years. The family business, his wife's family, is steel. Apparently, it's done obscenely well under his direction." He paused. "He and his family are here on a visit."

"They are here now?" Nigel repeated. A cruel shiver snaked up his back.

"Yes."

So. A debt had been amassed, the estate verged on collapse, marriage could solve it, and the bride-to-be was here. It was overwhelming. "I'm meeting my friends," Nigel said as he rose. He started for the door, and no one said another word as he left.

Chapter Three

igel had the driver drop him a few blocks away from White's thinking the walk would do him good, but apparently it hadn't since he'd failed to notice his friend Dabney Adams until he spoke. Dab had been waiting on the sidewalk for him. At six feet four inches tall with dark hair and eyes fringed with absurdly long lashes, Dab was not easy to miss. He was the most strikingly handsome of their group of friends. He was also the most enigmatic. He was an only child, but utterly closed off to and about his family. He rarely saw his parents. His tight group of friends seemed all that was important to him.

"You're late," Dab said when they were practically within touching distance.

Nigel gave him a look. "I believe I'm on time," he countered.

"Except you are always early, so to arrive on time makes you late," Dab reasoned as they started for the building.

"By the same reasoning, I suppose you're early?"

"Exactly. It's all a matter of expectations."

"What is your view on that?" Nigel asked.

"On what? Expectations? That's easy. Don't have them and do not offer them. Makes life simpler." He paused before asking. "You all right?"

Nigel gave a quick, if rather noncommittal nod. As they walked in the front door, JG waved them over. As if he was difficult to spot. John George Baillie was the heir apparent to the dukedom of Morguston, and the tag-along to their five. The five, Nigel, Dab, Hugh Pritchett and twin brothers Joel and Jonathan Stewart had been friends since meeting at Harrow as boys. Nigel,

Joel and Jonathan had gone on to Oxford while the others had attended Cambridge where they met and befriended JG.

The twenty-four-year-old JG stood five feet ten inches tall, had ginger hair and some fifteen to twenty pounds of excess weight snuggly packed around his middle. He tried too hard and frequently spoke up when it would have been better to remain silent, but he was a good fellow with superb connections. He had doors open to him that the other five, mere sons of barons, did not. He was their ticket into White's and sometimes into the most prestigious events of the season. "Already signed you in," JG told them stepping backwards. "We're upstairs."

"Uh—" Dab uttered as he grabbed JG's arm to keep him from backing into a man who then glared at JG.

"Sorry," JG muttered. He turned scarlet before walking on. Nigel and Dab followed him through the elegant foyer and past the morning rooms on either side to and up the imposing staircase. Billiard balls cracked from the back room of the ground floor.

"Is something wrong?" Dab asked Nigel quietly.

Nigel shook his head but avoided Dab's curious gaze.

"We got a table," JG said over his shoulder. "It's deuced crowded this evening."

They entered the card room and spotted the rest of their friends, Joel, Jonathan and Hugh, seated together as Jonathan shuffled a deck of cards. They looked up in cheerful greeting, but then Hugh's eyes narrowed thoughtfully at Nigel. Hugh's hair was the color of ripe summer wheat. He had a finely boned face that was apt to get overlooked because of the spectacles he wore to correct his near-sightedness. "What's wrong?" he asked Nigel as the newcomers took their seats. Joel and Jonathan glanced over the three before their gazes closed in on Nigel.

Nigel tried to sluff it off. "Who said anything was wrong?"

Dab stuck a finger in the air. "Saw it in your face."

"We're playing Faro," Jonathan said.

"Good," Nigel said, ready to have the attention off him. "I thought I was joining my friends, not a table full of nursemaids."

"So, play first," Jonathan said, "or spill it first?" he directed to Nigel.

An attendant came around with the glasses of whiskey they had ordered, and Nigel took one after giving Jonathan a look. If Dab was the best-looking member of the group, the twins were a close second. They were tall with dark hair and surprisingly pale blue eyes. The differences between the identical twins were that Joel, the elder by eight minutes, had a mustache, and Jonathan had a faint scar on his chin, the result of a childhood fall.

"Is it about your father?" Joel asked in a hushed voice when the attendant had gone.

Nigel's pulse jumped. "Is it common knowledge?"

"Is *what* common knowledge?" Hugh asked, looking between Nigel and the twins.

"No. Only rumors," Jonathan supplied.

"Why didn't you say something?" Nigel asked.

"We haven't seen you since we caught wind of it," Joel said.

"What's happened?" Dab asked Nigel.

A pair of older gents sauntered up. "You fellows going to use the table?"

"Yes, we are," Dab replied.

"Because you can jaw jack in—"

"We are, sir," JG seconded.

One of the men grunted and elbowed the other. "Let's join Fitzgerald's table," he said and then led the way.

Every other table was full, so Jonathan began dealing. "This is just for show," he said quietly.

"What are the rumors?" Nigel asked.

"Debt," Joel supplied quietly. "Gambling."

"What's the fact of it?" Hugh asked.

"Debt," Nigel replied. "Goddamn gambling. Apparently, my father can't control it." An uncomfortable silence fell over them during which Nigel felt his face heat.

"How bad is it?" JG asked. "Perhaps I could help."

The offer was touching. "Thank you, but no."

"We could all go in on it," Joel said.

"You are the best of friends, but no. Apparently the way out is marrying an heiress."

"Sign me up for the same," Dab said. "Although that is somewhat easier said than done, is it not?"

"Normally, yes. But my father has conveniently lined one up."

"Who?" most of them said in unison. The chorus dispelled the tension and made them laugh.

"An American," Nigel said. He rather enjoyed the shock of his friends. He sat back and looked at his cards. "I have not met her yet."

"How did that come about?" Hugh asked as he laid a card down.

Nigel shook his head. "I have no idea," he admitted. "I feel like I am the last to arrive at a lavish masquerade ball and every other guest knows who I am, but I don't recognize any of them. It is disconcerting to say the least."

Dab laid down an ace of hearts.

"We're not really playing at all?" JG asked, baffled by the discards.

"No," Dab said. "We're not. It's for show until we get the story."

Nigel put a card down and JG did the same.

"Well, give it some thought, JG," Dab scolded.

"You didn't give it any thought," JG retorted.

"I mean *appear* to give it some thought." Dab glanced over his shoulder before looking at Nigel. "An American," he puzzled.

Nigel nodded. "Someone my father knew from school left for America, did well and had a daughter."

"What's his name?" Hugh asked.

Nigel couldn't recall if he'd been told. Yes, he had. What was it? Weathers? Weatherby?

"More importantly," Dab said, "What do you know of the daughter?"

"Nothing, really. Only that I'll meet her soon. The family is here on a visit."

"So, she might be exquisite," Jonathan said with a shrug.

"Or she might have a face like a pug," Nigel returned. "I don't suppose it matters a great deal in the overall scheme of things."

"I doubt they'll force you to marry her if, say, she is repulsive," Joel spoke up.

"You're right. I suppose I could reject her and go find another heiress who'll fork over a small fortune for the privilege of marrying me."

That silenced the table again.

"Well," Dab said. "Perhaps meet her first and then see how dire the situation is."

JG nodded. "Besides, I'm certain there are worse things than having a wife with a face like a pug."

"Yes," Jonathan agreed. "For example, she could also be thick around the middle and have bowed legs. And a large gap between her front teeth."

Nigel grinned and took another drink. He was finally relaxing.

"Pug faced children, though," Dab commiserated. "With thick bodies and bowed legs."

"And she might be excessively loud," Joel added. "As Americans can be."

"What's on the menu this evening?" Nigel asked JG in order to change the subject.

"Roast duck."

"At least it's good timing," Dab continued.

"The roast duck?" Nigel asked wryly.

"Yes, exactly. The roast duck." Dab rolled his eyes. "With the season upon us, I mean. Perhaps some young lady will be launched that fits the bill admirably. Should the American not work out, I mean. And if that's the case, send the bow-legged dear my way."

Nigel looked at him, prepared for the jest that was to come.

"Even if she does have a face like a pug," Dab said. "I'm pretty enough to salvage the children, I think. And bringing a fortune to the match sounds marvelous."

"I'll keep it in mind," Nigel said.

"All right," Jonathan said, gathering up the cards. "Let's play for real."

Chapter Four

ocelyn knocked once and then went into the bedroom to find Alice lying flat on her back in the middle of the bed with a piece of paper over her face. Lying about her was the material she had been compiling for her book, plus a plate with crumbs from the macarons they'd purchased that afternoon. "I see a body and blonde tresses beneath a paper where a face ought to be."

Alice removed the paper, and her eyes were alight. "Rather than between a husband and wife or a man or woman, because I hadn't decided if I was going to make them married yet, the correspondence could come from a child," she said speaking rapidly as she always did when inspiration was fueled by too many sweets. "A boy of twelve when the rebellion begins," she added as her gaze drifted toward the ceiling where, apparently, a vision of this new character appeared before her mind's eye.

"He is too young to join," Alice continued. "His parents forbid it. They also make him feel responsible for working the farm and for his mother's safety. His father goes off to fight, and the letters are between the father and son with their simultaneous stories. The son … what shall I name him? Whatever it is, he will eventually get dragged into the fray. Because he would. How could he not by eighteen or nineteen?" Alice stopped speaking abruptly and looked at her sister who was standing by the edge of her bed.

Jocelyn gave a slow shake of her head. "I did not exactly follow that."

"I suppose not." Alice covered her mouth with the backs of her fingers and gave in to a yawn. "I'll explain tomorrow if it still makes sense to me."

Jocelyn recognized one of the copied letters on the bed. "This one is so moving," she said picking it up. "Abagail Adams, July 16, 1777."

Alice recognized the date without looking at it. "The stillbirth. Don't mix up the piles. I put them in a certain order."

Jocelyn held the paper closer and read aloud. "'Join with me my dearest friend in gratitude to Heaven that a life I know you value has been spared and carried through distress and danger, although the dear Infant is numbered with its ancestors.'"

"It was a baby girl," Alice said. "Think of it. It's been five days since the birth and Abagail is only now able to sit up, but she never feels sorry for herself. She worries more for her daughter who took it hard."

"It was never made clear what was wrong with the baby, was it?"

"Not that I've been able to discover. We know from her letters that she was ill beforehand. And she says it was apparent why the child had not lived, but that she dared not write it down in case it fell into the wrong hands."

"Here it is," Jocelyn said as she sat on the bed and began to read aloud. *"'It never opened its eyes in this world. It looked as though they were only closed for sleep. The circumstance which put an end to its existence was evident upon its birth, but at this distance and in a letter which may possibly fall into the hands of some unfeeling ruffian, I must omit particulars. Suffice it to say that it was not owing to any injury which I had sustained, nor could any care of mine have prevented it.'"* Jocelyn put down the paper and thought about it. "What do you think it was?"

Alice sat up. "I suppose there had to be some sort of deformation. What else is apparent?" She reached for the last of her drink. "I don't suppose you would fetch more punch and macarons," she said sweetly.

Jocelyn twisted around with a disdainful expression. "For once, you fetch them." She set the letter back down in its proper pile.

"I meant for us to share," Alice replied defensively.

Jocelyn gave her a look of reproach. "Granny's punch has quite the kick. I felt dizzy after one glass."

"So did I. But it grows on you. I can hardly wait for her next batch. Aunt Julia said there have never been two exactly alike."

"Ali, I need to talk to you. I think there's something strange about us being here."

"Here? In this house?"

"No, of course not. Here in London."

"What do you mean?"

"Oh, Alice. If you would get your nose out of your story for five minutes, you would see it, too."

"That's not fair. I haven't had my nose in my story the entire time."

"I am telling you, there is something secretive between father and mother and …whatever it is, it somehow involves you."

"What are you talking about?"

"I've seen looks pass between them," Jocelyn explained. "She's been the instigator. She gets his attention, looks pointedly at you and then back at him with … this look."

"What look?"

"As in …do something. Say something. He ignores it, but his expression—" Jocelyn paused trying to get the description right.

"What?"

"I'm thinking how to describe it."

"Well, while you ponder the matter, why don't you fetch us more punch and cookies?"

"Mama would say you've had enough punch and cookies."

"Which is precisely why I'm not asking her."

Jocelyn rolled her eyes. "You only use that sugar-sweet tone of voice when you want something."

Alice gasped in dismay but, a moment later, her expression cleared. "That's true, isn't it?"

Jocelyn nodded. *"Mm-hmm."*

Alice pulled a pout. "Why do you even keep me around?"

"Are you saying I have a choice in the matter? Seriously, though, as to the look on Papa's face, imagine that you and I are girls of ten and eleven. We've stolen into our sister's room and you have broken her music box, which we were not supposed to touch. Or I have broken it. It doesn't matter."

"Then let's say you broke it."

"Fine."

"Which sister?"

"Clara."

"Sophia would be more ferocious about it."

"Sophia, then," Jocelyn rejoined impatiently. "Later, we're all at dinner. This is before Sophia has discovered the crime. One by one, all the family clears out from the room except the three of us. I know I have to say something about the box, but I'm dreading it. You don't want to be blamed for it, so you give me a look as if to say *tell her.*"

Alice blinked when Jocelyn stopped speaking. "Is that it?"

"Yes. That's the look."

"Your imagination is as good as mine."

"Not quite."

"What would father have to feel guilty about?"

"I don't know."

"He wanted to come back for a visit and we wanted to come every bit as much. More so, in fact. So, again I ask, what is there to feel guilty about?"

Jocelyn shrugged and shook her head. "And again, I say I do not know."

Alice looked at her sister fondly. "If this intrigue you have imagined, while entertaining, is your way of telling me to pay more attention to everything around me, I will. I will try. I can't help the way my mind works, you know."

"I do think you should pay more attention to everything around you, but I am not inventing this."

"Well, time will tell. If anyone, it's Mother who should feel guilty. Always trying to change me. I swear, she won't be satisfied unless I marry Stanley Ingham."

Jocelyn could not disagree. "Mama wants the best for you, for all of us, and she will never feel guilty. You know that."

"Yes, I do," Alice admitted. "But you can't know how much I wish I'd never made that promise about accepting an engagement by age twenty-two."

"Before the age of twenty-two," Jocelyn reminded her.

Alice huffed. "No eighteen-year-old should be held accountable to promises made to her mother in order to be left in peace, but she means to hold me to it."

Jocelyn nodded in agreement. "With Stanley Ingham. She thinks he hung the moon in the sky."

"I can always run away."

"And join a convent?" Jocelyn teased.

"Exactly. That would show her. Guess what, Mama? I got married … to Jesus," she finished in a whisper.

"And before the age of twenty-two," Jocelyn laughed. "I did have to convert to a new religion first, but I kept my promise."

Alice groaned.

"You still have almost a year," Jocelyn placated.

"But the summer will go by quickly here and then nearly two months for the return trip home? My time will be up before you know it." Alice sighed, but then got off the bed. "I'm not going to think about it anymore tonight. Let's sneak down for more wine."

"In your stocking feet?"

"For stealth. Come with me. Be my co-conspirator."

Jocelyn accepted her sister's hand up. "I wouldn't be anyone else's."

~~~

The other members of the Weatherly family were downstairs in the parlour which was pleasantly lit by way of strategically placed lamps, both carcel and Argand. Richard Weatherly was reading The Times. Eliza Weatherly sat at the card table across from her sister-in-law playing Écarté while Mr. Weatherly's stepmother, indeed the only mother he had ever known, since his own died when he was still in nappies, Mrs. Emmanuel Thompson Weatherly was occupied netting.

Jeremy Alward, Julia's son, who was seventeen and fine looking with facial features that seemed more feminine than masculine, stood sketching on a large paper affixed to an easel in a corner of the room. No one was allowed to draw near and view his work without invitation. One could glance his way without incurring his umbrage. At the moment, one could even blatantly stare since Jeremy took no notice of anything or anyone as he worked. The poor lad was touched in the head.

Jeremy was strangely intellectual but not always intelligible. He sometimes stated facts one after the other and it was usually unclear why he felt those particular facts needed voicing. He seemed unwilling to make eye contact with anyone other than his mother, grandmother and the maid, Rose Fisher. Even their cook of the last seven years, Mrs. Halley, was not deemed sufficiently trustworthy for anything other than furtive glances. His pretty cousins fascinated him, but he observed them only when they were not looking at him. Naturally, they understood this and complied.

Julia Alward, who was five years younger than Richard, had never been more than attractive, but she had aged well. She had borne setbacks and tragedies with aplomb, trusting that providence was firmly in control. She believed in focusing on one's blessings, of which she had many. Her son, her mother, this house, mornings full of wonder, her extended family, lively card games, good books, fine wine. There were so many.

She generally slept soundly, woke early and slipped down to the garden, no matter what time of year it was. The garden, indeed, the world was so alive first thing in the morning. Why every human being did not rush out of doors of a morning to witness and enjoy the bountiful gifts of nature, she could not fathom.

She relished her nighttime ritual no less than her mornings. She ended each day savoring two maple-sugar fancies, a glass or two of her favorite port and a few chapters of a book. Then she topped it all off with a pinch of her powder just before bed. The powder, a remedy for a headache, sleeplessness or fullness of the head, was made from coca, mescal and other natural ingredients. She made a practice of transferring it from the canister it came in to a lovely snuff box from her late husband's collection. It had a silver base and a white enamel lid adorned with delicate hand-painted flowers and a swirling design of vines around the perimeter.

At the moment, old Mrs. Weatherly was peering confusedly at the project in her hands. The lady typically wore a lace cap and collar over a non-descript gown, usually of gray or lavender. It was for the sake of occupation that she netted; she no longer had the eyesight for embroidery. She had possessed quite a talent with the needle in her day, but she did not net well. They would never be able to rid themselves of the various reticules, purses and scarves she had netted, but it entertained her well enough.

"Hetero," Jeremy murmured. "Chrome. Chromia."

Eliza and Julia glanced over at him. "I beg your pardon, my love?" his mother asked.

"Different eyes. Alexander the Great had it."

"Had what?" Julia asked. "Two different colored eyes? Like Alice's eyes?"

"Heterochromia," was his only reply.

Julia looked at Eliza. "I didn't know it was called that."

"Nor did I," Eliza returned.

"It is," Richard said as he turned the page. "Didn't know that about Alexander the Great, though. I wonder what color his were?"

"Blue, brown," Jeremy said.

"Ah," Richard said.

"Are you drawing Alice?" Julia asked her son.

He did not reply or look away from his work. Julia knew the expression and went back to her cards. "Your girls look so different from one another," she commented. "Alice more like you and Jocelyn like Richard."

Eliza murmured agreement as she discarded. "The same as with their sisters. Clara resembles her father and Sophia looks like me, more so than Alice."

"I would have dearly loved to have seen them again."

"They have their hands full."

"Yes, they do." Julia picked up a card and then discarded another. "They are all so lovely."

"Alice's head is in the clouds too much of the time," Eliza opined.

Richard chuckled and the ladies glanced over at him. It wasn't clear whether he'd reacted to the comment or something he'd read. His lips were pursed, his gaze still on the paper. Julia and Eliza exchanged an amused glance and went back to their card game.

"It's a good thing you take the paper," Eliza said. "He wouldn't know what to do without it."

"I wouldn't be without it," Richard spoke up. "I would have started a subscription as I did last time I was here. I'm surprised you kept it up."

"Jeremy reads it," Julia explained. "Cover to cover."

"Reads it to me, sometimes," Granny said. "More entertaining than this damn netting, I can tell you."

Chapter Five

igel straightened his tie in the mirror and then looked himself over with a critical eye. The Weatherly family was on approach with his intended in tow. "We'll soon know," he uttered. He stepped back thinking of his elder brother. *If you were here, this mess would be on your shoulders,* he thought. He imagined Jamie's smirk and reply that he was not there. "No, you're not, so it's up to me."

Second best.

~~~

"Do you think we'll receive invitations to balls soon?" Jocelyn asked her father as they rode toward the home of a former schoolmate of his, a man named Walston.

"I should think so," he replied. "Especially after this evening."

Alice looked at him, curious. "Why is that?"

"The Walston's are well-connected," he replied smoothly.

"Were you Mr. Walston close in school?" Jocelyn asked.

"No. He had his friends and I had mine. He's not called Walston, though. He's called Merton. Lord Merton. He's the baron of Merton."

The ranks and titles of the English were so confusing. "Then," Alice pondered, "why not call him Lord Walston who is the baron of Merton."

"That's not the way it's done."

"Is Merton a place?" Alice persisted.

"Yes. I believe it's a village or small township in the county of Somerset. You'd heard of Bath?" Both girls nodded. "Bath is a city in Somerset."

"What do barons do?" Alice asked. "Do they govern their little fiefdom?"

"In a matter of speaking."

Jocelyn studied her father quizzically. "When did you and Lord Merton strike up a friendship?"

"I wouldn't say friendship exactly," he prevaricated. "We've had correspondence. When I mentioned our trip here, he invited us to dine with them."

"But how did the correspondence begin?" Jocelyn persisted.

"Good Lord, Jaus," her father playfully scolded. "You're not writing a book, too, are you? Not sure your mother and I can bear it."

Alice huffed.

"I am teasing," he said to Alice. Turning his attention back to his youngest, he said, "I believe the way it went was this. Lord Merton ran into my old friend Randall Page somewhere or the other and I was mentioned. You'll remember Mr. Page."

Alice nodded. She recalled an agreeable man with a handlebar mustache. He had done a trick pulling a coin out his ear that had fascinated her.

"After their encounter, Lord Merton wrote to me, and I wrote back."

"How is Mr. Page?" Alice asked.

"Not well, I'm afraid."

"What's wrong with him?" Alice asked.

"Alice," her mother objected.

"What? I liked Mr. Page. It would be nice to see him again."

"That's not likely," her father stated. "I will see him, but a friend is a different matter. His physicians believe it's an ailment of the liver."

"I'm sorry to hear it," Alice said. "You will pass on our best wishes?"

"Of course, I will. Now, back to this evening, the Walston's have two daughters about your ages and a son who is a bit older. His name is Nigel."

"What are the daughters' names?" Alice asked.

"I don't recall," he replied thoughtfully, "although one is exceedingly odd."

"The girl or the name?"

"The name. I don't know anything about the girl."

Alice looked at Jocelyn. "I can't wait to find out what it is."

Jocelyn smiled, but then her eye caught on something beyond Alice's window, and she gawked. Alice turned to see what it was as the carriage stopped in front of a beautiful home, a mansion, in fact. She blinked in surprise. "Is this it?"

"It is. They call it Larkspur House," Mr. Weatherly replied.

"Larkspur House sounds like a cottage," Alice said wonderingly. "Not this. Good gracious!" It was brick, four stories high and five bays wide. She was the first to alight from the carriage with the help of a Larkspur House footman. She was suddenly glad she had worn a new gown beneath her tippet. It was a pretty combination of blue and light purple muslin and silk with short, puffy sleeves.

Jocelyn joined her wearing one of last year's gowns. "Do you think they'll be frightful snobs?" Jocelyn asked quietly.

"Probably. I only hope we're found suitable to warrant invitations."

"So do I."

The front door was opened as they approached, and the grand foyer they were admitted into had a gilded ceiling twenty feet above, a wide staircase that curved in two different directions and a plethora of marble sculptures. "It's a palace," Jocelyn breathed so that only Alice would hear.

As the butler led them down a wide corridor lined with large paintings, Alice was cognizant of looking without gaping which was not the easiest thing in such a place. So this is how barons lived.

They entered a salon where the family had gathered. A fetching middle-aged man, obviously Lord Merton, stood with a welcoming smile and came to greet her father. "Weatherly," he greeted. "Good to see you."

"And you, Lord Merton," Richard returned, shaking the man's hand.

A handsome younger man, obviously the son, stood by the hearth. There was a resemblance between the Walston men, light brown hair and a pleasing countenance. Three ladies, one older and two younger, were looking at the new arrivals, most especially her with interest. *Please, may we pass muster so we can receive invitations to balls.* English balls were one of the things they had been looking most forward to.

"May I present Mr. Richard Weatherly," the butler announced, reading from the card he'd been given, "Mrs. Eliza Weatherly, Miss Alice Weatherly and Miss Jocelyn Weatherly."

Everyone on their feet gave a polite bow as their name was said.

"Thank you, Crichton," Lord Merton said in dismissal. "May I introduce my wife?"

"Lady Merton," Mr. Weatherly said. "Such a pleasure."

"The pleasure is mine, sir. Welcome to our home."

"Thank you."

"This," Lord Merton continued, "is our son Nigel. And our daughters Lakely and Ada."

Each bowed their head slightly as their name was said. The elder daughter, Lakely, was stunning with very dark hair and a look of astuteness. The younger had lighter hair and a sweet smile.

"Please sit," Lord Merton said. "It turned into a fine evening, did it not?"

They all agreed that it had. As a servant began circulating with glasses of sherry, Alice's gaze flicked to Lakely Walston, who was observing her. They each smiled.

"Your home is so beautiful," Mrs. Weatherly said.

"Thank you," Lady Merton said. "It was built for an ancestor of my husband's more than a century ago."

Alice accepted one of the small glasses of sherry. Jocelyn declined. Alice hadn't known what to expect of the evening, but Larkspur House was splendiferous. She wanted to absorb every, single detail of the home to be part of a future book.

"Are you enjoying the city, Mrs. Weatherly?" Lord Merton asked.

"Very much so," she replied. "I always do. It is the girls' first trip abroad," she said with a sideways glance at them. "So that is special. We brought our eldest daughters on a previous trip, but that was nearly ten years ago."

"And what do you ladies think?" Lord Merton asked cheerily addressing Alice and Jocelyn. "What's been your favorite thing?"

"All the normal tourist sights," Alice admitted. "The palaces. We don't have them at home."

Everyone smiled.

"And Vauxhall Gardens," Jocelyn added. "What an adventure it is."

Alice nodded in agreement. "I've enjoyed Hatchard's, the bookstore," she said, "And the confectioner shop called Parmentier's."

The Walston girls agreed.

"How are things in the United States?" Lord Merton asked Mr. Weatherly, to which Mr. Weatherly complied, primarily talking about business and growth. Alice sipped her sherry and glanced at Nigel Walston who was listening to her father with interest. Indeed, he was fine-looking.

"Have you had an opportunity to travel there, Mr. Walston?" Mr. Weatherly asked Nigel.

"I have. Yes. I visited New York with friends three years ago. It is very different from London."

Mr. Weatherly nodded. "I still remember my first reactions."

"But then it grew on you," Lord Merton observed.

"Oh, I liked it from the start," Mr. Weatherly replied. "I was ready for the change and the opportunities that came with it."

"I enjoyed it, as well," Nigel said. "I did not mean to indicate otherwise."

"When did you move to America, Mr. Weatherly?" Lady Merton asked.

"In seventy-nine. I was seventeen."

"So young," Ada remarked.

"Yes," Mr. Weatherly agreed. "That tends to be when we have the most courage."

"Did you know someone there?" Lakely asked.

"My father had acquaintances and he sent me with letters of introduction. They helped a great deal."

"The war was still on," Lord Merton realized.

Mr. Weatherly nodded. "Indeed it was. It was not an easy time, but I was fortunate to have hosts that made all the difference."

"Did you fight in the war?" Lakely asked him.

"Lakely," her mother rebuked.

"What?" she asked defensively. "It's a logical question."

"I don't mind answering," Richard said, directing it to Lady Merton. "I did," he said to Lakely. "On the side of the colonists."

"I would have done the same," Lakely replied.

"You don't know that," Nigel said to his sister. "You can't know that. So much has to do with one's duty and responsibility."

Mr. Weatherly nodded. "I agree," he said to Nigel. "For my part, I love this country, but I felt the colonies deserved the independence they sought. It's a shame it had to come to war."

"Why don't we turn to a happier topic," Lady Merton suggested lightly.

"Do you know about our messy situation with the king and queen?" Lakely asked Alice with a mischievous twinkle in her eye.

"Lakely," her mother admonished yet again. "That is hardly what I meant."

"I know, but you cannot deny it's interesting."

Alice wished she could ask whose side they were on, the queen's or the king's, but Lady Merton wanted the subject changed.

"Are you ready for the season to begin?" Jocelyn asked Ada quietly. Because the room had gone quiet, everyone heard and paid attention.

Ada beamed. "Oh, yes. It's my debut."

"How exciting," Jocelyn replied with a smile.

"Do you have a season in America?" Ada asked curiously.

"Nothing as grand as here."

Alice glanced at Nigel as he happened to glance at her. They both smiled in embarrassment and looked away.

At supper, Alice was seated between Nigel and Ada and across from Lakely. She was having a far better time than she had expected of a polite dinner with an old acquaintance of her father. Largely that was due to Miss Walston who was different than anyone she had encountered. Unrestrained was the description that came to mind. "Your name is unusual," Alice commented when soup was served. "It's lovely, but unusual."

"It is my mother's maiden name and my middle name," Miss Walston replied.

"Her given name," her mother said from the end of the table, "is Lara. And so she was called until she was four years of age and announced that her name was Lakely and not Lara. Naturally, we corrected her, but she was an untenably stubborn child. This went back and forth until the day she turned five and refused to answer to any name other than her middle name."

Lakely shrugged. "I knew it was my name."

Lord Merton smirked. "It took her mother some time," Lord Merton said, "before she gave in on a continual basis."

Lady Merton still seemed peeved about it. "I fervently wished we had named her something else, but it was too late."

"They do sometimes have minds of their own," Eliza sympathized.

Lakely caught Alice's eye, glanced toward their mothers, and made a pouty face, which Alice laughed at silently.

"What of your elder daughters?" Lady Merton asked Mrs. Weatherly.

"Clara and Sophia are both happily married with children. Three for Clara and Sophia is expecting their second in summer."

"How nice it must be to have grandchildren."

"Yes," Eliza replied with a smile. "It is."

The next course was a delicate fillet of sole with a lemon caper sauce and sautéed vegetables.

"What do you enjoy doing, Miss Weatherly?" Nigel asked.

"I have a passion for writing," Alice replied.

"Oh? Writing what?"

"Stories. I am working on a novel."

"What pastimes do you pursue, Miss Ada?" Mr. Weatherly asked, nearly interrupting Alice's reply.

"Music," Ada replied. "Listening, mostly. I do not play well. And I adore dancing. It's one of the reasons I am eager for the season to get underway," she directed to Jocelyn who smiled and nodded.

"What is your novel about?" Nigel asked Alice.

Lakely looked at her with interest.

"It revolves around letters written during the revolutionary war."

"A series of letters, then?" Lakely asked. "Of famous people?"

"No. The correspondences will be between five or six couples, I believe, starting at the beginning of the conflict and going through to the end. I want to give the reader a sense of the toll of the war from different perspectives."

Nigel nodded. He seemed interested.

"I've acquired actual letters, but the plan is to intersperse them with a story or stories of fiction."

"How fascinating," Ada said earnestly.

"It is to me," Alice replied. "I've been working on it for over a year. Mostly researching."

"Are your eyes two different colors?" Ada asked, just realizing it.

"Ada," her mother reprimanded. "Your manners."

"It's quite all right, Lady Merton," Alice said. She looked at Ada. "They are."

"Remarkable," Ada exclaimed.

Lakely rose and leaned in closer to see. "Oh, my!"

"Lakely," her mother huffed with exasperation.

"They are two different colors," Lakely marveled, utterly ignoring her mother.

Alice sensed Nigel looking, so she turned to him so he could see for himself.

"Fascinating," he said softly.

"And what pastimes do you enjoy, Miss Walston?" Mrs. Weatherly asked.

"I wish I wrote novels," Lakely replied. "I love to read them. Well, let's see. I enjoy good food and wine and travel and—"

"Creating a bit of havoc here and there," Nigel interjected.

Lakely shrugged. "Only when things need a bit of shaking up."

"The research you're doing," Ada said to Alice. "What's involved in that?"

"Finding and copying letters of the era and uncovering the stories behind them as best I can."

Ada nodded. "I see."

"That can't be the easiest thing to do," Nigel commented.

"No, but we're fortunate to have an excellent Historical Society at home that has been invaluable."

"I would think there is one here," Lakely suggested.

"I hope so," Alice said. "To me, it doesn't matter that the Americans and British were on the opposing sides; they all had their convictions and obligations. They all knew hardship and pain and love and courage."

"Yes," Nigel agreed.

"But I'm monopolizing—" Alice started to apologize.

"No," Lakely and Ada said at the same time.

"It is very interesting," Nigel said politely.

She looked at him and felt a queer little tickle in her center.

"If you need any help with your research," Lakely said, "I'd be interested."

"I'd help, as well," Ada offered enthusiastically.

"That's so kind of you both," Alice replied. "I do fear I'll run out of time and not get enough accomplished while I'm here." The expressions on their faces suddenly changed. In an instant, there was an odd strain in the air. Why? What had she said? As it did sometimes, everything seemed to slow around her, other than the beating of her heart.

She saw Lakely blink in surprise and then look at Nigel.

Lord Merton glanced at her father wonderingly.

Her father looked disconcerted, perhaps even embarrassed.

Oh, Lord! What had Jocelyn said? *I am telling you, there is something between father and mother and, whatever it is, it involves you.*

Nigel's gaze was fixed in front of him. He looked as if he'd been turned to stone. *Nigel.* This was about Nigel?

Lady Merton cleared her throat. "More wine," she said *sotto voce.*

Alice felt like she could not move. She could barely breathe. As Lady Merton's command was attended to, the lady took control of the conversation. "There's to be a ball at Buckley's the Saturday after next. I hope you'll be able to come. They are sending an invitation at my request."

"That would be most agreeable," Mrs. Weatherly replied smoothly. "Thank you."

Lady Merton gave a slight inclination of her head. "Later, we should discuss the girls' presentations at Almack's."

"Oh, indeed," Lakely said quietly, directing it to Alice. Apparently, she had recovered from whatever shock Alice had caused earlier. "Because the world revolves around the approval of the patronesses of Almack's. Or so they believe. And we all have to pretend it's so."

Alice was not following, not only out of ignorance of British society, but from the jolt of what now seemed appallingly clear, that she had been left out of a plot that very much involved her. Or was her overdramatic mind conjuring the notion? But the more she observed the others to discern what they knew, the more she was convinced that something of significance was in play.

Lakely looked riveted by her.

Ada looked embarrassed and apologetic.

Nigel seemed stoical and somehow offended. Was this the famed English stiff upper lip she had heard so much about? But what precisely had her offense been?

Neither her mother or father were meeting her eye, which conveyed culpability. Jocelyn was trying diligently to converse cheerfully, which meant she had some understanding of the situation. It was rather humiliating. Alice had always fancied herself a perceptive study of people, so how had she missed whatever this was?

The next course was a salad. The next was beefsteak with a red wine sauce and a side of potatoes. Alice nibbled at each course and felt as if she'd been struck dumb. Cheeses were served and finally a torte with a berry filling. The food was delectable, but how much had she actually tasted? With the meal concluded, the men excused themselves. Alice felt a dull panic. Was she to languish the rest of the evening not understanding what everyone else seemed to know? She helplessly watched the men file from the room.

Seconds passed, but she could not stand it. "Will you excuse me a moment?" she directed to Lady Merton before rising and leaving the room, purposely not looking at her mother. Had she even gotten a response from Lady Merton? She couldn't worry about it at the moment. She reached the corridor and saw her father and Lord Merton walking several yards ahead. Where Nigel had gone, she did not know, but it was her father she needed to speak with.

The memory of Jocelyn's warning kept step with her. *I am telling you, there is something between father and mother and, whatever it is, it involves you.* She must have been blind not to see it. While she had been in her own little world, they had been scheming behind her back. "Papa," she called.

Mr. Weatherly stopped. He asked Lord Merton to be excused for a moment, to which their host was gracious, adding that the smoking room was just ahead. Lord Merton then continued on his way while Mr. Weatherly walked back to his daughter with an irked expression. He gestured to an empty room, a study, and she walked in and turned back to face him.

"Alice, this simply isn't done," her father stated irritably.

"What isn't done?" she challenged.

"You should not have left the ladies to come after us."

~~~

Upon exiting the dining room, Nigel excused himself and ducked into the library to collect his wits. In the last twenty-four hours, he'd thought himself put upon. But to realize that his *intended* had no idea that she was the prize to tempt him? Why in Heaven's name had she not been told? No wonder she had been so relaxed. Earlier, he'd noticed her looking the salon over and it had occurred to him that she was probably deciding how she would redecorate once she got her hands on it.

Why did the situation suddenly feel so insulting? He began to pace, stopping short when he saw Alice go by in the hall. Before he had decided whether to follow her or not, Lakely also passed, moving furtively. Had she been a spy against the French, the war would have undoubtedly ended sooner. He trailed after her. Ahead, Alice went one way, toward their fathers, and Lakely went another, in the direction of the servant's hallway. He followed his sister who opened the door and slipped inside the passageway. By the time he reached the same doorway, he saw that she had quickened her pace to a near run. He did the same.

She glanced behind and saw it was him, but neither of them slackened.

She began peeking in doorways. The narrow, dimly lit hall they were in had been designed for discreet access and egress of the servants. Spying was wrong, absolutely wrong, but Nigel had a sudden, burning need to learn what he could. Lakely, now only a yard ahead of him, stopped abruptly. A line of light from the crack in the closed door marked her. He reached her and looked over her head and into the study where Alice and her father stood facing one another. Alice lifted her chin in what looked like defiance.

"Is this some matchmaking attempt between me and Nathaniel?" she demanded. "Oh, whatever his name is. Nigel."

Nigel's eyes widened at the insult. He was aware that his sister held her breath and drew her lips inward in an attempt not to laugh.

"We will discuss this later," her father replied in a low voice.

"It is, isn't it?" Alice insisted.

"I thought you would enjoy meeting him. All of them. Lakely and Ada are close to your ages, and Nigel Walston is amiable and impressive. Now, please, get back to the ladies before they're convinced you are just another American without the slightest notion of proper behavior. Do not embarrass me any further than you already have."

The slight must have robbed her of breath and her father took advantage of her speechlessness and quickly left the room. Alice huffed to herself.

Nigel and Lakely watched Alice's turmoil. "Well?" Lakely breathed as she drew back.

"Well what?" he whispered back, unable to tear his gaze away from Alice.

"Get in there," Lakely said, shoving him in the door.

He gasped and nearly stumbled, startling Miss Weatherly who stared at him with wide eyes and a slightly dropped jaw. He hastily shut the door behind him, wishing he could swat his sister's head the way they'd done as youngsters. "Hello," he said to Alice. "I beg your pardon for interrupting, if I am." He cleared his throat and fought an urge to smooth his jacket and hair. Fidgeting would make him appear even more guilty and awkward than he already did.

"Did you hear the exchange between me and my father?"

It would be absurd not to admit it. "I did. For which I apologize. I had no intention of eavesdropping, but I went the back way to join our fathers and came upon …you. It. That." Her coloring, he noticed, was rising even higher. "You needn't feel badly for having a snit fit," he said as he came further in. "I did when I learned of it."

She drew back. "I did not have a snit fit, sir! If and when I ever do have a *snit fit*, which I am relatively certain I have never done, on principal, but if I do and you conveniently happen to be in the vicinity of hearing it, you will know." She paused and lifted her chin. "What sort of man has a snit fit anyway?"

Obviously not an American man who was all swaggers and muscles. "It was a figure of speech," he retorted. "Suddenly I'm at fault here?"

"I did not say that, but it is a ridiculous figure of speech, if you'll pardon my saying so."

By damn, she was pretty when she was angry. "I beg your pardon for appearing ridiculous I must say that is the first time I've been accused of such. Especially in my own home by a guest—"

Her expression altered to one of profound regret. "I beg your pardon," she said. "That was unforgivable."

He studied her a moment. It was ridiculous to like her so soon, especially given the wild contrasts of her personality, but she was refreshingly direct and ingenuous. She said what she felt. He couldn't fob it off on being American, because he had known American ladies that were as restrained as any gently bred English lady. Even Jocelyn seemed utterly different than her sister. And to be fair, Alice had been taken unaware. "Let's not be too dramatic, Miss Weatherly. Unforgivable is a strong word."

She smiled wanly and looked down at her hands as she clutched them beneath her breasts. They were nice breasts, and it took an effort to keep his eyes off them.

"I feel as if we're playing blind man's bluff," she said, "and I'm the one blindfolded and fumbling pathetically."

He recalled his masquerade ball reference and relinquished the last of his touchiness. "I understand."

"I'm not sure that I do," she admitted. "I thought this evening was merely a visit to an old school chum of my father's. But it was meant to be more," she said haltingly, half statement and half question.

"Yes. It was meant to be an introduction."

"Between us?"

"Yes."

"But why?" she blurted.

He barked a laugh at the bluntness of the question. He felt heat creep into his face.

"Why me, I mean?" she clarified.

"Are you questioning your worth, Miss Weatherly?" he asked lightly.

"No. I'm confident in my worth, Mr. Walston. It's more our … suitability I question."

That stymied him.

"Not that we know one another," she added. "But—"

"There you are," Lakely said from the main hall door.

Nigel noticed she was a touch out of breath, likely from the mad dash she'd made after listening to most of their conversation. He glared at her to establish the blame she was due and would be hearing about later, but she only had eyes for Alice who had turned to her.

"I thought you might enjoy a breath of fresh air before we join the others again," Lakely said to her.

"Yes," Alice said. "I would." She turned back to Nigel and dropped into an elegant curtsy, avoiding his gaze. "Mr. Walston," she said demurely.

He bowed. "Miss Weatherly."

~~~

As Alice walked beside Lakely, she felt confused by the encounter with Nigel. Something had passed between them, but *what*? She felt blind as to what was right in front of her and off balance because of it. Lakely led the way into a withdrawing room and closed the door behind them before going to the far end of the room and opening French doors that led to a moonlit courtyard. Alice came closer, drawn by the fountain in the courtyard. The spraying water shone and splashed. Behind her, Lakely went and poured wine for them.

"To a new friend and a good Bordeaux," Lakely said as she handed one of the glasses to Alice.

"Thank you." She sipped. "It's delicious."

"I know. I always keep a bottle stashed away for just such occasions. Don't you get fed up with the watered-down varieties ladies get served? As if we can't be trusted to gage our own consumption." She paused. "So. You seemed inquisitive earlier."

Alice's spirit plummeted. "Did I make a ninny of myself?"

"No! Of course not."

"I thought this was going to be an uneventful dinner at the home of an acquaintance of my father's."

Lakely murmured sympathetically. "Does it feel a bit as if you're the main course at supper and our fathers are sharpening their carving knives?"

"Oh, my," Alice laughed.

"I say shocking things, I know. Most of the time, I do it on purpose."

"What would be the purpose now?"

"To make light of the situation, I suppose. Make it easier for you to ask what you really want to know."

Alice hesitated.

"Go on," Lakely urged. "I'll tell you whatever you want to know if I have knowledge of it. Which I probably do. As Ada would tell you if she was standing here, I am in incorrigible snoop."

"Does everyone expect a match to be made between your brother and myself?" Alice asked.

"Not expects so much as hopes."

Alice blinked. It was a surprising, but rather nice sentiment.

"Now that we've met you, I hope for it," Lakely continued. "I had thought having a sister-in-law would be a drudge and now I see what pure delight it could be. Of course, that all depends on the sister-in-law, doesn't it?"

"But why me?"

Lakely shrugged. "You fit the bill nicely."

"How so?"

"You're lovely, healthy and bright."

Me and a hundred others, Alice thought. "Would an English lady not suit better? One with perfect manners and knowledge of your society and a more restrained tongue?"

"Good God! I hope not."

Alice gave her an imploring look.

"As I said, you fit the bill quite nicely. Lovely, healthy, bright …and rich."

Rich? How odd to hear it stated as if it were fact. She had never thought of her family as rich. Her father was successful, and they had a nice home, but it was nothing like this one. Neither she nor her sisters had ever wanted for much, but their family was ordinary in their own society. "Your family is far richer. Truly, I never thought of my family as rich."

Lakely walked to the doors to look out on the night. "Appearances are not always what they seem."

Surely Lakely was not insinuating they were not rich. It would be absurd.

"May I share something in confidence?" Lakely asked, turning back to face her.

"Please."

"We have property, title …and debt," she finished in a whisper.

Alice thought about it. "Did Nigel cause the debt?" Would marrying her be punishment of some sort?

"No! My brother has an excellent head on his shoulders and control over his impulses. He's fairly wonderful all the way around; although please never mention I said so."

The idea that her dowry could satisfy the debt of the family who owned all this was incomprehensible. "I would have thought eligible young ladies would be standing in line for a chance to marry your brother. Ladies of noble lineage. Isn't that important here?"

"To be the daughter of a peer never hurts but, at the moment, an influx of capital is of paramount importance to my father. He is the one who has a passion for gambling and acquired the debt."

"I see," Alice said softly.

"While, to your father—"

Title. Alice suddenly saw it. This was about her acquiring a title, something he had always coveted. Tears sprang to her eyes, so she looked away before it was evident. The situation wasn't exactly a betrayal, except perhaps of her trust, but it did feel like a conspiracy with a fair amount of deception.

"Please, don't be sad, Alice. You and I will be friends even if you don't want anything to do with my brother."

Alice smiled and nodded. She dabbed the corner of an eye before turning back to her hostess. "I'm not sad. It was a surprise. That's all."

"We expected that you would know."

Alice shook her head.

"I want to help you with your research if you'll allow it."

"Of course, I will!"

"First, I will have to go in search of my brain and dust it off and make sure it still works. Now, let me think, when was the last time I used it?"

Alice laughed. "There is no question that it works."

"Let's go rejoin the others. They'll be wondering where we are."

"Thank you, Lakely," Alice said meaningfully.

"You should know the truth. We all should. I sincerely hope that you will consider getting to know Nigel. Don't allow this business between our fathers put you off before you've gotten to know him." Lakely gave a delicate shrug and shook her head. "After all, he has done nothing but try to live up to his responsibilities."

Alice felt goosebumps along her arms. Fortunately, Lakely didn't notice as she downed the last of her wine, set down her glass and started for the door. Alice set her glass down on the same table and followed still pondering the statement and wondering why it so bothered her.

~~~

The four younger ladies played whist while their mothers sat across the room conversing with surprising ease as if they were old friends. When Alice heard the men returning, she felt a surge of warmth in her face and silently cursed her tendency to blush. Nigel was the last to walk in.

"Mr. Walston," Jocelyn said as she set her cards down. "I've lost again. Do take my place."

The game was not even halfway over, but Lakely took the cue and quickly gathered up cards saying, "Better luck next time," with a gleam in her eye.

Alice looked up and met Nigel's gaze at what seemed the precise moment he glanced at her.

"Would you mind?" Nigel asked her.

"Not at all," she answered honestly.

Ada rose. "Why don't I show you around?" she offered Jocelyn.

"I'd like that," Jocelyn returned.

Lakely shuffled the deck as the girls left the room. "I think they're going to be good friends."

Alice tried to relax, but she had become aware of the width of Nigel's shoulders and the way his hair brushed against the starched neck of his shirt. He was handsome, wealthy and a future Lord something or the other while she was just an American without the slightest notion of proper behavior. Why would the two of them be matched? Even if Lord Merton had debt, how much could it matter to people who had all this? It made no sense.

"Do you play Euchre?" Lakely asked her.

Alice snapped back to attention. "I do."

"Good. We can play that with three."

Across the room, their parents shared some joviality and, once again, Nigel and Alice glanced at one another at the same moment.

"No cheating, Nigel," Lakely said as she began to deal.

"Remind me of the last time I cheated?" he asked dryly.

"Just because I haven't caught you yet, doesn't mean you are not cheating."

"Miss Weatherly," Nigel said. "Does that make sense, I ask you?"

Lakely looked at Alice. "He wins too frequently, so he must be cheating."

Nigel shook his head. "If you require sound logic," he said as he picked up his cards. "You'll want to seek someone other than my sister."

Alice was glad of the lighthearted teasing. Dinner had been spoiled for her, but there had been pleasant aspects to the evening. She liked Lakely and Ada very much and she certainly did not dislike Nigel Walston.

~~~

By the end of the evening, Nigel and Alice each felt uncharacteristically shy with the other. There was some reluctance and yet also a measure of relief to say goodnight; they had both become so self-conscious. Nigel watched the Weatherly carriage drive away while the rest of his family discreetly observed him.

"What do you think?" his father asked.

"I don't know," Nigel replied quietly. "Not what I was expecting." He turned and went back inside without looking at anyone.

Lord and Lady Merton followed, which left Ada and Lakely peering out at the starry night. "Not what he was expecting," Ada mused. "Does that mean Alice was not what he was expecting, or the evening was not what he had been expecting?"

"Or both," Lakely said. "Perhaps a certain feeling within himself was not what he was expecting." They looked at one another and grinned. "Maybe it will be just as it should be after all."

"How wonderful that would be," Ada marveled. "Fate seems so unfathomable, but perhaps it's surefooted. We simply don't recognize it until it has laid a path."

Lakely started back inside. "I think it's a bit soon for that."

Ada lingered a few moments more with a wistful smile on her face.

<u>*Chapter Six*</u>

*A*lice stared out her carriage window while her father, seated next to her, stared out his. No one had spoken since they left the Walston home, not for several blocks.

"I liked them very much," Jocelyn said to break the silence. Unfortunately, it only broke it for the time she gave words breath. "The tour Ada gave me was fascinating," she tried again. "There are a dozen bedrooms for family and guests and there is a ballroom."

"Everyone knew," Alice blurted. "Everyone knew that the idea of a match between Nigel Walston and myself had been bandied about. Everyone but me." She looked accusingly at her mother and then at her father. "Can you at least appreciate why I felt foolish?"

"If you had not commanded so much of the attention," her father began. "Talking of writing novels."

Alice's jaw dropped.

"That's not fair," Jocelyn objected.

"Stay out of it," Mr. Weatherly said to his youngest.

"I was answering their questions," Alice snapped. "That's the first thing. And I *am* writing a novel and proud of it! That is the second. You were not honest with me. Point number three. Why?" She looked at her mother. "And that is a question for both of you. Why was I left out of a discussion about *my* life? As if anyone other than me has a right to pick and choose whom I will consider as a suiter, much less a husband!"

"Besides which," Jocelyn offered. "How could she not command attention when she was under scrutiny? Which is understandable when you think someone may be joining your fam—"

"Jocelyn," her father barked.

"She is in this family," Alice cried. "She is my sister and I do not wish her to be silenced! Indeed, *she* was astute enough to recognize your sneakiness when I was too stupid and blind."

"I never said sneakiness," Jocelyn said with a rapid shake of her head.

"No, you did not," Alice agreed. "She did not."

Mr. and Mrs. Weatherly exchanged a look.

"Why didn't you say something?" Alice demanded.

"You are not being forced to do anything, Alice," her father stated coolly. "This is not an arranged marriage you've stumbled upon. If you never want to see Nigel Walston again," he paused and shrugged. "So be it."

"But you did discuss a marriage settlement with Lord Merton," she accused. "The discussion went that far. Correct?"

"If it did, it was just a discussion. One he initiated."

She huffed and looked back out the window. Had she completely overreacted to everything and everyone? Why did it suddenly feel as if she had blundered pathetically and made a fool of herself?

"Alice," her mother said.

Alice looked at her but didn't trust the strength of her voice.

"Lady Merton has been very gracious in offering to set up invitations to special events. The balls you and your sister have repeatedly mentioned? If you do not want to take part, let me know and I will make our apologies."

Now it felt as if they were mocking her, but Alice wasn't certain of anything, so she didn't reply. It was all she could do to hold back the childish tears that threatened. She looked back out the window and counted the gas lamps they passed. When they arrived back at home, she went straight upstairs to her room without a word.

~~~

Jocelyn lingered behind in the foyer. After a few minutes, she trailed after her parents who had gone into the drawing room. She glanced in and saw that the rest of the family had retired for the night, so she walked on. If battle lines had been drawn, and she hoped that was not the case, but if they had, she had to be aligned with her sister. She had never used the word sneakiness in regard to their behavior; it was a most distasteful word, but nor had her parents been forthright.

Then again, if her parents had been perfectly candid …

Jocelyn stopped at the base of the stairs and considered the thought that had just occurred to her. There had been countless opportunities for her parents to have discussed the correspondence between men, but if they had, Alice might have resented and resisted it. At the very least, she would have gone into this evening guarded if not downright apprehensive. Instead, she had gone there as her inimitable self.

Jocelyn started up the steps. Alice had taken the entire Walston family by surprise. She had taken them by storm *because* she'd been able to be herself. It was a point Jocelyn needed to make to her sister, although now probably wasn't the time. She reached the second floor and looked left to the closed door of their room.

"Hello," Jeremy said, causing her to jump. She looked the other direction to find Jeremy perched in the window seat at the far end of the hall, his dark form silhouetted by the moonlit sky. "Hello," she returned. He stood and so she started toward him with a tentative step.

"There's a full moon," he said. His hands were clutched together, and he swayed side to side in a slight manner. "Luna."

She stopped a few yards in front of him. "It's beautiful, isn't it?"

"The insane get flogged."

Jocelyn blinked. "I beg your pardon?"

"To keep the madness down. They are chained and flogged."

She grimaced at the thought. Was it true? "That is horrible."

55

"Luna. Lunatic. No one really goes mad."

"No," she agreed. "But the belief remains, doesn't it? People going mad and howling at the full moon. Oh, and werewolves taking form." She was unsure what else to say. She and Jeremy hadn't exchanged a dozen words before now. "I always just think how beautiful it is."

"Do …you want to see?"

"The moon?"

He shook his head and moved past her to an archway that housed the staircase to the third floor. He started up.

She hesitated a moment and then followed. At the base of the stairs, she blinked in surprise at the effusion of light from the wall-mounted sconces. Because of the design of the tin candleholders, light was either directed upwards or downwards in pretty patterns. At the top of the staircase, she drew in a breath of surprise. She had imagined a cramped space with a bed and a table full of art supplies. Instead, a neatly made bed, a table holding a bowl and ewer, and a wardrobe were the only furnishings that bespoke of a bed chamber. The rest of the room was an elegantly appointed artist's studio.

There were dormer windows along the front wall and a round window at the far end. Floor lamps and mirrors stationed here and there provided additional light. "This is lovely,"

Her eye was drawn to two finished paintings on easels. Another easel was turned to face a tall stool next to a table with painting implements. Jocelyn moved closer, lured by the image in the first painting, a gentleman extending his hand before a waiting carriage while a lady inside the conveyance leaned forward to peer out. The focus was on the woman inside the carriage, but also the mystery of the man and his upturned hand. A small brass plate at the base of the frame was etched with the words, '*The invitation*.' The painting fascinated her. Who was the lady and what was she thinking? Who was the gentleman? "Jeremy," she breathed. "I had no idea. You are a master!"

The other painting was an unframed bucolic image featuring a boy of ten or so with a length of rope in his hands. He stood, his legs slightly apart, staring out as if lost in thought. In the background was a cottage with an open door where a woman stood watching the boy warily. Jocelyn cocked her head as she studied their expressions to discern what they were feeling. She turned to her cousin. "These are brilliant! They are as good as any I've ever seen." Jeremy was looking at the floor but smiling. His smile gave her heart a lift.

A glass-front cupboard had shelves of stoppered cruets of oils and neatly stored jars, each with a smear of color on each front. There were stone mortar and pestle sets and bowls of various sizes. On another table were containers of paint brushes and knives, and a linin cloth with pieces of chalk. There was white chalk, black chalk and red chalk, as well as charcoal. It was all neat and orderly and fascinating. Clearly, painting was not a mere diversion for him; it was a passion that he excelled at. "To think we have been living under the same roof with an artistic genius. I can hardly wait for Alice to see it. Oh, I do hope you will show her. She will love it as much as I do. You know that she writes stories."

He nodded.

"She creates stories with words while you create them with images," she said looking back at the paintings.

Jeremy moved to the third easel and turned it so she could see the work in progress. Her breath caught to see her own image as well as that of Alice. The painting showed them standing close together as if they had been sharing a secret before looking at the viewer. She was facing forward while Alice's body was in profile with her head slightly inclined. It was fully sketched, the painting on it just begun. Their faces were flesh-tone and her hair had layers of gold and brown. "It's wonderful! That you have done this in so short a time is ... well, it is astonishing. All of this comes from your mind? No one posing?"

He shook his head. "No."

"You captured the color of my hair."

"Mummies," he said.

"I beg your pardon?"

He went and selected a jar and handed it to her. The label said Egyptian Brown. "Made from mummies. Crushed."

Her jaw dropped. "No!"

He nodded.

"You're saying the brown paint is from ...it's made of crushed up mummies? From Egypt?"

He nodded again.

She swallowed and handed it back. The thought made her queasy. "Oh, my." She looked at the painting again. Not only had he managed to capture their likeness, he had captured their closeness, their utter trust in one another. "I don't suppose I could watch you work sometime?"

He ducked his head. "I won't see you."

"No, I know," she said. "You lose yourself in it, don't you?"

"Lose myself. I lose myself," he repeated as if enjoying the words.

"Alice does it, too, when she's writing. I can be in the same room with her, and, after a fashion, she'll be oblivious to it because she is seeing whatever she's writing about. It's as if she's there."

"Lost in it."

"Yes." Jocelyn looked at the sketch again. "Thank you for showing me. It is remarkable." She glanced around the room. "All of it."

"Cousin. We're cousins."

"Yes, we are. And I hope we'll be good friends, as well."

He looked uncertain but nodded.

"Goodnight, cousin," Jocelyn said. She started from the room.

"Goodnight. Cousin," he echoed when she was midway downstairs.

She felt a wave of compassion and sadness for him that made tears rush to her eyes. Alice was in bed and turned onto her side facing the window when Jocelyn slipped into the room. She readied herself for bed in silence and then walked around and blew out her candle before getting under the covers. She knew Alice was not sleeping. There was ample light to make out the tension in her sister's posture. "Are you all right?" she asked tenderly.

Alice turned over to face her. "Did I make a fool of myself?"

Jocelyn frowned in confusion. "Of course, you didn't. When?"

Alice blinked in surprise. "At dinner. And after."

"Honestly, I thought it went well. Everything considered."

"What does that mean? Everything considered?"

"Only that it became evident that there had been some discussion about a match between you and Nigel."

"Yes. It became evident between bites of fish. I don't think a fillet of sole will ever taste quite the same."

Jocelyn grinned.

"But what about when I left the dining room?"

Jocelyn shrugged. "I thought nature had called. You asked to be excused. And then Lakely left right after. I assumed to make certain you found where to go."

Alice shook her head. "No. I went to speak to Papa."

"You did?"

Alice nodded. "I needed to understand what was happening. I saw the men walking ahead and followed them. Well, not Nigel. I don't know where he'd disappeared to. But I caught up enough to call for Papa who then came back to speak to me, although he was displeased about it. We went into an empty room where he scolded me for behaving like an American who would not know a good manner if it walked up and bit me on the ankle."

"He said that?"

"I'm paraphrasing. And right after he left again, Nigel suddenly appeared and we had words."

Jocelyn's eyes widened. "You had words with Nigel?"

"He took me by surprise. He'd overheard part of my conversation with Papa, if it can be called a conversation," she added with a roll of her eyes.

"In this conversation, if it can be called that, with Papa, had you said something bad about Nigel?"

"No," Alice replied sheepishly.

"Well, what did you say to Nigel? And what did he say?"

"I don't remember what I said exactly. But then Nigel said something about me throwing a *snit fit*. That did not go over well and I—"

"You what?" Jocelyn asked when Alice stopped speaking.

"In a nutshell, I was rude. He reacted to it, and I apologized. He was gracious about it, kind even, and then Lakely came for me. She and I left and had a talk. It was she who told me the truth of things, that Lord Merton has acquired debt, I assume a large debt, from gambling," she added in a hushed voice. "And Papa offered a substantial bride price for me."

"Did he?" Jocelyn looked thoughtful. "He's enamored by the title, isn't he?"

"It has to be that." Alice replied sadly.

"Also, they live in a palace of sorts," Jocelyn said. "I suppose it's not their only house either. But *bride price,*" Jocelyn said with a comical frown. "What a terrible expression. It's very off-putting."

"It's a terrible concept," Alice agreed. "You need a bride? Here, take my offspring. By God, I'll pay you to take her off my hands."

Jocelyn chuckled. "But think of it, Ali," she said with a waggle of her brows. "You would be a baroness one day."

"All I've ever wanted," Alice rejoined dryly.

"Tease as you will. You do like him. I knew the moment he came back from their smoke."

"I do not dislike him," Alice hedged.

"He does not *dislike* you either. So, tonight was a success, all things considered."

"Success," Alice fretted. "I'm not sure what that's supposed to mean."

"It means we had a nice time and met some new friends. That alone makes it a success. And now invitations to parties and balls and other fancy dinners will begin for us." She paused. "Good gracious, you don't have to marry him, but you do like him well enough, so let's enjoy everything that unfolds. Because of Lady Merton, we will be presented at Almack's, whatever that means, and we'll have fittings at the most in-demand modistes that we couldn't get into before."

Alice groaned. "I hate fittings. I can feel my hair growing as I stand there. I can feel the blood running through my legs."

"That is your over-active mind at work, and you know it. The important thing is we'll get beautiful new things."

"We have enough things. Don't you see? A life of fittings and formalities and titles is not for me. I'd rather wear sackcloth and be left alone to write."

"Sackcloth," Jocelyn repeated. She sighed and collapsed on her back dramatically. "I give up." She looked at her sister with a look of defeat. "It *has* occurred to you that we're in London at the beginning of the season?"

Alice fluttered her eyes. "We are?"

"Yes, we are. The only one we'll probably ever have. Oh, by the way, Jeremy is an artistic genius. He showed me his paintings."

"He did?"

"Yes. He is working on a painting of us. He has an *amazing* talent."

"When was this?"

"Tonight. When we got home. I just left him. You will not believe your eyes. His work is worthy of being in a museum of art."

Alice huffed softly in surprise.

"We had a nice talk. I mean … for Jeremy. And the attic is a wonder."

"That is not what I pictured," Alice remarked.

"Nor I. The picture of us is fully sketched and he's started to paint it. He captured the colors of my hair perfectly. Oh, and guess what? The brown paint he used for it comes from crushed up mummies. It's called Egyptian brown. Isn't that a revolting thought?"

"Yes, it is."

"Well, goodnight."

"Does the paint smell?"

Jocelyn made a face. "I didn't smell it, for goodness sake. I don't want to think about it."

"I will have to smell it," Alice said.

Jocelyn groaned and turned onto her side, ready for sleep.

Alice leaned over and kissed her cheek. "What would I ever do without you?"

"We'll probably never know. If you marry Nigel, I am coming along. There is plenty of room in Larkspur House and Ada and I would have such fun."

"Getting ahead of yourself, aren't you? All I said is that I did not dislike him."

"*Mm-hmm.* Goodnight."

~~~

Three a.m. Alice suspected it was the witching hour and it was confirmed as she listened to the mantle clock's tinny dings. She'd slept earlier, but now she was wide awake. She got out of bed, went for her journal and left the room, silently shutting the door behind her. In the upstairs parlour, she pulled the door to and turned on a lamp. Writing was a release, although it fueled her mind rather than calmed it.

She sat at the desk wondering what was bothering her. Was it that her parents had been secretive or was it that she instinctually liked Nigel and resented it? Lakely's comment about Nigel living up to his responsibilities bothered her. She did not want to be a mere solution to a financial difficulty, and she didn't want a match arranged for her, either. The nerve of her father thinking that he could. It was the sort of behavior she was used to from her mother, not him.

Alice leaned back with a frown, but the memory of Nigel grinning over his cards softened her ire. She rose again and paced around the room. Yes, she liked him, but she would not be manipulated and that was that. She alone would choose the man she loved when she loved him, and if that was not by the fateful day she turned twenty-two, so be it. Her mother had strong-armed a pledge from her that she should not have, nor should she have agreed to it.

She sat on the settee wondering about the bride price offered for her. She could not recall a single conversation about their dowries over the years. Had one been paid for Clara? For Sophia? Had the other young men who had asked for her hand the last few years expected one or been offered one? The concept of a dowry was distasteful. If anything, a man should pay to acquire a bride.

She curled up, wondering what Nigel had thought of her. Did he find the sight of her different colored eyes bothersome? Would he consider that any child she bore might inherit the defect? How odd had he found her? She had realized long ago that many people found her unusual. She was interested in all sorts of things a lady should not be and not at all interested in most things a lady ought to care about. She did not want to stitch samplers or to play the pianoforte or paint china. She wanted to write stories and research what she did not know and read about things that had happened and were happening, even morbid things. Especially morbid things. She wanted to know what crushed up mummy paint smelled like.

The reality was that she could not choose to have a normal mind any more than she could choose to have one-color eyes.

Chapter Seven

The next morning, Mrs. Weatherly bustled into the dining room where Alice and Jocelyn were finishing breakfast, having slept later than usual. "Here you are."

"Good morning, Mama," Jocelyn said. "Did you sleep well?"

"Well enough," her mother replied as she stopped at the table, "except I dreamed the boys were here running around playing some game. I was upset because I couldn't remember having brought them with us. I kept trying to remember if I'd told Clara we were bringing them. I knew how fearful and livid she would be if I had not. I said so to both of you and then Alice gave me this strange, scathing look and informed me that the family was all here. Then I began worrying about where we were all going to sleep. Even once I woke, I kept trying to figure out where we could all sleep in this house."

Jocelyn chuckled and even Alice gave in to a smile, but she avoided her mother's gaze.

Eliza pulled back a chair and sat. "So," she said to Alice. "You have had an opportunity to sleep on the *revelations* of yesterday," she said almost tongue in cheek. "What do you think? And before you answer, just let me just say that as far as I'm concerned, we can pass a quiet few months seeing the sights and visiting our family. There are public balls we can attend and the theatre and so on." She paused. "If we affiliate with the Walstons, there will be private balls and events and more of them. But these things are not of importance to me or your father. It is up to you."

"Jaus and I would like to affiliate with the Walstons," Alice replied evenly. "We enjoyed the company of Lakely and Ada."

"And she did not dislike Nigel," Jocelyn added.

Alice was sorely tempted to state again that she did not appreciate the secrecy her parents had employed, but she refrained. She noticed her mother did not look particularly pleased as she nodded and rose. "Are you disappointed?" Alice asked curiously.

"Darling, I'm neither glad nor disappointed. This is a pleasure trip. It should be pleasant and, if you wish, busy and eventful. As I said, it is your choice. I never expected you would form an attachment to Nigel Walston. The notion was something your father got into his head. I tried to tell him."

Ah-ha! "You thought I would rebel against the notion," Alice accused.

"You did rebel against the notion. I think I know my own daughters."

"And I imagine you thought that a certain American gentleman might suddenly fare better in my estimation?"

"Alice, I do not wish to argue. Do you?"

Alice took a moment to reply. "No."

"Good. You girls could help copy recipes. Mrs. Halley has shared hers."

"Ooh," Jocelyn said. "Her bread pudding?"

"Yes, and a hundred others. Granny and Julia and I are going through them."

"I'll help when I finish breakfast," Jocelyn said.

"I have to get back to writing," Alice said.

"Of course, you do," Mrs. Weatherly said, and she turned and left.

Alice and Jocelyn exchanged a look. Jocelyn shrugged and Alice rolled her eyes in disgust. "Do I look like a puppet to you?" she asked quietly.

"You know she can't help herself."

Alice leaned back with a stubborn frown.

~~~

"Ali, it arrived!" Jocelyn exulted an hour later as she practically danced into the upstairs parlour where Alice was working. "The invitation arrived!" She read it aloud. "The Buckley Ball. Your company is requested for an evening of entertainment at Steadfield Manor on Saturday, the 29th inst. nine o'clock." She looked at Alice. "What does inst. mean?"

"It means instant. As in this month. Instead of saying April."

"May I keep this? Mama says I can if you agree."

"That's fine. If I can have the next."

"Agreed," Jocelyn said happily. She left the room with a light step. "We're invited!" she cried happily.

Alice smiled. Admittedly, it was exciting.

Chapter Eight

There were many advantages to being affiliated with the Walstons, but no one in the Weatherly household was certain that Miss Robina Rathke, whom Lady Merton had referred in order to tutor the girls in social graces, was one of them. It felt one part insulting to three parts amusing or perhaps the other way around. On a Thursday afternoon, they sat across from Miss Rathke at the table in the parlour with paper and pen at the ready should the need arise to take notes.

Miss Rathke was middle-aged, unsmiling and thin. Her body was thin, her face was thin and her tightly bound dark hair looked thin. She spoke slowly and looked back and forth between Alice and Jocelyn with one thin hand laid atop the other on the table. The girls' mother, aunt and grandmother were also in the room, each occupied, Julia reading, old Mrs. Weatherly netting, and Mrs. Eliza Weatherly embroidering curly pink lips on one of the rag dolls she was making for her granddaughters. Miss Rathke paid them no mind. She had her assignment, and she took it seriously. After all, should the girls go forth and blunder from this day on, it might reflect badly on her. One never knew about Americans.

Miss Rathke had begun the tutorial asking questions about their upbringing. Once she was satisfied that they were not complete philistines, she began a reminder of the most basic concepts taught to every girl by the age of eight. These rules formed the groundwork from which they could sally forth and perhaps reach great heights.

She held up a single thin finger. "A young lady must never be alone with a gentleman." She stuck a second finger in the air. "Unmarried ladies must be chaperoned when in public." A third finger went up. "A young lady should listen a great deal." At this bit of wisdom, she gestured toward her ear before gesticulating from her lips outward. "And speak sparingly."

"What if we are asked a question?" Alice asked ingeniously, having decided she might as well have a little fun with the session. After all, it would be two hours out of her day that could have been spent writing.

"Naturally, you answer, my dear, but temper your reply. Do not speak at length or with alacrity. Softly stated and inoffensive should be your objective at all times."

"Ah," Alice replied. "That will be a change, at least for me."

Miss Rathke gave a regal nod, as if acknowledging the almost incalculable value of her advice. By this point, Alice and Jocelyn were painfully cognizant of the necessity of not looking at one other. If they did, they would dissolve in unladylike hilarity.

Miss Rathke had them curtsy for her, which she found acceptable. She examined their calling cards and found them satisfactory. "Always leave a card on a visit, but an unmarried lady never leaves a card for a gentleman."

The girls nodded politely.

"A lady should not make a morning call before eleven. Most morning calls are reserved for close acquaintances. As for afternoon calls, accept tea and refreshments when offered. Partake slowly and with unimpeachable manners." She paused before adding, "I feel certain it goes without saying that one's utensil should never scrape one's plate," she said with a curl to her lip. "Nor should you ask for seconds."

"Not even if it's delicious?" Alice asked.

"No, Miss Weatherly. If they offer, then it is fine. But pray, do not ask."

Alice bent to write the note on a paper, which seemed to please Miss Rathke.

At the appointed time, Fisher brought a tea service, per the protocol they had been given for the session. Once served, Alice had a strong urge to slurp her tea just once but resisted. A doltish question here and there made the time pass faster, especially knowing how Jocelyn was struggling not to react, but slurping was going too far. Still, there was something about being thought a bumpkin that made her want to act the part.

Miss Rathke enjoyed the petite sandwiches and used the break to make inquiries of her charges as well as throw out nuggets of knowledge. "You know never to reach for a dish during a dinner party."

"Yes, Miss Rathke," Jocelyn replied.

"Indeed," Alice added, timing her response to Miss Rathke selection of another sandwich. "It is the same in our ... society." Miss Rathke had not seen Alice mouth the word *barbaric* in the sentence, but Jocelyn had, which made it nearly impossible to hold in a titter of amusement. However, a lady never snickered, guffawed or spit. Surely, these instructions were about to be made. Elsewise, how would they know?

The lesson continued. They should not leave the house without a bonnet or hat during daytime hours, but a bonnet or hat should not ever be worn to a ball. "Some decorative headdress, feathers and such are fine for evening affairs," the lady stated, adding that if they had questions of taste about a specific piece, she would be happy to see it and opine on its appropriateness.

"But not one feather straight up on the head," Alice said sweetly. "Correct? At least not for us. Someone might think we adopted the style from the Indians that surround us at home."

At this, their mother looked up sharply, Julia pulled in both lips and trembled in an effort not to laugh while poor Jocelyn could only hold her breath and dig one thumbnail into the opposite palm in the same effort.

Miss Rathke took no notice of any of these reactions as she pondered the question. She blinked once, twice, and then drew breath. "There should be no concern there, Miss Weatherly. Feathers are the fashion. Almack's often requires them and will even specify the number you are to wear. I understand you are to be presented there?"

"We understand the same, Miss Rathke," Alice replied.

"Then I shall tell you about the patronesses."

That lecture, one Miss Rathke had obviously made countless times, took at least fifteen minutes, during which Alice helped herself to seconds and offered the plate to Jocelyn, who did the same. That was followed by a lecture on how one addressed each member of the peerage. Alice, at this point in time, was making up a poem in her head.

Your Grace, my Lord and My Lady and such. A kiss to their ring is the proper most touch. It is all very silly, at least, to us. Dear Lords and ladies and Dukes and such.

Miss Rathke finally concluded the lesson with a staunch warning to adhere to the proper times to shop, ride and so on. "I have it all written out," she said sliding a brochure onto the table.

"Thank you, Miss Rathke," Jocelyn said.

"Yes, thank you," Alice echoed. "This has been vastly helpful."

"I do hope so. You are charming girls."

"Thank you," the girls said in unison.

"I shall take my leave now."

It was Jocelyn who showed Miss Rathke to the door. Alice sat back down with her back to her elders and doodled on her paper, suddenly apprehensive about the scolding she would soon receive from her mother. Admittedly justifiable, yes, but what a ridiculous and insulting waste of nearly two hours!

When Jocelyn returned, holding herself stiffly and ardently avoiding her sister's gaze, her elders' reaction began with laughter from Granny. The sound of it was shocking enough that everyone looked at her before being swept into the madness. Tears were running down old Mrs. Weatherly's face and she was doubled over, as far as she could slapping the side of her chair. The mirth had only just gotten under control when Granny fumbled for a handkerchief to wipe her face and blow her nose.

"Oh, Eliza," she said. "Why did you never tell us you were surrounded by Indians?"

This renewed the laughter.

"How will we ever keep a straight face when we see a lady wearing a single feather?" Jocelyn asked.

"Bloody hell, if I haven't gone and wet myself," Granny remarked, which started the laughter yet again.

~~~

"How was the tutoring today, girls?" Mr. Weatherly asked at dinner. He was adding peas to his plate, so he did not notice the grins all around, even from Jeremy who had been let it on the experience.

"It was not terribly instructive," Jocelyn replied.

Alice agreed. "We already knew not to pick up peas with a knife."

Mr. Weatherly noticed the amused expressions of everyone. "Ah. Somewhat insulting in the content?"

"You could say that," Alice replied.

"I do wonder," his wife said. "How base do they fear we are?"

"I don't think they fear that," Mr. Weatherly rejoined. "Not at all. It wouldn't surprise me if their own daughters hadn't been schooled by the lady."

"I seriously doubt that," Alice said as she selected a piece of ham from the platter.

"I doubt it, too," Julia agreed. "Or if they did, it was when the girls still had their milk teeth."

Alice grinned. "Even then, Lakely would have made a debate of it."

"Pass the potatoes, sweetheart," Granny said to Jeremy. "A lady can't reach, you know."

"By the way," Julia said, "Alice and Jaus, I found something for each of you." She held up two feathers from her lap. Everyone laughed except for Mr. Weatherly who looked at them as if they had all gone a bit mad.

Friday, April 28   𝔞𝔚𝔢

Morning: *9:00 Fitting with Madame Neveah*
Afternoon: *Rework second chapter*
Evening: *7:00 Family dinner at Rules*

This morning seemed intolerably long. Although I detest fittings, I will admit that the dressmaker's operation was fascinatingly well run and the experience was better than usual. Madame Neveah is clearly an astute lady of business with a half-dozen helpers each of who stayed busy, measuring, recording or sewing. The large shop had thick carpets, velvet upholstered chairs, gilded full length mirrors and perfumed air.

Dinner this evening was truly special. The family went out to a restaurant called Rules, which has been in business for more than twenty years. The food and service were excellent. Jeremy went with us. Granny and Aunt Julia seldom have an evening out, but it is almost unheard of for him. Jaus and I were so glad. He tasted our food and we tasted his, which amused him greatly. It is what we do and have always done, but he is an only child, plus isolated in his uniqueness.

Ever since Mama's dream about the boys being here, our family in Boston has been on my mind. I miss them, but this is our family, too, Granny, Aunt Julia and Jeremy. I will miss them dreadfully when we go back, but how could I live away from my parents, elder sisters and the children?

I couldn't.

The Buckley Ball

Your company is requested for an evening of entertainment

Steadfield Manor

Saturday, the 29th inst. nine o'clock.

-Sir Horatio Buckley

Chapter Nine

The Weatherly carriage was admitted into the line of vehicles steadily approaching Steadfield Manor for The Buckley Ball. Jocelyn peered out Alice's window trembling with anticipation. Since they were seated three on one side, Alice could feel it. Julia, on Jocelyn's other side, was nearly as thrilled as they were. Their parents sat across from them. "How many times do you think you'll dance tonight, Aunt Julia?" Alice asked.

"I expect gentlemen will line up for their chance," Julia replied. "Five. Ten. Who can say? I only hope I don't wear holes in my shoes."

Jocelyn reached over and squeezed her aunt's hand. This was their first ball and would be the least formal they would attend, or so they had been told, but Steadfield Manor was splendid, light-colored stone with white stucco and a many-pillared portico. Clearly the ball was not being judged by the magnificence of the home.

It had been explained by her father that Sir Horatio Buckley had distinguished himself in the war with the French and consequently been made a baronet, which was not to be confused with a baron. He was not a peer. That led to an explanation of the peerage and who ranked where and what they were called and what their wives were called and what their children were called and who inherited what. Good gracious! As if any of it were important. And yet the way her father's eyes lit up when he spoke of it!

The carriage rounded the bend in the curving driveway and a footman opened the door and saw to the stairs. Alice was helped out first. As she waited for the others, she observed the throng of guests going inside and those standing about in clustered groups conversing on the spacious veranda.

Jocelyn joined her, her eyes sparkling with wonder. "Don't you feel like Cinderella?"

Alice smiled as she unbuttoned her spencer jacket.

"I do," Jocelyn added.

"You also look the part," Alice said. Jocelyn's gown was pale gold with a layer of fine net over the skirt that was a shade lighter and lent it dimension. With her golden dress, flushed cheeks and shining eyes, she looked lovely.

"So do you," Jocelyn returned.

"Two Cinderellas," Alice mused. "That changes the story a bit." Now that she thought on it, it was fitting in a way. Not that they had ever dressed in rags or worked in servitude, but nor had they ever attended the balls of a London season dressed to the hilt. The evening did have an enchanted quality to it. When the entire family had alighted from the carriage, the girls put their jackets back inside and went toward the house passing other carriages whose occupants were descending. Jocelyn kept her gaze in front of her, but Alice could not help noticing the looks of curiosity from guests they passed. She heard, "who are they?" more than once.

The foyer was crowded and so the level of sound and warmth rose substantially. They made slow progress making their way through. Midway through the large room, Alice sensed something to her left and looked through a clearing of people at Nigel as he looked over at her. Both smiled and nodded to the other. As she looked away, she felt heat in her face. How strange! She'd felt his presence as if some invisible string drawn between them had been twanged.

Jocelyn touched her arm. "Lakely."

Indeed, Lakely was nearly to them wearing an emerald green gown a cut above anything they possessed. It was gorgeous. Their gowns, while pretty, were simple by comparison. Hers had a pale blue bodice with a white skirt. Silver embroidery at the bottom of the skirt was the only embellishment.

"We'll be inside," their mother said as they continued on.

"There you are," Lakely said when she reached them. "You look fresh as daisies."

Hopefully, they did not look as provincial as daisies, but in comparison to *that* gown?

"Hello," Ada said as she came up behind her sister. "We've been watching for you."

"It took some time to get in," Alice explained.

"It is always crowded," Lakely said. "Why don't we introduce you to Nigel's friends before we go inside?"

"They are like brothers to us," Ada added. Her gown was the color of a ripe peach with short, puffy sleeves. "Nigel has known them since they were boys. They went to school together. Well, JG didn't go to Harrow, but he's not even here this evening. Do you want to hear about the rest of them?"

Alice and Jocelyn both nodded. "Yes," Jocelyn replied without hesitation.

"Joel and Jonathan are twins and very handsome. And very nice. Hugh is the one with spectacles and he is thoughtful as the day is long. And then there is Dab, who is more handsome than is good for him or anyone." She paused before adding, "He's rather a lost soul, really."

Lakely gave her a wry look. "That's a tad melodramatic, wouldn't you say?"

"No," Ada replied sincerely.

"You both look so lovely and sophisticated," Alice remarked.

"This is from last year," Lakely replied in a bored tone. "I couldn't get away with it at other events—"

"And our mother was less than pleased that she wore it tonight," Ada interjected.

Alice couldn't imagine not wearing a gown from the previous year. "Do either of you have your eye on a special gentleman?"

"I do not," Ada spoke up. "I suspect my sister does, but she refuses to admit it."

"She is right on both points," Lakely stated. "She does suspect that I do, and I do refuse to *admit* it, as she puts it."

"Ah-ha," Ada exclaimed. "Meaning that you do!"

"No, it does not mean that."

Ada rolled her eyes. "She talks in circles and riddles when it pleases her."

"I am not talking in circles or riddles. When you can provide no sound reasoning for a suspicion that—"

"Except that I know you," Ada interrupted.

Jocelyn murmured her support for the statement. "One does know her own sister. Nearly as well as we know ourselves."

"Yes," Ada agreed. "We do."

"Come on," Lakely said to Alice. "There is a ball in progress." She took hold of Alice's arm and led the group toward Nigel and two other men his age. The muscles in Alice's stomach tightened.

"Miss Weatherly," Nigel greeted when they reached them. "Miss Jocelyn." He bowed and they curtsied. "Delightful to see you. May I present my friends, Hugh Pritchett," Nigel said, indicating a fair-haired man with spectacles standing next to him. "And Joel Stewart," Nigel gestured to a dark-haired, light-eyed man with a mustache. Both men bowed their heads when introduced.

"Pleased to meet you," Jocelyn said, stammering in her nervousness.

"So," Nigel said swiftly. "Your first English ball."

Alice got the impression he had spoken up quickly to cover her sister's embarrassment and she felt a keen appreciation for it. "Yes."

"It will be an easy one," Joel Stewart said. "It's more like a country dance than a ball, really."

"Which I infinitely prefer," Hugh Pritchett said.

"You don't care for balls, Mr. Pritchett?" Jocelyn said, once again stammering in her nervousness. She could hardly be faulted. They were so handsome.

"I don't care for stuffy," Hugh replied, wrinkling his nose on the last word.

"Where are the others?" Lakely asked.

Joel glanced around. "Getting another drink probably."

"Joel has a twin named Jonathan," Lakely said as if it had not already been explained, "And Dabney Adams is the final member of their ferocious five."

Mr. Pritchett chuckled. "I've never heard us called that."

Nigel had a smile on his lips. "She has several names for us, and I assure you they are not all flattering."

Lakely smiled sweetly at Mr. Pritchett. "The ones for you are all flattering, Hugh."

"Thank you," he said dramatically.

Joel slapped a hand to his chest. "Lakely! I am wounded."

"I feel certain you will recover," she teasingly rejoined.

Joel's pale blue eyes were arresting, they were in such contrast to his dark hair.

"But shouldn't it be six something or other?" Hugh asked. "Mustn't leave JG out. It would hurt his feelings."

"I'll think of something," Lakely said.

"Here they are," Ada said as two other men walked up. The circle expanded to admit them, and Nigel and Alice were pushed closer, something she felt acutely aware of.

"Alice, Jocelyn," Lakely said, gesturing to them as she said their name, "Meet Jonathan, the twin," Lakely said.

"I adore being called that," Jonathan remarked drolly.

"It's all you've ever wanted to be in life," his twin teased. "Isn't it?"

"Indeed," Jonathan returned.

"And this is Dabney Adams," Lakely continued. "Whom, if I did not already warn you about, I will later."

Mr. Adams grunted. "I would object, but I can hardly disagree." He smiled at them. "A pleasure to meet you ladies."

"A pleasure to meet you," Alice replied, understanding what Ada had meant in saying he was too handsome for his own good. He was breathtaking.

"So, Miss Weatherly," Hugh said to Alice. "I understand you write prose."

"I do. Yes."

"A bluestocking, eh?" Dabney Adams asked.

Alice was unfamiliar with the term.

"A lady with a brain," Lakely explained. "A very frightening concept."

"Actually," Nigel said, "it was a society of ladies who were advocates of education and literature. It's not even around anymore. Now, we tend to call any lady who is intellectual a bluestocking."

"Ah," Alice replied. "I suppose I am," she said to Mr. Adams. "At least, I would like to think so. Although I am more creative than intellectual. But I love to read and research and write and learn."

"What exactly do you write?" Dab asked.

"Fiction, although my current project is as much non-fiction."

"How so?"

"It revolves around letters written during the revolutionary war."

"Fascinating," Hugh commented. "Actual letters?"

"Yes."

"How did you find them?" Jonathan asked.

"Perhaps she can explain another time," Lakely said to him before turning to Alice. "Shall we go in?"

Lakely led her away. It had been eleven days since Alice had last seen Nigel. Had she realized how considerate he was? Not to mention fine looking. Her heart was beating at a rate sufficient to make her breathless. "They are very nice," she said as calmly as she could manage.

"They are," Lakely agreed. "Of course, you have to get to know them to really know that. Especially Dab."

~~~

"If you decide you don't want her," Dab said to Nigel.

Nigel gave him a look. "Thank you for *not* finishing that utterance."

Dab chuckled.

Hugh nodded at Nigel. "She's special."

79

"She is," Nigel conceded. What he didn't know was whether she thought the same of him.

Hugh clapped Nigel's shoulder and the five filed toward a ballroom teeming with color and movement. Inside, an orchestra played a lively tune while a crowd of dancers stepped to a quadrille, and onlookers talked and laughed loudly enough to be heard over all of it.

~~~

"I stuttered like a moron," Jocelyn agonized as she and Alice waited for Ada and Lakely to return from the refreshment table with libation.

"You did not," Alice returned.

"I did. And the way Nigel spoke up to cover it? I like him, Alice. I really like him."

"So do I."

Lakely handed Alice a glass of punch. Ada handed one to Jocelyn, and Lakely stuck her glass in the air. "To a memorable evening."

The girls toasted, drank and shifted to watch the dancers on the floor. Jocelyn's earlier embarrassment seemed forgotten in the moment. Alice found herself watching for Nigel. She could hardly believe she was, but she was. She attempted discretion, but she was looking for him. Her breath caught when she noticed him headed toward them, and then she noticed a beautiful lady also spot him.

The lady had auburn hair. She wore a white gown with pewter-gray trimmings. A small, sparkling tiara looked perfect in her hair. Corkscrew curls spilled over one shoulder. The cut of her gown displayed pale shoulders. Time seemed to slow as Alice focused on the lady closing her fan. The tip of it went to her chin a moment before she reached out and touched Nigel's arm. He had passed by without noticing her, but he turned back. She smiled and said something.

"That is Therese St. Clair," Lakely said.

Miss St. Clair and Nigel were conversing easily, and the interest Miss St. Clair felt was evident. "She is exquisite," Alice remarked.

"I dare say she is," Lakely agreed. "Her uncle is an earl, but he has sons to inherit so it doesn't benefit her other than the connection." She sipped her punch. "She is unfailingly pleasant. Very gently bred."

"Is she in love with your brother?"

Lakely pressed the backs of her gloved fingers to her lips and grinned. "You say rather shocking things, too. Only you don't mean to, do you?"

Alice was puzzled. "Why is that shocking?"

"Because my brother is *your* suitor. Or he will be if you'll have him."

It was far too soon for such a statement. Ridiculously too soon. "What I meant was, before I arrived, before anyone knew of me, were the two of them likely to—"

Lakely shrugged in a non-committal way. "It's possible."

Alice looked away. Was she actually experiencing a fluttering of jealousy? How preposterous! She had only just met Nigel Walston. Still, she could not help herself looking back over. Not that it mattered. Other people had gotten between them. So. Therese St. Clair. The niece of an earl. She looked wealthy. Beautiful and wealthy. Surely, her dowry would have sufficed. That union would have made sense.

When Nigel joined them a few minutes later, he seemed unflustered. Alice wished she felt as composed as he appeared.

"May I have the honor of the next dance, Miss Weatherly?" he asked.

If he had any pangs of guilt or regret where Miss St. Clair was involved, she did not see it in his face. "Certainly, Mr. Walston. I'd like that."

"Shall we make our way toward the floor?"

He extended his arm and she accepted it. Had she done it slowly or was her mind going into molasses mode again?

~~~

Therese St. Clair watched Nigel and the fair-haired stranger walking toward the dancefloor with a feeling of unease. Nigel had been as polite as ever, but not as attentive.

"Who is she, I wonder," Miss Diana Fletcher said. "I've never seen her before."

"Nor have I," Susan Moorcroft, the third member of their group concurred. "A friend of his sister's perhaps."

Miss Fletcher was attractive with brown hair. Miss Moorcroft was petite, fair, and of average looks. Miss Moorcroft's breath caught to see Dabney Adams coming their way. "Dabney Adams approaches," she announced.

"Mr. Adams," Diana Fletcher called when he was a yard away.

He smiled a polite if somewhat strained smile and walked over to join them followed by his friend Hugh Pritchett. "Good evening," Dab greeted.

"Hello," Hugh echoed. "You ladies look lovely this evening."

"Thank you," Therese replied, lowering her gaze modestly.

"Yes, thank you," Miss Moorcraft said. She looked from him to Mr. Adams with an adoring expression.

"And you both," Miss Fletcher spoke up, "look debonair," she commented with a seductive movement of one shoulder.

Miss Moorcraft tried to commit Diana's gesture to memory in order to practice when she got home.

"Kind of you to say," Hugh replied.

"It's true," Miss Fletcher rejoined. "It's rather a wonder we all dress so finely for such a rustic affair, don't you think? Although I notice not everyone is wearing something new. I feel certain I saw Miss Walston in that gown last year."

Hugh's expression remained unperturbed. "That is not the sort of thing a man notices. Oh, the gown perhaps and how a lady looks in it. But this year's fashion as compared to last?" He shook his head. "No. We have no idea and no care for it either way."

"I am certain that's true," Therese St. Clair said sending Diana a sideways look to encourage silence on the matter. These were Nigel's close friends, which meant they would have loyalty toward his sisters.

Miss Moorcraft caught the look. "Oh, look," she said to change the subject. She nodded toward Lady Gosforth, a portly lady of sixty standing next to a slight young woman of seventeen or eighteen. The girl wore white with a pink ribbon around the waist. "Lady Gosforth is here with her ward. The girl looks very sweet and young, don't you think?" she asked, wanting to say something pleasant.

"She's not a ward," Therese St. Clair said. "The Gosforths are sponsoring her for the season. My understanding is that she is the daughter of a close acquaintance."

Miss Fletcher raised her brows. "*Hmm.* I wonder. Is it out of generosity or merely the appearance of it?"

Hugh and Dab exchanged a look. "If you will excuse us," Dab said. "We should rejoin our party."

"May we ask," Miss Fletcher spoke up to stop them. "Speaking of Miss Walston—"

"Were we?" Dab asked with a curious expression. "Speaking of Miss Walston?"

"Of course, we were. In last year's gown? But that's not the point. We were wondering who she was just standing next to. The lady now dancing with Mr. Walston?"

"That is Miss Weatherly," Hugh replied. "Alice Weatherly. Her younger sister, Miss Jocelyn Weatherly, is standing with the Miss Walstons now. They are from the United States."

"America," Miss Fletcher said with derision. "No wonder we haven't seen her before."

Hugh gave a brief nod. "Mr. Weatherly went to school with Lord Merton."

"Ah," Therese St. Clair said with a smile. "They are old friends then, I suppose." She paused before asking, "Have they been in London long?"

"Not very," Hugh replied.

"Have you met her?" Miss Moorcraft asked.

"Yes. This evening. She is delightful. Intelligent and clever."

"Really?" Miss Fletcher said drolly. "An American? It makes me wonder how many responses she has prepared. Is she truly clever or is every reply planned for, studied and practiced?"

"Excuse us," Dab said pointedly.

"Oh, don't go," Miss Fletcher inveigled. "I promise to curb my tongue and be less wicked."

"Wicked," Dab repeated. "Is it true wickedness, Miss Fletcher?" he asked coolly. "Or merely an excellent impression?"

Hugh nearly choked on the sip he'd just taken. Dab flashed a smile at the others, murmured, "Ladies," and walked away.

"Touché," Hugh said under his breath as they walked away. "And bravo."

Dab shook his head with disgust. "I could come up with a few different words than wicked."

"Yes, but this is a nice, rustic affair, so do mind your language," Hugh jested.

~~~

"Lord Merton."

Lord Merton turned to the man who had spoken, a twenty-three-year-old with rather long fair hair and a finely featured face. "Mr. Bower. How nice to see you," he said despite the fact that he was the one who had gotten the young man included in this evening's festivities.

"And you, sir," Harrison Bower returned. "May we speak privately?"

"Of course." Lord Merton led the way to a secluded alcove of the room and looked at the man expectantly.

"I look forward to meeting Miss Walston," Mr. Bower said meaningfully.

"So, you could agree to the terms of a possible engagement?" Lord Merton returned quietly.

"I find the sum you mentioned rather exorbitant, but I will agree to it should things progress that far."

Lord Merton nodded. "I was going to have my son make the introduction, but he's occupied at the moment, so let's go find her." Harrison Bower nodded agreeably, and Lord Merton made his way to where he had last seen Lakely. He could see no reason she would object to the match. She did not have her cap set for anyone and Harrison Bower was a handsome fellow from a well-heeled banking family. He had an income of seven thousand a year and would one day inherit a tidy sum and property. "There she is," he said when he spotted her.

Harrison Bower had only admired Miss Walston from afar, but her beauty stayed with a man. Haunted him.

"Hello ladies," Lord Merton greeted when he reached Lakely, Ada and Jocelyn.

"Hello, Papa," Ada said. Her curious gaze flicked to Mr. Bower.

Lakely's gaze went directly to Mr. Bower. When she looked back at her father, her expression was suspicious if not downright accusing.

"May I present Mr. Harrison Bower of the Bower-Vasey Bank of London?" Lord Merton said without missing a beat or any sign of recognition as to Lakely's reaction.

Mr. Bower bowed. "Ladies."

"Mr. Bower," they murmured.

"This is my eldest daughter, Lakely, and my youngest, Ada, and this is Miss Jocelyn Weatherly from America. Miss Jocelyn's sister, Alice, is on the floor with my son at the moment."

"A great pleasure to meet you all," Mr. Bower said. "Speaking of dances," he added, looking to Lakely. "May I have the honor? The set has just begun."

"Certainly," she replied coolly before turning and walking toward the dance floor.

Mr. Bower bowed his head to Ada and Jocelyn and then followed. Ada's gaze snapped to her father's, hers full of wary inquiry.

"Your mother and I will be leaving soon," he said. "I'll send the carriage back for you. Enjoy yourselves." He turned and walked away, leaving Ada to stare in his wake.

"I believe he's up to it again," Ada said confidentially. "And Lakely will not like it one little bit." She looked out to the dance floor. "Mr. Bower is fetching though, isn't he?"

Jocelyn murmured her agreement. She could think of nothing further to add, but she was distracted anyway by a man stepping too closely by, a man in his mid-twenties with reddish-blonde hair and a friendly face. "Ladies," he said. "Hello!"

"JG," Ada replied cheerfully. "I didn't think you were able to make it this evening."

"I snuck out of the Sarasin affair," he admitted. "I knew this would be more fun. You're all here."

"May I present Miss Jocelyn Weatherly from America?" Ada introduced.

"Ah! You're her," he returned enthusiastically. "The heiress from America."

"JG," Ada objected. "No! That's her sister Alice who is on the dance floor with Nigel."

"Oh!"

"And we are not heiresses," Jocelyn added with a shake of her head.

"I beg your pardon. Was that offensive?" he asked with a look of genuine remorse. "If I could go but one day and not put my foot in my mouth ... I would probably wonder why my jaw felt so free."

Jocelyn laughed. "I am not offended, but we are not heiresses."

"Jocelyn," Ada said, "This is John George Baillie. He will be a duke one day."

"I am the presumptive heir," JG said comically. "Although my grandfather does not plan on going anywhere near the pearly gates until he can be assured that they serve excellent port and quality cigars there."

Jocelyn laughed again. He had quite a personality.

"He has another title now," Ada said. "He is the marquess of Blairwood,"

He nodded. "So, you may hear me called Blairwood. In that event, please do not feel I've misrepresented myself."

"I would not think so," Jocelyn assured him. "I must admit, though, I find the array of titles and ranks confusing."

"So do I," JG exclaimed.

She laughed again.

"Think of nobility as a ladder of sorts," he explained. "A duke is the top rung, but he's likely garnered other titles on the way up the ladder. In which case, his son or sons or, in my case, grandson, is given the title or titles under his. While he lives, I mean to say."

Jocelyn nodded. "That helps. Thank you."

"You're welcome."

"What are you going on about?" Hugh asked JG playfully as he joined their group. Dab was right behind him.

"I was explaining the peerage," JG said.

"Ah," Dab said. He looked at Jocelyn. "JG here is the top ranking amongst us by far. The rest of us are lowly SOB's ... sons of barons," he finished with his head lowered deferentially, although the smirk on his face refuted the veneration. "At least, that's what we always called ourselves. Joel is a full-fledged baron since his father passed."

"In formal introductions," Ada said to Jocelyn, "Barons are referred as The Honorable." She directed the last of it to Dab with a sly look.

"Ada," he exclaimed. "Tell me you are not insinuating that I am less than honorable?"

"No. Never, Dab! No matter what rumors we hear. I always say, 'Excuse me, but we have long known the man, and Dabney Adams is ... honorable."

"Thank you, dear Ada. It is gratifying to know that I have supporters."

Nigel and Alice rejoined the group flushed and slightly breathless from the dance. "JG," Nigel greeted. "We didn't think you'd make it tonight."

"This is so much more fun than the other," JG returned. "I'm already having a marvelous time."

Nigel turned to Alice. "This is our friend JG." He paused. "Lord Blairwood."

JG bowed. "It is a great pleasure to meet you, Miss Weatherly."

"And you Lord Blairwood."

"JG, please," he replied. He noticed the color of her eyes and leaned in closer. "What fabulous eyes you have. Two different colors! Like a pale sapphire and a pale emerald." He whirled around to Jocelyn and studied her eyes.

She shook her head. "Boring brown."

"With an amber center," he mused. "Not boring at all."

She blushed and dropped her gaze.

"Shall we get some refreshments?" Nigel asked Alice.

"Yes," Alice replied. "Please."

"What a splendid couple they make," JG remarked when the pair had walked away. "Why it was just days ago—"

"JG," Dab interrupted.

"That they met," JG rejoined. "I was only going to say that they met." He looked at Jocelyn with a sad expression. "It's that foot-in-mouth trait again. Even if I'm not doing it, people assume I am about to."

Jocelyn smiled. JG was considerably different than the others, but she liked him. He was vastly entertaining.

Jonathon joined the circle. "This place is too crowded," he complained. "Even worse than last year."

"I agree," Dab replied. "Shall we make our way to the card room?"

"Yes," Jonathan exclaimed.

"Where is Joel?"

"First, he was snagged by Lady Lynn and her brood, and then Uncle Harold got hold of him. I also noticed Miss Fletcher weaving a web to get to him. As polite as he is, he'll be trapped for at least a half hour."

"No worry for you on that account, eh, Jonathan?" JG spoke up.

"Politely enduring company I loathe? No. I caught one glimpse of my uncle and headed the other way. He means well, I suppose, but he is full of opinions on everything. Most of them wrong. And I would have dropped to my belly and slithered away before I let Miss Fletcher get a hook into me." He looked at Jocelyn. "My advice is to avoid her. She is a devious sort."

Jocelyn had no idea who he was talking about.

"Have any of you danced this evening?" Ada asked. "You know you should before you go."

"The dancefloor is ludicrously crammed," Jonathan complained. "They are packed in elbow to elbow. If they want us to heed social dictates, they should invite less people."

"Who is Lakely with?" Hugh asked curiously as he noticed her making her way toward them followed by a fair-haired man. She looked peeved.

"Mr. Bower," Ada replied. "Of the banking Bower's. Father just introduced us."

"She looks none too happy about it," Hugh said.

When Lakely stopped next to JG, she was outwardly calm, but inwardly seething. "Where is Nigel?"

"They're getting refreshments," Ada replied.

Lakely walked away at once.

"And hello to you, too, Lakely," JG said under his breath.

"Ada," Hugh said. "Before we head off to play cards, would you care to dance?"

Ada smiled. "I would, Hugh. Thank you."

He offered his arm. "Now, I may have to have this back," he teased before mockingly jabbing with both elbows. "To make some room on the dance floor."

"That's fine. I don't mind a little violence if it means more space to dance."

The pair walked on.

"Miss Jocelyn?" JG spoke up. "Would you care to dance?"

"Thank you, I would."

As they walked off, Dab look around. "Where's a tray of drinks when you need them?" he muttered to Jonathan. "Let's go."

"I am right behind you."

~~~

Lakely was fit to be tied, although few would have had the nerve to try it. In the wee hours of the morning, Ada watched her sister pace the length of the salon, ranting with every step about the gall of men who believed they could choose each and every path a female could and would take.

"As if I would allow our father or any man to choose for me!"

After the ball, Ada had returned home with Nigel, who had wisely gone directly upstairs to bed. It was well past two in the morning, and she was tired enough to slump over and fall dead asleep, but she'd made the miscalculation of checking on her sister. Lakely had left the gala the very moment the carriage returned in order to have it out with her father; only she had arrived home to discover he had gone to his club. Frustrated, she'd opened a bottle of wine and consumed glass after glass, determined to wait up for her father. Once she finished the bottle, she started on his prize port, and still he did not return.

"I have to go to bed," Ada said as she rose. "I am done in. Goodnight."

"He's probably not even coming home tonight," Lakely raged.

"Probably not," Ada agreed as she started from the room, carrying her shoes. "You should go to bed, too." She kept walking because she could not make her sister do anything. No one could. It had been foolish for Lakely to have left the gala. It had been extraordinary, and she'd had a completely, magnificently wonderful time. She smiled and bit on her bottom lip as she made her way up the stairs.

~~~

At the same moment, Alice and Jocelyn lay in bed giddily recounting every impression of the evening. "I am so tired," Jocelyn said, "but I don't know that I will be able to sleep. My mind is all awhirl."

"Like mine when I wake in the wee hours of the morning and start writing in my head and can't stop."

"Yes. I imagine like that."

Alice turned on her side with a sleepy smile on her face. "Sorry to leave you all awhirl, but I'm going to sleep now. Night-night."

"Night," Jocelyn returned as she stared at a dancing squiggle of light on the ceiling. It existed because of the placement and proximity of everything in between her and the moon. Maybe it meant nothing at all, but maybe it meant everything. Or was she tipsy? *Because of the moon and the trees and the wind that stirred the leaves.* She smiled at the rhyme she'd concocted.

Jocelyn had always imagined marrying a man like Clara's husband, Ross. Roscoe Linfield had created his own success. He had gone to work at fourteen to help support his family and now he was part owner of a large brick manufacturer. As a youth, despite working a grueling day, he had continued to study and improve his mind when he could. Ross had a pleasing look but was not particularly handsome. He adored Clara, and he was a wonderful father to their two young sons and baby girl. Clara and Ross's union had an abundance of affection and friendship that she wanted in her own one day.

Sophia's husband, Paul Timmons, was handsome. He was an attorney with a thriving practice. He was a pleasure to have at any get-together, and Jocelyn sincerely liked him, but that marriage was capricious. Sophia and Paul seemed madly in love one day, but angry the next. They were outwardly affectionate on one occasion but would barely look at one another the next. The dynamics seemed exhausting. They had a three-year-old daughter, Lola, and were expecting their second child. They both adored little Lola and Jocelyn had no doubt they would love the baby, as well, but they did not seem to enjoy her as Clara and Ross enjoyed their children.

Never in a thousand years would a man like JG have come to Jocelyn's mind when she thought of potential suitors, but she liked him so well. He had been attentive, considerate and he'd made her feel special. With a contented sigh, she curled up on her side and closed her eyes to sleep. "It was such a good night," was her final whisper.

Chapter Ten

S eated in the morning room, frowning over a letter that had arrived that morning, Lady Merton looked up as her husband walked in with a grim look on his face and a letter in his hand. "What's wrong?" she asked warily.

"On my breakfast tray this morning," he began, "was my usual fare, the paper and *this*." He handed it to her.

"And you need to read this," she said, handing hers over. Lydia glanced at the signature of the letter writer before reading the contents. When finished, she looked at her husband, as perplexed as he was.

"They won't be up for hours," he said. "They came in about two."

She looked curious. "When did you get back in?"

"Oh, I never left. I only said so to avoid Lakely's inevitable tirade. For someone as inexplicable as she is, she can be quite predictable."

"I agree with inexplicable. I might go so far as to say incomprehensible." She sighed. "Well. I have calls to make and Lady Putnam's garden party to attend."

"Let's get on with our day then and leave the message that we will have a mandatory family meeting at tea."

She nodded in agreement. He handed back the letter she had given him and left. Lydia looked from one letter to the other and shook her head. She was flummoxed. It was as if their plan had disintegrated only to be reformed into a butterfly that now fluttered enticingly. Of course, it might still fly away leaving an odd stench in its wake.

~~~

JG walked into the dining room to find his grandfather glowering at the paper. "Good morning, Granddad." His grandfather merely grunted, his typical reaction when absorbed in the paper. JG filled a plate from the selections on the sideboard. Rich muffins with slabs of butter, slices of fatback, and apple compote. He sat and poured himself a cup of tea. "Anything interesting?" he asked before taking a bite.

His grandfather made a sound of disgust. "Damned rantings of Hobhouse," he scoffed. He brought the paper closer to read aloud. "'He was astonished that any man of common sense and common knowledge could suppose for a moment that the bill would be treated with anything like impartiality in the House of Lords. He did not mean that the Peers were *worse* than common men, but he did maintain that they *were not better*—'" He slammed down the paper with a look of repugnance. "Not better!"

JG refrained from comment. His grandfather was of another era. The old guard. The king was God-ordained, and peers were superior among men. Absurd or not, and it was, no one would ever convince him otherwise.

"It will be you in the House of Lords one day soon," his grandfather said warningly. "You ought to be going more. Sit in the gallery. Observe. Listen. Learn."

JG nodded obligingly to mollify his grandfather. It worked as usual, and the old man went back to scowling at the newspaper. "I received an invitation from Lady Toomey," JG said. "Apparently, select couples will be dancing a waltz at her ball, a performance of sorts, and there's to be an audition for it." He paused, but his grandfather did not respond. "It's unusual, I know. But I thought I might try."

"Tea," Lord Morguston barked. As the butler snapped to attention and refilled his cup, he studied his grandson. "What did you think of Runyon's niece?"

That she was plain and dull with an overbite. "I thought she was nice."

"I noticed you disappeared early," Lord Morguston said.

"There was another ball."

"Which ball? Not Buckley."

"Yes. Buckley. I had a very nice time."

"A good time with your *friends,*" the old man said despairingly.

JG set his cup down and pointedly looked at his grandfather. He did not appreciate the tone or the insinuation. "That's right."

"Buckley is a baronet," Lord Morguston snapped. "You should be spending your time with your equals."

The comment was not worthy of response and JG was determined not to lose his composure. Anytime he went up against his grandfather, he did not fare well.

"In the next few years, you will take a wife, JG. The *right* wife who can produce an heir or hopefully two or three of them. Life is not a party. You will be at the helm of our empire—"

JG could have groaned.

"It will happen before you know it. You will wonder where the time went. So, we will throw a soiree soon. Invite Runyon and his niece."

"I am not interested in Runyon's niece."

Lord Morguston's eyes narrowed. "After so little consideration? Why is that? Is there someone else?"

"There does not have to be someone else to know I am not interested in her."

"I asked if there is someone else," his grandfather stated suspiciously. "You are turning red, JG. You have never been difficult to read."

"All right, since you mention it, I have met someone and enjoyed her company very much."

"Who?"

"It's no one you know. She's from America."

His grandfather gaped.

"Her name is Miss Jocelyn Weatherly, and she is lovely in every way. Nigel is courting her elder sister."

Lord Morguston harrumphed. "Oh, I see. An American with money, no doubt. I could tell you what that is about if you do not already know. Merton is a fool and he has gotten in hock, that's what. Shameful, that's what it is. Shameful!"

"Perhaps he has," JG replied levelly, "I couldn't say. I can tell you this much, Both the Miss Weatherlys are beautiful, intelligent and—"

"Enough! None of that business has anything to do with us. Look in a mirror, JG. You will be the eleventh Duke of Morguston. This family has three centuries of noble blood. You will not be the one to end that." He pushed back in his chair and rose. "You will join me in the House of Lords today and you will start living up to the legacy."

JG sat motionless as his grandfather left the room with a limp. Apparently, his gout had flared.

Good!

~~~

At four o'clock in the afternoon, Lakely sailed into the parlour looking formidable, but only her brother and sister were in attendance. Tea had been set out with a tray of delicate sandwiches and squares of cake. Her siblings were both partaking and took no notice of her. She walked over and sat carefully. She had consumed too much wine last night and had needed until the afternoon to recover. Under normal circumstances, she would have filled a plate and fixed her tea, but she needed her full focus on what was to come.

The fact that her parents thought that their offspring could be married off to benefit themselves was enraging. It was just shy of a miracle that Nigel's proposed match had turned out to be Alice, but even if Alice had not been captivating, marrying was far less of a sacrifice for a man than a woman. A married man could get about town and do as he pleased while the woman was stuck at home raising children and representing her husband. She was

subject to her husband's whims and moods and rights. *Rights.*
The word infuriated her.

"Are you not having tea?" Nigel asked her.

Before she could reply, her father walked in, and her mother
followed a moment later. The two of them did not sit. Lakely
squeezed the arms of her chair waiting for her father to begin.
She fully expected him to look at her and say, 'I know this is not
what you want to hear, but it is time you did your duty for your
family.' Just let him get those words out! She was ready. She was
trembling, she was so ready.

Instead, her father looked at Nigel. "Did you enjoy yourself
last night?" he asked conversationally.

"I did," Nigel replied lightly although he looked suspicious.

"I'm glad to hear it. And you?" he asked Ada.

Oh, I see, Lakely thought. *We're going around to each of us,
are we?*

"Oh, I did," Ada said with a bright smile. "I had a marvelous
time."

Lakely chewed on the tip of her tongue. It was her turn next.
Here it came.

"Ada," her mother spoke up sharply. "Did you dance with Mr.
Bower?"

"Yes, Mamma," Ada replied sweetly.

"Three times?" her mother asked angrily. "Or was it four?"

Lakely looked at her sister with surprise.

Ada looked down and picked at an invisible thread on her
skirt. "Was it that many?"

"According to the note I received from Lady Filmore," her
mother continued, "who *lives* to gossip, it was at least three times
and possibly more." The sentence ended in a virtual shriek. Lady
Merton drew in a long breath, exhaled and then looked away to
compose herself.

"The music was so lively," Ada explained. "And he was a
good dancer. The place was crowded so I—"

"Where were you?" Lord Merton interrupted, directing it to Lakely. "She is your younger sister. You could have stopped her from blundering."

Ada gasped. "Blundering," she exclaimed.

Lakely lifted her chin. "I came home to find you. I suspected you were pushing Mr. Bower at me, very likely for your own financial gain, and I wanted the truth of it. At least you warned Nigel before thrusting Alice in his face."

"As a matter of fact," her father replied coolly, "Mr. Bower voiced a desire to meet you. He approached me, presented his credentials and asked for an invitation."

She scoffed. "How many zeros did his credentials have?"

"You will watch that tone with me," Lord Merton warned.

"I will not be pawned off!"

"You needn't worry," he retorted scathingly. "Mr. Bower has no further interest after meeting you."

It was a staggering statement. For a moment, she couldn't move. The room had grown uncomfortably silent.

Lord Merton looked at his youngest daughter. "He now asks to court you."

Everyone looked at Ada.

"I like him very much," she said.

Lady Merton shook her head. "You know you cannot dance with the same man three different times in one evening," she scolded. "Now everyone believes you are engaged."

Lakely made a sound of disgust. "It is eighteen twenty, Mamma. That is such backwards thinking."

"No, it is not!"

"Lady Filmore has nothing better to do than stir up rumors," Lakely added. "And *this* is what has you up in arms?"

"I don't even know who Lady Filmore is," Nigel commented.

"But you have just turned eighteen," Lakely said to her sister. "You cannot possibly know what or whom you want yet."

"I can," Ada rejoined tenderly. "I am not you. I am no firebrand. I like Mr. Bower immensely. We spoke at length and we laughed and … yes, we danced. I am not saying I will marry him, but I'm pleased he wants to court me. I, too, wish it."

Her father nodded. "I will give my consent."

Ada smiled. "Thank you, Papa."

Lakely shook her head and exchanged a look with Nigel.

"Is there some financial compensation should they marry?" Nigel asked warily.

"Yes. A quite generous one," Lord Merton replied.

Ada blinked. "Are you saying he will pay to … marry me?"

Lakely drew breath to object. It was bad enough her younger sister was consenting to be courted after just meeting the man. But marriage? But her father had gone on.

"Yes. And you will have a handsome income of your own."

"What of my dowry?" Ada asked in confusion.

"There will be none," he said in a low voice. "I realize that is unusual. Naturally, this is all confidential."

Lakely was flabbergasted that he could be so naïve. Everyone would either know or suppose. In the *ton*? There was scarcely one of them that did not live to gossip and denigrate.

"He'll pay to marry me," Ada marveled happily.

"Should it come to that," Lakely snapped, giving her sister a look of both warning and alarm.

Lady Merton came and sat by her youngest. "There will be no pressure exerted for you to marry Mr. Bower," she said. "However, should it occur, it will benefit the family greatly."

Ada nodded. "I understand."

"Wait a minute," Nigel objected.

Lakely's fists were clenched in her lap. Had she been holding a teacup, it might well have shattered.

"Would Papa's debt be satisfied?" Ada asked.

"That is not your concern," Lakely said to Ada.

Lady Merton glared at her eldest daughter. "And you certainly will not make it your concern, will you?"

"This is not right," Nigel interjected. "This burden should not be put on my sisters."

"No, it should not," his mother agreed.

"No, it should not," his father echoed. "But this young man was not recruited. He came to me."

Lakely bit her tongue in order not to say, *Ah, but you negotiated for the most advantageous deal, did you not?*

"For God's sake," Nigel complained, "Ada is eighteen!"

"Nigel," Ada said soothingly. "It's fine." She turned to Lakely. "It is what I want. I do not feel forced in the least."

"Promise me you will take it slowly," Lakely pleaded. "Do not make any assurances to him or anyone until you are absolutely certain what you want."

"I promise." Ada looked to her father. "Papa, may we be candid for a moment?"

"What is it?" he asked tenderly.

"Is there a date when the debt must be cleared?"

He took a moment to reply. "For the most part, they are debts of honor. But a few of them are due by the first of the year at the outside."

"I see."

Lakely looked at her father with reproof, but he refused to meet her gaze.

"If you'll excuse me," he said before leaving the room.

Lady Merton reached over, squeezed Ada's hand and then followed him out.

As Nigel and Lakely sat frozen, Ada helped herself to more tea. "I think I'll have another sandwich," she said cheerfully. Her siblings both looked at her. "What? They're delicious." She dropped sugar cubes into her tea. "Nigel, will you write and invite Mr. Bower to dine with us on Tuesday? The Weatherlys are coming again, and it will be a perfect setting for our first family dinner."

Lakely and Nigel exchanged another astonished look.

"*Um,*" he uttered. "All right."

Monday, May 1

Morning: 10:00 Riding in the park
Afternoon: Work on Martha's story. Better dialogue!
Evening:

I felt happy and content the entire day. Happy and content are different things, but I felt them both all day.

We rode in the morning. It was perfect weather and the park was crowded. My horse was an older mare named Calliope and she was a delight. I will ride her again. Nigel has arranged for us to ride their horses whenever we wish. He asked to read some of my work. I did not commit, but I may bring it to dinner tomorrow. It depends on how courageous I'm feeling. I wonder if he realizes, if anyone truly realizes, how terribly personal one's writing is. My stories are an extension of myself.

This afternoon, I wrote while it rained. We had dinner at home and played games. It was my favorite sort of day.

Chapter Eleven

O n Tuesday evening, it occurred to Jocelyn that the salon of Larkspur House and its occupants would have made an interesting painting. Parents sat at a card table at the far end of the room, while Alice and Nigel sat at a table for two in the corner perusing her work and talking. Jocelyn, Ada and Mr. Bower were enjoying a game of *vight et un,* while Lakely, who'd been unusually quiet, worked on a puzzle, having declined to join the game.

Jocelyn found herself wondering what Jeremy would have caught in each person's expressions that belied their inner thoughts. The painting of a less introspective artist would have shown the privileged class at their various pursuits, but Jeremy would have captured far more. The flushed excitement in Ada's face and the keen attentiveness in Mr. Bower's. A growing awareness and responsiveness between Nigel and Alice. And what would be in the faces of their parents? Jocelyn wasn't certain what any of them felt.

"Jocelyn?" Mr. Bower asked since he was the dealer of this round.

Her cards, a three, a six and an ace equaled twenty. "I stand," she replied.

"Ada?" he asked.

She considered a moment. "I also stand."

"As do I," he said. "All right. Show them."

Ada turned hers over. They tallied seventeen.

"Eighteen," Mr. Bower said of his own tally.

"Twenty!" Ada said when she saw Jocelyn's cards. "You win."

"You should have taken another," Mr. Bower said to Ada.

"I was afraid to go over." She got a devilish grin on her face. "What would it have been?"

He waggled his fingers as he slowly reached for a card. He turned the top card over revealing a four of hearts, and they all laughed.

"I would have won," she agonized playfully.

"And the pot is so rich, too," Mr. Bower teased.

Lakely glanced over at them, but her expression was unreadable. Hers would have been the most interesting expression if Jeremy had painted them. A maid circled the room with refills of port for the men and a mild elderberry wine for the ladies. Lakely, when the maid got to her, said she would have port. The maid hesitated a moment, but then went for another glass. Lady Merton looked at her daughter with disapproval, but Lakely did not acknowledge it if she saw.

"I see," Nigel said to Alice. "You typically begin with a letter and then follow up with whatever the letter writer is doing."

"In this version. Yes. Although it may be better to begin with story and then go to a letter."

"So, it's not precisely fiction," he mused.

"The letters are not, but the rest of it is. That's why I get permission if family members are still living. I'm basing the fictionalized account on facts, as far as I can discern them, but that only goes so far. Eventually, there is no choice but to take over each story. Become each person. I'm also going to add a completely fictionalized section."

"And you've organized it by names. Horace and Catherine, James and Martha, John and Abagail—"

"Adams," she said. "The former president and first lady."

"Ah."

"Their letters are magnificent."

"How did you come by them?"

"The Historical Society. The letters were turned over when she passed on a few years ago. You can spend the whole day perusing them and even copying them. I'll show you."

As Alice turned the material she'd brought back toward her and went through it, the maid brought Lakely a glass of port, and the card games continued. Alice found what she was looking for and showed him. "This is a facsimile of an actual letter written by Abagail Adams, misspellings and cross-outs and all. I even attempted to copy her penmanship."

He looked over it.

"And this is the translation, which is easier to read." He leaned closer and craned his neck to see. "I tried to keep the translation as faithful and literal as I could, but also to condense and occasionally even correct. My plan is to explain that at the beginning of the book and then add a copy of the actual letters at the end."

"What a lot of work you've put into it," he marveled. "It is very impressive."

"Thank you. It hasn't seemed like work, exactly, because I enjoy it. It may take another year or ten years to complete. I only know I want it to be perfect in the end."

"I'm sure it will be."

She smiled at the avid interest in his expression and then picked up another letter. "This one is also from Abagail Adams," she said. "Written November twenty seventh of 1775. Shall I read the translation?"

"Please."

"You can see the copy of her actual letter on this page."

He leaned forward to read along.

"*'Tis a fortnight since I wrote you a line,'*" she began reading at a moderate pace so that he could follow the authentically copied letter. "'*during which, I have been confined with the jaundice, rheumatism and a most violent cold. I yesterday took a puke which has relieved me, and I feel much better today.*'"

"Oh my," he said with a self-conscious grin.

"*'Many people who have had the dysentery are now afflicted both with the jaundice and rheumatism. Some it has left in Hecticks, some in dropsies.*'"

His grin had vanished as he concentrated on the words.

104

"'*The great and incessant rains we have had this fall, the like cannot be recollected, may have occasioned some of the present disorders. We have lately had a week of very cold weather, as cold as January, and a flight of snow, which I hope will purify the air of some of the noxious vapours. It has spoiled many hundreds of Bushels of Apples, which were designed for cider, and which the great rains had prevented people from making up.*'"

He looked at her with awe. "I can imagine it," he said.

She nodded. "She paints a very clear picture."

"Of such a difficult time," he said. "People so sick that there's a stench in the air bad enough to cause apples to rot." He grimaced.

She nodded again, understanding the reaction. "John and Abigail Adams had the most remarkable friendship. They call one another 'friend' all the time. My dearest friend. And it's not just words. You feel the bond it in their correspondence. They were partners. True partners. He sees her ...they *both* saw her as his equal." She recalled something and flipped through pages until she found what she was seeking. "This is her advice on what should be included in the constitution for the country, which was being created at the time."

He leaned closer to see what she was reading.

"It's from March of 1776. She says, *'Remember the Ladies, and be more generous and favourable to them than your ancestors. Do not put such unlimited power into the hands of the husbands. Remember all men would be tyrants if they could.*'"

He let out a breathy laugh.

"*'If particular care and attention is not paid to the ladies, we are determined to foment a rebellion, and will not hold ourselves bound by any laws in which we have no voice or representation.*'"

She looked at him to find him grinning at her. Her hand slipped back and came to rest against his, but she withdrew it, suddenly aware that they were the center of attention, although it was a discreet examination.

He reached for his glass of port. "I think Mrs. Adams would have made an excellent vice president for her husband."

She picked up her glass. "Or *he* would have made an excellent vice president for her," she teased.

He laughed and they touched glasses before sipping. "Jocelyn," he said, looking over at their table. "One day I would like to get your impression of your sister's mind."

"Happily," she agreed.

"I think I should be a party to that," Alice laughingly objected.

"Well?" Nigel said to Jocelyn with a playful smile. "Now is as good a time as ever."

Jocelyn turned her chair to face them. "All right. Since we're between hands."

"Plus we all want to hear it," Ada said.

Even Lakely shifted in her seat to see Jocelyn.

"My sister has the most unique mind of anyone I know," Jocelyn said. "It's both a blessing and a curse, I think."

"How is it a curse?" Alice asked.

"Well, this is the real world," Jocelyn said, gesturing around the room. "And sometimes you are not in it because you are in your world," she finished with a light tap to her temple.

"Ah," Alice replied. "That is true."

"I will say, her world is a magical one," Jocelyn continued. "I would have one, too, if I could."

"So would I," Lakely agreed.

"In a crowd," Jocelyn continued, warming to the subject, "if she is bored, she will imagine each person she sees in another time and place, each with their own story."

Lakely looked at Alice. "Would you please put me in another time and place and with my own story? I'm bored enough for both of us."

Nigel gave his sister a look.

"That is intriguing," Mr. Bower said. "It would be vastly interesting to be in your mind for a few moments, Miss Weatherly."

Nigel grinned. "I suspect it might not be for the faint of heart. Lots of intrigue and danger and adventure, I imagine."

"Indeed," Alice replied.

"Come play cards with us," Ada said to Nigel and Alice. "You too, Lakely. Six can play this game."

Lakely rose. "All right, but I plan on winning."

"You always *plan* on winning," Ada returned mischievously.

Nigel looked inquiringly at Alice, got a nod in return, and they rose to join the game. "Thank you for sharing that with me," he said quietly.

"You're welcome," she replied no less quietly and with no less interest in her gaze.

Chapter Twelve

O n a rainy afternoon, the Weatherly ladies sat around the table in the dining room where there was plenty of room for the tea service, Eliza's daily planner and a stack of invitations. They were choosing which events they would attend. Lady Merton had been instrumental in both acquiring the invitations and determining an agenda. She had gone so far, in fact, to star the 'must attends.' Granny reached for another scone.

"Mamma," Julia scolded light-heartedly. "Should you be having a third?"

"Why not? I'm too old to be watching my girlish figure." Granny waggled her brows at Alice and Jocelyn who were both tickled at her. The sound of pattering rain was pleasant, and the scent was fresh as it wafted through the room.

"Looking at the week of the twenty-second," Eliza said.

"Then the schedule is all set for the next two weeks?" Jocelyn asked.

"Yes. You are writing them in your books, too?"

"Yes," Alice replied.

"I should make sure I've gotten them all," Jocelyn admitted.

"You know I keep my daybook on the drawing room desk upstairs," their mother reminded Jocelyn. "Until Alice moves it. But so far she's put it back."

"Yes, I have and yes we know," Alice said. "And if there is an A beside it, I'm to write the acceptance or regret, and if there is J, you are," she said to her sister.

"I haven't had a blow to the head and forgotten everything I've ever learned," Jocelyn protested. "I only asked if the next two weeks are set."

"They are and they are exceedingly busy," her mother stated. "Now on the twenty-third, a Tuesday, there is a flower show in the afternoon at the same time as a lecture on the status of modern science."

"Flower show," Jocelyn replied quickly.

"Lecture," Alice said.

"That's what I thought you'd both say," Mrs. Weatherly replied.

"Flower show," Old Mrs. Weatherly said from behind her napkin as her mouth was not quite empty.

Jocelyn grinned. "Which do you prefer, Mama?"

"The flower show."

"I'll go the lecture," Julia offered.

Alice looked at her. "I wonder if Jeremy might like to go with us."

"We can ask."

Eliza said, "Your father may want to go, as well. Julia, if you would prefer to attend the flower show, I'll insist he accompany Alice to the lecture. I know you love flowers."

"I do, but flowers are flowers and I'm happy with our garden. I enjoy its sense of natural disorder."

"All right." Looking back at her book, Eliza said, "That night is the symphony. Oh, here is another conflict. On the evening of the twenty-fifth, it is either the theatre to see The Merry Wives of Windsor or a fashion gala featuring gowns by the House of Leroy. Some Frenchman."

Jocelyn looked at her sister. "Fashion," she appealed. "Please!"

Alice shrugged. "That's fine with me."

"Granny?" Jocelyn asked. "Aunt Julia? Do you want to go?"

"No, thank you, dear," Granny replied. "My fashion is well set."

"I might," Julia mused. "It could be amusing."

Eliza made a note of it. "There are invitations to two different dinners on Saturday, but I'll ask Lady Merton's advice on that.

There is also a ball that night with a late supper, although I suppose we could do both."

"Begging your pardon," a girl said from the door. It was Dinah, Fisher's niece. "My aunt said to ask if you'd be needing anything?"

"We don't need a thing, dear," Julia replied. "But thank you."

The girl turned to go.

"Dinah," Jocelyn said.

The girl turned back.

"Would you care to join us for tea?"

"No, Miss," the girl stammered. She bobbed an awkward curtsy. "Thank you just the same."

When she had gone, having practically dashed away, Julia gave Jocelyn a tender look. "I've not had any better luck drawing her out."

"They seem to be doing well below stairs," Alice said. "I've come down when they're playing a game or working at the table."

Granny nodded. "They'll be having this same spread downstairs where they're more comfortable." She reached over to pat Jocelyn's hand with sticky fingers. "Don't you worry."

~~~

"Read it," Joel urged Dab as he chalked the tip of his pool cue. The six friends were in a billiard's room of Boodle's and Dab and Nigel had just lost a game to the brothers Stewart, whom few could beat. Now the twins were taking on Hugh and JG.

"I didn't bring it," Dab said, "but the gist of it is that the highly esteemed Lady Toomey, who spent the last months in Vienna getting inspired, invites me to partake in an audition next Tuesday."

"Audition?" Nigel repeated.

"Yes. The goal being to dance as one of a select number of couples for a performance at their ball."

"How special," Hugh said tongue-in-cheek.

"Isn't it? She desires participants who are attractive and who possess vitality to demonstrate the vibrancy of today's aristocracy."

"What she desires," Jonathan spoke up, "is a spectacle that will have everyone talking about her event for weeks to come."

"That too," Dab agreed.

"I received an invitation, as well," JG said as he concentrated on his shot. He looked up to see the others looking at him with bemused expressions. "I won't get picked," he added quickly. "I'm sure she felt she had to invite me."

"I doubt that," Nigel said.

JG shrugged and went back to studying the table.

"I wrote back," Dab spoke up again, "suggesting all of you."

Jonathan and Hugh harrumphed.

"Come on. It will be fun," Dab rejoined. "You needn't have a dance partner. She's chosen lovely young ladies to audition and she's looking forward to pairing up couples. In fact, if you wish for a particular young lady, you have to get approval."

"Oh, Lord," Joel said under his breath. "Pardon me if I pass."

"I will not. Come on! One for all and all for one."

"Old Harrovians make anything fun," the others joined in and then laughed.

JG took his shot and missed.

"How could you miss that?" Hugh complained.

"Practice," JG replied.

"I feel certain she invited the participants she wanted," Hugh said to Dab.

"As a matter of fact, she sent a message back saying you are all welcome to join."

"Pass," Hugh said as he circled the table looking for his best shot. "But thank you."

Nigel looked thoughtful. "I wonder how particular Lady Toomey will be in accepting a lady as a partner," he mused. "Do you think an American would pass muster?"

"Depends," Jonathan replied. "Is the American lovely and clever with two different colored eyes?"

Nigel experienced an unexpected pride. "She might be."

"Alice could charm a curmudgeon," Dab said. "You should go for the two near the corner pocket," he said to Hugh.

"It could be fun," Nigel mused.

"Have your mother write and request Alice," Dab suggested. "I doubt Lady T will refuse Lady M."

"Look at you," JG said to Nigel. "All lit up at the thought."

Hugh leaned in for his shot. "I seem to remember you distressed at the prospect of the dreaded American." He hit a ball into a corner pocket.

Dab nodded. "And if you remember, I said you should meet the lady first and then decide how dire the situation was."

Jonathan smirked. "Yes, Dab, and the very fact that you said it made it all work out."

Dab looked at Nigel. "You're welcome."

All work out. Nigel mulled the words over as his friends continued the game. Would it all work out? Up until a matter of weeks ago, he had envisioned choosing a lady for a wife who was right in the most fundamental ways, meaning attractive, of agreeable temperament, from a good family and well-spoken. He had never harbored fantasies about falling in love. He hadn't imagined being equally amused, bemused and fascinated by a woman's mind while also being wildly drawn to her on a physical level. Alice had changed everything.

What marriage could be was suddenly blindingly clear. It could be a passion-filled true partnership that enriched one's life immeasurably. He knew Alice liked him, but he wanted her feelings to go so deep that she could not imagine being without him. If that did not happen, if she returned home to Boston, he would be left behind and changed forever, longing for the union they might have known. He was feeling too much too soon. Somehow, he needed to rein in his feelings until he gauged hers.

Falling in love was an irrational state of being. In made no sense to be both happy and miserable at the same time. Vulnerable and yet bold enough to risk everything. It made no sense to be equally hopeful and fearful. Falling in love was for the birds – and, apparently, he had feathers and wings he had never known about.

Chapter Thirteen

On Friday, the twelfth of May, Eliza Weatherly sat alone in the morning room. Her daybook was open on the desk in front of her. Tonight was the Ladd Ball in Mayfair and tomorrow they would attend the opera. There was scarcely a day or evening that didn't have an event. Fittings. Teas. Garden parties. Balls. The theatre. The opera. Concerts. The girls were having a wonderful time, but she found the schedule draining.

Julia had offered to chaperone whenever needed. Eliza did not want to take advantage, but she had accepted her sister-in-law's assistance today. Julia was chaperoning Alice and Mr. Walston during a walk in the park. Jocelyn had also gone along.

There was a tap on the door and Eliza looked over to see Fisher with a tea pot. "I thought you might want some fresh tea," the lady offered.

"That would be lovely. Thank you."

The lady walked in, poured hot tea in Eliza's empty cup, and switched out the pots. "Nice to have a bit of time to yourself?"

"Yes, it is. We don't keep this social pace at home."

"I imagine you're missing your other girls and grandbabies."

Eliza nodded. "I do miss them."

"I've been wanting to tell you how much I like your girls."

"Thank you. I like them, too," Eliza said with a smile.

"I know you do. What a grand job you've done raising them."

Eliza leaned back as she considered the statement. "I don't know how much credit I can honestly take." It was a subject she had often pondered. "They are all so different. All four of them."

"Are they?"

"Yes. It's as if they came into the world with personalities of their own that only needed time to unfold … like the petals of the flower. Only when it's blooming do you know what sort of flower it is and how best you can tend it."

Fisher chuckled. "What sort of flowers are they?"

Eliza pondered a moment. "Clara is a rose with very few thorns," she replied thoughtfully. "Sophia would have to be a wildflower. Perhaps a passion flower."

"I don't know that flower."

"We have them at home. They are rather dramatic. They have tendrils. They vine." She smiled at the silliness of the exercise, although it was interesting to think about. "Jocelyn would be a sweet pea."

"And what about Alice?"

"She would be something surprising like a dahlia or a tulip, I think. Although I could make an argument for a sunflower. Bright, bold, unyielding in her stance."

"And your grandchildren?"

"They are all different as well. Samuel is eight. He is quiet and studious, like his father. Stephen is five and precocious, far more likely to get into mischief than his brother ever was. Little Annabel is almost two and I do believe she's going to be more like Stephen than Samuel. She is a little chatterbox. Sophia's little girl, Lola, has a head full of curls. She is shy."

"And Sophia will have the new baby before long," Fisher said.

Eliza nodded. "End of the summer."

"Can I get you anything else?"

"No but thank you. I am perfectly content."

Fisher left, and Eliza rose and went to the window. Both the top and bottom sashes were open, admitting a fragrant breeze from the garden. It was a day full of sunshine and birdsong, ideal for a stroll through the park. Eliza frowned as she mused over Alice and Nigel Walston. That Alice liked him as well as she did was disturbing. There had been numerous suitable young men interested in her the last few years and she hadn't shown interest in any of them, no matter how attractive or excellent a prospect they were.

Stanley Ingham was the perfect age, height and pedigree. He was a fine-looking man who enjoyed excellent health, a good income, an agreeable personality and temperament. He was smitten with Alice, but he would not wait forever. The most vexing thing was that Alice either could not or would not give a satisfactory reason for her lack of interest in him. When pressed, she would say she liked him but that her feelings went no further. She had given similar responses to Terrance Mickelson and Bart Johnson and Jim Whitehall. Eliza had once thrown up her hands and declared that real life was not romantic fiction. Alice, to her infinite annoyance, came back with, "You would not wish me to marry for less than love, would you?"

It was true, of course. Eliza did want love for all her daughters. However, love could be built, provided the right foundation. Please God, let it not be the case that love had been stumbled upon here. She had known her husband had a notion about Alice marrying into nobility, but she'd expected Alice to rebel against the interference. Her third-born had certainly chaffed anytime she had an opinion.

This London holiday was only meant to be a spring to midsummer excursion. Their lives were in Boston. Perhaps, in the back of her mind, she had secretly hoped that this trip might make Alice more amenable to Mr. Ingham's attentions when they returned home. Eliza sighed and squeezed her eyes shut for a moment. *Just let it be a passing fancy with Nigel Walston. Please!*

~~~

"Our second walk of the day," Jocelyn said to her aunt as they strolled along the broad foot path alongside Rotten Row, the gravel road that the gentry of the city traversed in fine carriages or on horseback.

"This is no walk," Julia replied. "This is meandering. The only exercise is of the neck, turning to see who is here and what they are wearing."

"It is fun though, isn't it? It would be an even greater enjoyment if I knew more people. Have you noticed the looks Alice and Nigel are getting? He must be well-known."

Julia's gaze flicked to Alice and Mr. Walston walking several yards ahead of them. "Indeed." The park was beautiful, in sight of both the Serpentine River and Kensington Gardens.

"I think she's in love with him," Jocelyn confided.

Julia blinked in surprise. "I can see that she likes him, but it seems rather too soon for that depth of feeling."

"Do you not think you can fall in love in a single day? Or even in an hour if it's the right person?"

"I don't know. I would not say it's impossible. I never did." She paused. "Has Alice said she's in love with him?"

"No, but she wouldn't. Not yet, anyway. She would think it's rather too soon for that depth of feeling."

Julia grinned. "She has a good head on her shoulders. And so do you."

"I've always thought so and yet the right man can turn your knees to jelly and your mind to giddy wonderment and daydreams."

"Oh my! What a description."

"What was my uncle like?"

"He was a nice man. Ordinary, I would say."

"But what did you think when you first met him? Did you find him dashing?"

"I married when I was in my mid-twenties, not eighteen," Julia replied with a tender expression. "And he was forty-one, a widowed man. So, no. I didn't find him dashing. I found him acceptable. He proposed and I wanted to be married. I fervently hoped we would be able to conceive a child. He and his first wife had not been blessed with children."

"And then came Jeremy."

"Yes." A young couple rode by them on a sporty gig. It was followed by two ladies riding in stylish habits, one in blue and one in yellow. They wore shortened top hats, one with a feather atop. "I knew there was something different about Jeremy from the time he was two or three, but I never loved him the less for it."

"Of course, you didn't."

"Nor did his father."

"How old was Jeremy when his father died?"

"Almost six. That was a difficult time. Peter's death was a terrible shock. It was a heart seizure."

"I'm sorry."

"I remember the morning it happened so clearly. Peter was not feeling well. He kept complaining of a pain in his arm. It confounded him how he had managed to pull a muscle there. Jeremy was at the kitchen table drawing a picture that he wanted Peter to take to work with him. I remember a very particular smile Peter gave me before he went up to get his jacket. He said he would take his time and not leave until the picture was done." Julia paused. "Not long after that, we heard a clatter upstairs."

The ladies had come to a halt.

"He was gone," Julia said softly with a shake of her head. "By the time I got upstairs. I ran as soon as I heard the fall, but ...he was gone. It was so sudden." She swallowed. "So sudden," she repeated in a whisper.

Tears had sprung to Jocelyn's eyes, but she held them back. If her aunt wasn't crying, she didn't have the right.

They started walking again. "Peter was a clerk," Julia continued, "so there had never been a great deal of money in our household. We'd gotten by without hardship," she added quickly, "but we rented the house we lived in. Fortunately, I had a home to return to and a mother who welcomed us with open arms. We really have been so fortunate."

"I hope I can always emulate your attitude, Aunt Julia. You are so optimistic."

"I'm not merely putting a good face on," Julia rejoined.
"Truly. My life is one I chose and would choose again. I've been
blessed with the people in my life. Think of it. I could have had a
less loving upbringing, a less kind mother, a less generous
brother, and everything would have been different. The house
belongs to your father, you know. Naturally, Mamma has a life
tenancy, but Richard assures me I should think of myself and
Jeremy of having the same."

"Of course! It's your home."

"It is your home, too, if ever you need or want it."

Jocelyn smiled affectionately at her aunt. "Thank you, Aunt
Julia."

"We relish having you here. You have brought life and joy
into the household. You and Alice have made a difference in
Jeremy I would not have believed possible."

The words tugged at Jocelyn's heartstrings. She thought it was
the nicest compliment she had ever received. "We love him. And
we like him, which are very different things."

"Yes, they are."

"Now, sometimes Sophia—" Jocelyn said teasingly. "Let's
just say we always love her."

Julia laughed.

~~~

"It occurs to me," Nigel said to Alice. "I have been remiss in
something."

Alice looked at him. "What's that?"

"Asking to court you."

She stopped with a sharp intake of breath.

"Too much was taken for granted," he added.

"It was an unusual situation," she said haltingly.

"Oh, I don't know. All marriages used to be arranged, you
know. This boy," he said, affecting a voice, "shall marry this girl.
But, sir, they are still in their cribs. No matter. They will marry

and be happy. Or perhaps they will not be happy, but they will marry."

"Did you feel that was being said? Marry this girl and be happy. Or don't be happy, but marry her."

"No. Not at all. The idea of marriage was never foisted on me. It was suggested, but not forced."

She wondered if it was true. No woman wanted to be forced upon anyone. She wanted to be loved and appreciated for exactly who and what she was. If only marriage had not been discussed between their fathers before they had ever met. If only a financial settlement had not been discussed. The fact that it had cast a pall over the relationship. What if she didn't have a substantial dowry? Would he be asking to court her? Would he be considering marrying her? *Marrying her.* Spending the rest of their lives together. Good heaven, what a thought! Especially in that she would live so far away from her family.

"I would like to," he said.

His statement snapped her from her reverie and caused a moment of alarm. "Like to what?"

"Court you. I would like to court you, Miss Weatherly."

She was relieved he was not referring to marriage.

"Are you amenable?" he asked.

"Yes," she replied thoughtfully. "I am." She paused before adding, "As to the rest of it, I need time."

"Of course," he replied. "We both do."

She tried not to react, but the words felt like a bit of a slap. Which was not at all reasonable. "There is so much I don't know about you that I would like to," she said.

"Such as?"

"Well … what do you do most days?"

"A fair question. By the way, please feel free to take my arm if you wish. We are courting, after all."

She slipped her hand around his arm, and the feeling of walking as a couple was exhilarating. She had walked with other gentlemen, but she had never experienced this strange thrill.

"I am not obligated to be in the House of Lords yet," he said, "but I will be. And I enjoy politics to a point. The workings of parliament are important. After all, they make the laws, address issues of the day, control taxes. So, I spend a day, sometimes two, in the gallery of the House of Commons or the House of Lords listening and learning. It really depends on what's happening."

Alice nodded.

"I do not yet control our family finances yet, but the subject is of great interest to me. My Aunt Rosemont, my mother's youngest sister, had me take over the financial management of her estate a few years ago. I don't make big decisions without her, but I make recommendations and they've done well. Monty, my aunt, insists I take the same percentage of profits that any other manager would take. So, with that sum, I began making some investments of my own and they have done well."

It occurred to her that if they were married, she would be able to discreetly stroke his arm. Or hug herself to it. The idea was titillating. It *held* too much appeal, in fact. It was not ladylike to have such yearnings.

"I engage in physical activity a few days a week," he continued. "Boxing, fencing, rowing."

That explained the strength in his arm.

"And I typically join my friends once or sometimes twice a week at a club for cards or other amusement." A couple went by in a curricle and the man lifted a hand in greeting. Nigel waved back before looking at Alice with a curious smile, "On a completely different subject, do you waltz?"

"That *is* a different subject. Yes, I love the waltz."

"There is a rather unusual event next week and I would enjoy taking part, if you feel the same."

"I'm intrigued."

"I'll tell you all about it. That's the Cake House ahead."

She looked at a pretty brick cottage in the distance with people milling about it. The river shone behind it.

"They serve snacks and drinks. Shall we stop and have a syllabub?"

"That sounds perfect."

"Good. I am thoroughly enjoying this day, Miss Weatherly."

"So am I, Mr. Walston."

Friday, May 12   a𝔚𝔢

Morning: 10:00 Walk in the park
Afternoon: Rework James and Martha scene.
Evening: 9:00 Ruston Gala

Today, Nigel asked to court me and I said yes. Yes!
I should be writing, because I am not pleased with
chapter two, but I cannot clear the thought of him from my
mind. It was an excellent outing although the way people
overtly observed us seemed odd. I must admit to some rather
unladylike yearnings where Nigel Walston is concerned. It
is probably that we have no brothers, but they seem like an
entirely different species than us. One I like more than I
realized.
    Nigel James Walston.
    ~~Mrs. Nigel Walston.~~
    ~~Lady Merton.~~
    ~~Lady Alice Merton.~~
    ~~Alice Walston.~~
I just realized my initials would remain the same.

LADD

PLEASURE BALL

The Weatherly Family

IS CORDIALLY INVITED TO THE RESIDENCE OF
LORD FITZROY LADD
SATURDAY, THE 13TH OF MAY AT EIGHT O'CLOCK
NO. 11 CHARLES STREET

Chapter Fourteen

On the way to the ball, Alice and Jocelyn were strongly advised to dance with a gentleman one time only unless she wanted it rumored that they had an attachment. Apparently, Ada had forgotten herself at the last ball and now found herself inexorably connected with Harrison Bower.

Jocelyn, wearing a gown of dusty-rose, and Alice, wearing pale pink, listened without comment. They had witnessed the attraction between Ada and Harrison at the Buckley ball, and they had seen the developing fondness and commitment since, so if the couple was being used as the subjects of a cautionary tale, it was not terribly effective.

Alice had been at the ball more than an hour, socialized appropriately, and danced with two different gentlemen before the Walstons arrived, having had a previous dinner engagement.

"My mother and her musts," Nigel grumbled when he finally stood with Alice. "It's either go along with it or never hear the end of it. We must attend this dinner. We must attend that recital. My sisters must keep two afternoons for formal calls and stay in on Thursdays to receive."

Alice knew all this from Lakely's complaints.

"But now I am free and ready for some enjoyment," Nigel said. "Shall we dance?"

"If it is your dance of choice," she replied coyly. "I can only dance with a gentleman once or twice, you know. Otherwise, people assume there is a connection."

"Ah! So that's how it goes?"

She nodded. "I have it on good authority."

"But we do have a connection. Our families are the best of friends."

"Two dances, then," she returned. "As long as they are not back-to-back."

"Never back-to-back," he played along. "That might imply an engagement."

Alice looked over to discover Lady Merton watching them. The lady smiled smugly before turning away.

~~~

Nature had called and Jocelyn had been forced to answer. She was returning to the ballroom after a trip to one of the retiring rooms when she saw JG waiting in the corridor outside the ballroom holding two glasses of champagne. He beamed at her, and she could not help but smile back. "Hello," she said as she reached him.

"Hello." He offered a glass to her. "I bribed the help to bring these."

She accepted. "Thank you."

He lifted his glass. "It's wonderful to see you again."

"You, as well." She touched her glass to his and they sipped. She'd never tasted finer champagne. "Did you really bribe someone to bring it?"

"I did. And I suggest we drink it out here before going back in there. And not only because I desire a few moments alone with you. Alone-ish, I should say."

The corridor was far from empty and yet standing there with him felt clandestine somehow. "Did you just arrive?"

"Yes. With my grandfather."

A burst of excitement went through her. "Oh!"

JG looked uncomfortable and then leaned slightly forward. "He's not the nicest person," he confided. "A dreadful snob, I'm afraid."

Her smile dimmed because of the apprehension in his face. She sipped again to have something to do. It seemed his grandfather did not care to meet her. It was her first taste of a limitation being imposed because she was not of noble birth. It

did have a distinctly bitter quality. No wonder her father had
developed such sensitivity about it. She could imagine the
frustration of always being evaluated because of something you
had no control over. Worse, being dismissed because of it
without any real consideration of your character. "There is
something I would like to discuss with you," she said.

He brightened and nodded.

"My cousin, Jeremy. He is …different from others. Not
comfortable with many people. But he is a magnificent artist."

"Is he?"

She nodded. "Yes. He is young, only seventeen, but I believe
his painting could sell. Would sell. But we have no idea how one
would go about getting his work in front of the right people."

"Is it something he wants?"

"I think so. Yes. His father died when he was young, and his
mother, my Aunt Julia, was not left with much of a financial
settlement. So, to have an avenue of income would not only be
appreciated in their household, but it would also make him proud
to contribute. It would set him up for independence one day
should his paintings prove to be a success."

"I'd be glad to help. I will have to make enquiries, and I would
need to see his work first. Would that be possible?"

"He doesn't leave the house a great deal. You would … have
to come to us."

"I'd be glad to," he said eagerly.

"Perhaps for tea?" she suggested shyly.

"That would be excellent. Name the day."

"It should be at your convenience. Early next week, perhaps?
Tuesday?"

"Perfect."

She smiled. "It's in Bryanston Square. Number fourteen."

"It is committed to memory. I look forward to it."

"So do I."

He noticed a gentleman give him a pointed look.
"Unfortunately, we'll need to go back inside the ballroom
separately, but I'll find you later, if that's all right."

"Of course."

"For a dance, I hope?"

"Yes. Thank you again for the champagne."

"Seeing you again is cause for celebration."

She blushed, but her heart lifted. He lingered as if he had something more to say, or was she supposed to be leaving first?

"You've been on my mind since we met," he admitted. "Brown eyes with an amber center."

Her blush was deepening, so she turned and went back into the ballroom. Or was she floating? Her heart felt as if it was soaring, lifting her entire being. Perhaps JG was wrong. Maybe his grandfather would like her. Every good thing in the world suddenly felt a possibility.

~~~

Lady Merton watched Lakely conversing with friends across the room. Her eldest daughter wore red this evening and the gown stood out in the roomful of light-colored dresses. Lakely was so beautiful, and she could be perfect in her social graces when she chose to be, but there was an underlying unhappiness within the girl that had worsened the last few months. Ada suspected it was due to a matter of the heart, either someone Lakely loved that did not return the affection or someone who was unavailable. A married man perhaps?

Lakely was not easy to be close to, at least not for her mother. Oil and water, her husband frequently remarked. His conclusion was that they were too much alike. Lakely and Ada were close, but it was easy to be close to Ada. She was not temperamental and argumentative. Lakely lived to argue a point. It could be amusing to watch if the dispute was with her father. He would usually halt the debate by declaring "Enough! Lakely! That is enough!" To which, Lakely would self-assuredly accept his withdrawal as a win in her favor. Nigel sometimes took his sister to task for the fun of it. The two of them bantered, but rarely heatedly.

Lady Merton wondered if Lakely's melancholy had to do with Ada's attachment to Harrison Bower. It was difficult when a younger sister found a match before the elder. Or perhaps it was distress over the thought of losing the daily companionship of her younger sister. When Lakely looked her way, Lady Merton motioned for her. Lakely excused herself and started toward her.

"Hello," Lakely said when she reached her. "Are you enjoying yourself?"

"Well enough. I wanted to tell you that you look beautiful tonight. I love that color on you."

The compliment seemed to surprise Lakely. "Thank you." She glanced around. "Where is your husband?"

"My husband who would be your father?"

"Unless there is something you want to tell me," Lakely returned innocently.

Lady Merton chuckled despite herself. "I don't know where he is at the moment. In all truthfulness, I wanted to speak to you because I've been worried about you."

"Why?" Lakely asked levelly.

There it was again. The invisible wall between them. It had slammed into place again. Lakely stood before her regal and unreachable. "I wish you were happier," her mother stated.

Several moments passed before Lakely replied. "So do I."

Was that a small give in the wall? "Is there someone you've set your heart on?"

Lakely mused over a reply. "Yes, but he is a ghost. Or else I am. I'm not altogether certain which it is. We cannot seem to connect because he has his world and I have mine although they swirl around one another. Occasionally even collide."

Lady Merton was not following. Was it a married man? Unfortunately, the Meltzer heir stepped up and asked Lakely to dance. She accepted and moved toward the dancefloor with him, leaving her mother at a complete loss. Had she been given an answer of sorts or had the strange reply been more of Lakely's game-playing to keep her at arm's length? She truly did not know.

Chapter Fifteen

*E*liza Weatherly put a bookmark in place and shut the novel, a tragic and rather frustrating story Alice had purchased a week ago and had already finished. This was the second quiet evening in a row for the family, and she was grateful for it. Richard was spending the evening with his friend Randall Page, and everyone else had already retired to their rooms. She relished the quiet.

When she retired upstairs, she saw Julia standing outside the entrance to the third floor. There was something about the way her sister-in-law stood with her arms folded, her head bent forward, the back of one hand pressed to her lips. Was she crying? Eliza moved closer, but Julia looked over and Eliza saw that her expression was one of joy. Eliza was about to speak when Julia pointed to the third floor. As if on cue, there was laughter from their children.

"I promise," Alice said. "Smashed right into the poor man."

"And him with his overfull glass of red wine," Jocelyn added.

There was more laugher.

Tears shone in Julia's eyes. "Just listen to that," she said quietly. "The girls have been a Godsend."

Eliza touched Julia's arm and nodded. "Goodnight," she whispered.

"Goodnight."

At the door to her room, Eliza glanced back to where Julia was still listening, enraptured by the sounds of amusement. It was a moment she knew she would recall as one of the most touching of the trip.

~~~

"What will you wear to the Derby?" Jocelyn asked her sister at the same moment.

"I don't know yet," Alice replied absentmindedly as she continued to look through a magazine. It touched on most every topic, politics, fashion, editorials. She and Jocelyn were lounging in Jeremy's room with a half-consumed carafe of wine. They were keeping their cousin company while he worked. "My beige and red perhaps. Or the blue I wore to the Shoemaker wedding. Would that be all right for a race, do you think?"

"Blue," Jeremy said.

Alice grinned. "One vote for the blue."

"Two votes for the blue," Jocelyn agreed.

"What about you?" Alice asked her. "What will you wear?"

Jocelyn smiled sweetly. "Your beige and red?"

Alice rolled her eyes, flipped the page and read on. "Speaking of fashion, listen to this. '*Fancy, Fashion's Prime Minister, with her creative touch,*'" Alice read in an affected voice, "'*…still continues to inspire, aided by her handmaiden, Invention, the active priestess of the toilet.*'"

"Toilet," Jeremy repeated.

"'*With light and rainbow wings,*'" Alice continued, making her voice even more comical, "*they continue to hover over different establishments devoted to the adornment of Beauty.*' Beauty has a capital B, mind you."

"So may I wear it?" Jocelyn wheedled. "The beige and red."

"I suppose. It looks better on you than me, anyway."

"Then may I have it?"

"No!"

Jocelyn turned to Jeremy. "Are you're sure you won't go with us on Wednesday? It will be fun."

He shook his head and reached for another brush.

"Tell me if I can help you do anything," Jocelyn offered. She got up to pour herself more wine. "I particularly like the grinding part. There's satisfaction when it starts to get smooth."

Alice made a face of confusion. "This says another favorite head-covering for a carriage ride is the Caroline hat of red lavender satin. Red lavender? What is red lavender?"

"I don't know," Jocelyn replied.

"A mix of lavender oil and rosemary," Jeremy said without looking away from his canvas. "And red sandalwood."

"You're saying it's a real color?" Alice asked.

"Nutmeg," he continued listing ingredients. "Cinnamon bark."

"Sounds tasty," Jocelyn commented. She walked closer and leaned over Alice's shoulder to see the illustration. "It's pretty. I like it."

Alice continued reading. "'*For half-dress, a new material called Baltimore crape, which is sprigged, has lately made its appearance; the colour is that of the dried date leaf.*'" She looked up at Jeremy again. "I suppose you know what color that is, too?"

This struck him as humorous and he laughed so infectiously the girls couldn't help but join in.

Chapter Sixteen

On Tuesday afternoon, the day of the dance audition, Alice climbed inside the Walston's carriage where Lakely sat alongside a lady of forty-five or so who looked very like her. The lady's dark hair had one silver streak that looked so perfectly placed, it was almost theatrical. "Hello," Alice said.

"Hello," Lakely returned. "Alice, this is Aunt Rosemont, Lady Vinton, whom we call Monty. Aunt Rosemont, meet Miss Alice Weatherly whom we have talked about in great length."

"Pleased to make your acquaintance, Lady Vinton," Alice said as the carriage started in motion.

"Call me Monty. Everyone does. I already feel as though I know you, my dear."

"Monty is the most amusing of our entire family and the one I am closest to, save Ada, of course."

"As it should be," Lady Vinson stated.

Lakely looked at her. "Except it isn't with you and my mother."

"Well … no. But, of course, I care deeply for her, and I love her children." She looked at Alice. "I didn't have my own, you see, so I have occasionally borrowed my nieces and nephew to appease those rogue maternal urges that surfaced out of nowhere." She grinned mischievously. "Afterwards, I was usually thankful I didn't have children all the time."

Lakely laughed.

"Is Nigel meeting us there, I suppose?" Alice asked hopefully.

Lakely replied to the affirmative. "He had some business with Father and then he was meeting his friends and going with whichever of them is joining in this lark."

Lark. Was it a lark? "I'm a bit nervous," Alice admitted.

"Don't be," Lakely rejoined. "Lady Toomey has a vision in her head for this performance and she will choose exactly who she wants to carry it off. I think it's probably half political and half ... well, I don't know what. It should be an interesting afternoon, though."

"Oh, yes," Lady Vinson agreed.

"Who will you dance with?" Alice asked Lakely.

"I have no idea. Lady Toomey will pair people up unless they got permission for their own coupling."

Alice felt her face heat at the evocative term, which was silly. As usual, she was reading too much into something. "I hope there is nothing different about the way you do the waltz from what I know."

"Well, let's see," Lakely said impishly. "Back, side, close. One, two, three. Up, side, close. One, two, three. Does that sound right?"

Alice laughed. "It does.

"I wouldn't be concerned," Lady Vinton said to her. "Nigel is only thinking of the amusement of it, even if it is just for today."

When Lakely announced that they were close, Alice realized they were near the park again, which meant they had come out of their way to fetch her.

"That one belongs to the duke," Lakely said pointing at a mansion beyond a brick-pillared and wrought iron fence. "Apsley House."

"The duke?"

"Wellington."

Ah. Of Waterloo fame. The home of Lord and Lady Toomey when they arrived was no less grand than Apsley House. Carriages were steadily arriving, and stylishly attired occupants were disembarking. Was she dressed well enough?

Lady Vinson leaned forward. "It is a gorgeous home, yes," she said kindly. "Pretend that you live in one that's very similar, and then go in and be yourself and have a wonderful time." The carriage door opened. "Are you ready?" Lady Vinson asked.

Alice nodded. "I think so." They were each assisted from the carriage, and they moved toward the steps leading up to the front veranda. There had been a time, not long ago, when she would have been absorbing every detail of the place for use in her writing. Now her full focus was spent on comparing herself to the other females making their way toward the same destination.

They entered a large, mostly white foyer. The only bursts of color were from a flower arrangement in an oriental vase on a table, a round rug and an upholstered bench in scarlet velvet. They joined a line of ladies to be checked in by a gentleman seated at a desk.

"That's her secretary," Lakely whispered discreetly. "Goes most everywhere with her," she added suggestively. When they reached the man, Lakely said, "Miss Walston and Miss Weatherly."

"Very good," he said checking off their names. "If you would please, Miss Walston, attach this to your gown before the audition." He handed her a wide white ribbon with the number 26 embroidered upon it. "You must be Miss Weatherly," he said to Alice.

"Yes," she said with a nervous smile.

He handed her a ribbon with 47 upon it. "Here you are."

"Thank you," Alice said.

He cocked his head very slightly and smiled, probably noticing her eyes or perhaps responding to her accent. "You are most welcome."

Alice and Lakely followed the convocation toward the sound of stringed instruments warming up. Alice had always enjoyed the sounds of instrumentalists warming up before a performance. It never failed to provide a stirring of excitement. "I suppose you've been here before?" Alice asked.

"Every year. They have two ballrooms side by side. We're in the smaller ballroom today," she said as they entered a cavernous room that measured no less than thirty yards long by twenty wide.

This was the smaller of the two? At least a hundred people had gathered, beautiful women, impressive looking men, plus their chaperones. Some seating had been set out and half of it had been claimed by chaperones. There was a centrally placed long table with three chairs behind it, but no one sat at it yet. A violinist and a cellist warmed up in the orchestra balcony.

A middle-aged lady bustled up to them offering assistance in affixing their ribbons. She quickly and efficiently attached both and said they would be getting started soon. Alice fidgeted as she looked around in search of Nigel. She did not see him – and then she did, at the same moment he saw her from across the room.

"What is that smile for?" Lakely asked.

Alice had not meant to burst into smile. "Your brother and I have a habit of seeing one another at the same instant."

"Of course, you do. And is it my imagination or are violins suddenly playing?"

Alice laughed to herself as Nigel joined them along with Dabney Adams.

"Where is the rest of the merry band?" Lakely asked.

"Jonathan may be coming," Nigel replied. "But we haven't seen him yet. Joel and Hugh flatly refused to participate, and JG had something else to do."

"JG," Dab said, "is convinced he doesn't stand a chance of being chosen, so he's not taking part at all, and I don't think Jonathan will show."

Lakely leaned closer to Alice. "As to who is who," she said. "Considered the catch of the season in the lady's category is …standing to our left, lighter hair than yours."

Alice glanced over and saw a beautiful young woman in a pale blue gown.

"Lady Meredith Hill. Her father is Lord Graveston, a duke. The only thing larger than her dowry is her vanity. Walking up to her is Miss Baldwin. Constance Baldwin."

Miss Baldwin was attractive, but not remarkable.

"Her father has the touch of Midas, and she will be an heiress," Lakely said. "Next, we have—"

She was interrupted by the banging of a spoon against the glass. They looked over to where a tall, thin man with a curling mustache stood in the center of the dance floor. "If I may have your attention," he called in a voice that carried well.

The room quieted. Alice noticed the three ladies seated at the table prepared to judge. She clutched her hands together to stop their trembling. It was about to begin.

"Royalty, indeed," Lakely whispered as she also noticed the panel. "Lady Toomey is in the middle, Lady Castlereagh is to her right and Lady Jersey to her left."

The mustached man was speaking again. "Lord and Lady Toomey were recently in Vienna." His voice was one of affectation with perfect modulation. "There, they were greatly inspired by the music and dance. At their annual ball this year, there will be a waltz performed by those of you who are selected. I am Phineas Skeffington, dance master," he added with a slight bow. "I will be the master of ceremony at the ball, and I have choreographed the dance." He paused. "I trust you will forgive the crassness of assigning you a number, but it is the easiest manner to be certain of selections. You may think that everyone knows you, and perhaps they do, but how would it have looked if we gave everyone a number except for you?"

There was a general chuckling.

"We will have couples dance a simple waltz ten at a time, beginning with numbers one through ten. When the song ends, you will either be given this gesture ..." With two fingers, he made a flinging gesticulation. He did this repeatedly, turning his body for all to see. "That indicates we have seen enough, and you are excused. Being excused implies neither acceptance nor rejection, only that we have seen what we need. If, however, you get this gesture," he paused as he motioned towards himself, "Please remain behind to possibly dance again. Very simple, is it not?"

No one signified to the contrary.

"You will receive word in regard to participation by the end of the week. Is everything understood?"

And so it began, although not smoothly. The first ten couples paired up, but some needed to be switched around because of a too-marked difference in height. When the first set of dancers finished, Phineas Skeffington conferred with the panel and dancers were either excused or directed to stay behind. Alice had become aware of scrutiny she was receiving from a few women in the crowd, one in particular. She tried to ignore it, but it was distracting.

Dab was part of the second group. Afterwards, he was directed to stay behind, as were several others. Lakely was part of the third group. Unfortunately, her partner was a red-faced young man without sufficient grace to compliment her or himself. When the music ended, he was excused while she was asked to remain.

"That was painful," she muttered when she returned to Alice. "Why couldn't I have danced with Dab?"

"You have a better partner," Nigel said to Alice with a teasing smile.

She smiled, but it faded when she saw the female who had been staring at her taking the floor. "Who is the lady on this end?" she asked Lakely. "Wearing green."

Lakely made a face of distaste. "Diana Fletcher. She has some good friends; I'm not sure how, but she is best avoided. We dislike each other intensely, so if you're with me, avoiding her will not be difficult. She will not come within ten feet of me. I once told her what I thought about some remarks she had made. It was in the presence of others and then word spread like wildfire. She left early that night, as well she should have."

The music began again and Miss Fletcher, who had a strong partner, danced with confidence and poise. She was excused afterward, probably because she had been selected without hesitation. Some of the best dancers had been excused.

When it was finally their turn, Nigel offered his arm and led Alice to the dance floor. Theirs was the final group. In fact, they had the last number.

"I couldn't care less if we're selected or not," he confided. "I just wanted to dance with you today."

That helped relieve her anxiety. The music started and they moved together easily and enjoyed themselves. When the music ended, the dance master once again conferred with the ladies and then made the pronouncements. Nigel and Alice were excused, but Mr. Skeffington quietly asked that they stop by the table. Nigel led Alice there, bowing when they reached the table. "Ladies, may I have the honor of introducing Miss Alice Weatherly?"

"How do you do?" Alice said.

"Miss Weatherly," Nigel said, "this is Lady Jersey, Lady Toomey and Lady Castelreagh."

"It's an honor," Alice replied.

"We were pleased to have you," Lady Toomey said to her. "How is your visit going?"

"It could not be better."

"That American accent," Lady Jersey said with an amused expression. "But you are lovely, and you danced beautifully. Both of you. We found you enjoyable to watch."

"Are you two engaged?" Lady Castlereagh asked in a hushed voice.

Alice tried to remain expressionless.

"No," Nigel said. "Not ... not at this time," he stammered. His awkwardness seemed a source of amusement for the ladies, although they were discreet about it. As they walked off, Nigel asked. "How many times did I just say the word not?" he whispered as if in pain.

Alice laughed silently. "Did you say it more than once? I didn't notice."

They found seats next to Monty, who complimented them on their dancing, and watched as the audition continued.

~~~

"Mr. Baillie to see Miss Jocelyn," JG said, handing the maid his card.

"Of course, sir," Fisher said, stepping back. "Please come in."

He stepped inside as an attractive lady reached the foyer. "It's Lord Blairwood, is it not?" the lady asked agreeably.

"It is." He bowed.

"I'm the girl's aunt. Welcome."

"Mrs. Alford," he said. "It's a great pleasure to meet you."

"And you. The parlour is this way."

Jocelyn smoothed her skirt nervously. She had heard every word and now she listened to their footsteps getting closer.

"Here we are," Julia said, stepping inside.

JG and Jocelyn exchanged a smile and a bow.

"If you'll excuse me a moment," Julia said "I'll let Jeremy know you're here. Perhaps, he'll join us."

As Julia walked away, Jocelyn gestured to a chair. "Please."

He walked over and sat. "How are you?"

"Very well, thank you. And you?"

"Tip top."

He seemed nervous and Jocelyn fleetingly wondered if she should apologize for the irregularity of the invitation and being left alone together. For being American and not of nobility and already being half in love with him and—

"I've always liked this square," he said.

"So do I. Especially because my father grew up here."

"Is he at home?"

"No. He and my mother had an engagement. I didn't realize it when I suggested today."

"If it's a problem," he said quickly.

"No! Not at all. For me. But I realize the culture we came from is less … structured than this one. I want to behave correctly, of course."

"You do. Please never feel otherwise. I adore your … may I say freshness? There is an ease and honesty about you and your sister that makes one feel good to be around."

The thought gave her a lift. "I also did not remember that today was the day of Lady Toomey's audition."

He shook his head. "That held no interest for me. The ball itself will be excellent, but I have no desire to be on display during it." He cringed. "The thought of it. I can see myself stumbling over my own two feet, turning the color of a beet, and probably tripping my unfortunate partner and anyone around me."

She couldn't help laughing.

He gave a mock shiver.

"I very much doubt that would happen," she rejoined. "We have danced. Remember?"

"I would never forget."

She had already relaxed, she realized. She smiled at her aunt as she reentered the room. "Jeremy is not coming down?"

"No, but he's looking forward to meeting you," Julia said to JG.

"Shall we go to him?" Jocelyn asked JG.

"If it's all right with your aunt," JG said.

"It is," Julia assured him. "We'll have tea afterwards."

Jocelyn rose and led the way out. On the second floor, she slowed her step. "My cousin is highly intelligent," she explained softly, "but most people make him uncomfortable." She stopped entirely and faced him. "He may not look at you or speak directly to you. He may rock back and forth."

"Do not worry about me," JG replied just as softly. "I can accept a person as they are, however they are. I am not easily wounded by any slight. I've had a lifetime of practice at it."

The statement so saddened her, she had an urge to reach out and touch his arm, but this was not the time to pursue the thought and she could certainly not be so bold as to touch him in such a familiar manner. "It's on the third floor," she said before she led the way up to the attic.

Jeremy had moved the three easels to form a curve facing them, so the paintings were the first thing they saw. JG was clearly astonished at what he saw. "Oh my," he exclaimed as he came closer.

Jeremy stood to the side watching him furtively.

"I thought," JG began. He shook his head. "I thought perhaps you may have been unduly biased because of your affection for your cousin, but these are magnificent. Look at the light in this one. The way it casts the water green, but still with a translucent quality. And this one. The reds are so …primal. It's a tipped vase of flowers in a disorderly room, or is it much more? Is this a rose petal or a drop of blood? I can't help wondering what's happened here."

Jocelyn caught Jeremy's eye and smiled. It was wonderful to see JG caught up in the paintings, and Jeremy enjoying his reaction.

"They are so powerful," JG remarked as he turned to the third. "The expression on his face," he murmured, gesturing with his hands. "Is it a moment of enlightenment? Fury?" He suddenly looked over at Jeremy. "Oh, do forgive me. I got so riveted in your work, I completely forgot my manners. I'm Jocelyn's friend, JG."

Jocelyn's breath caught; she so loved the words. Jeremy bowed and the sight of it tugged at her heartstrings. The bow was something they had practiced.

"How do you do," Jeremy said with his gaze on the floor.

JG bowed. "I am very well. Thank you. And you?"

"Very well."

"Just out of curiosity, have you been to Somerset House?" JG asked, glancing between them.

"No," Jocelyn replied.

Jeremy shook his head, but he was still avoiding JG's gaze.

"Ah, you must! It was a palace intended for Princess Charlotte, but then she died. Which was very tragic."

"In childbirth, wasn't it?" Jocelyn asked.

"Directly after. They say the birth was horribly botched. The babe was born dead, and she died a few hours after. The physician in charge killed himself."

"Two years ago," Jeremy said.

"Yes," JG said. "The whole nation went into mourning," he said to Jocelyn. "But I mentioned Somerset House because it's the sight of the Royal Academy Exhibition. It is something to marvel at for anyone, much less an artist."

"You have seen it, then?" Jocelyn asked.

"Oh, yes. I go every year. The exhibition room is very large and filled top to bottom with paintings of all sizes. The ceiling must be a hundred feet high and there are enormous domed windows. There must be sixty feet of paintings one on top of the other in a room the size of this house." He paused and looked at Jeremy. "I hope you'll allow me to take you this year." He glanced at Jocelyn. "And you and Alice." He looked back at Jeremy. "And perhaps your mothers. We have a town coach that can seat six comfortably. We could make an afternoon of it."

"It sounds wonderful," Jocelyn said. She noticed Jeremy had begun rocking slightly. "However, my cousin does not particularly enjoy crowds, so—"

"Ah, but," JG said so abruptly that Jeremy stopped rocking and looked at him. "Imagine that we are there, and all of these walls are huge and filled with paintings. Yes, there is a crowd, but everyone is doing this." JG stared at the wall, moving his head up and down slowly as if taking in each painting. He steadily moved closer until he was next to Jeremy, and then stepped by him without looking at him, saying, "Pardon me," in a distracted fashion.

Jeremy seemed to be imagining it, so Jocelyn played along. "Oh, look at that one," she murmured to herself as if taking a gander at a large painting. She, too, moved closer until she stood next to Jeremy, but she didn't look at him. Then she did, but only to give him a polite dismissive smile and step around to study the next section of paintings.

"Do think about it, Mr. Alford," JG urged. "Or may I call you Jeremy?"

Jeremy nodded. "Yes."

Progress! Jocelyn thought excitedly.

"Now my next question is this. Do you want to sell your paintings?"

Jeremy nodded. "Yes." He looked at JG. "Will they?"

"Will they sell? Honestly? Yes. I believe they will sell. I think they are brilliant, and I will be happy to assist. Perhaps contact a gallery owner?"

Jeremy nodded again. "Please."

"I would need to show him your work. May I take a painting or two with me? Perhaps even three?"

"All right. Yes."

"Which ones? Or do you want to give it some thought? I can certainly come back." He looked at Jocelyn.

"Yes," she replied enthusiastically.

"Think about it," Jeremy murmured. "I'll think about it. Which ones. Three."

"Good. Then I'll come back and I will look forward to it. It was a great pleasure meeting you and seeing your work."

Jeremy bowed his head. "P-pleasure."

"Do think about the exhibition. I would love for you to see it."

Jocelyn caught JG's eye. She didn't want him to push; it had gone so well.

"Goodbye," JG said. He turned and followed Jocelyn.

"Goodbye," Jeremy said when they'd reached the stairs.

JG turned back and smiled. "I'll see you soon."

Jocelyn was glad she was in the lead, so JG did not see her expression. Hopefully, she would be able to rein in her fiercely beating heart before he saw her full on. She felt proud of JG. She did not have the right to feel so proud of him, but she did. They reached the second floor and started toward the other staircase, but she stopped before they reached it and turned back to face him. He looked at her expectantly. "Thank you," she said meaningfully.

His expression was tender. He took hold of her hand, lifted it to his lips and pressed a kiss to it. "There is nothing to thank me for."

Her shoulders quivered. She managed to inhale quietly, which felt like a feat.

"His work is astonishingly good," he said. "What it makes you feel. The way you are drawn into the image. I will be delighted to help. He is such a handsome lad. I wonder if a bit of mystery could be created to stir up interest. His work, his looks, his illusiveness."

She was thrilled beyond measure that he was willing to help. He was such a wonderful man. "Shall we have tea?"

"Absolutely."

~~~

As the clock struck ten at night, Julia lay in bed, as usual, but she could not concentrate on her book. She had seen a few of her son's paintings earlier. She was no judge of great art, but his paintings seemed genius to her. Where had the talent come from? She had no artistic ability and, as far she knew, Peter had not possessed one either.

She reached for her port and sipped. She had always meant to do her best by her son, but had she? Had she unwittingly held him back by overprotecting him? He had never been asked to run errands. She purchased whatever he needed and brought them home to him. She had tried to make his life as pleasant as possible, but had she, in fact, held him back without realizing it?

Alice and Jocelyn accepted him wholeheartedly and encouraged exploration. They had given him the strength to leave the house and share in activities. Dinner out at a restaurant. A carriage ride. A walk. A trip to a coffee house. He was even considering attending the Derby tomorrow. Was the girl's success with Jeremy because they were close to his age or had they simply bolstered and inspired him the way she should have done all along?

Her thoughts flitted back to Peter and all the things she did not know, would never know about him. But one thing was certain. "You'd be proud of him," she said wistfully. "So proud."

Chapter Seventeen

The Derby! Jocelyn pressed a gloved hand to her stomach and walked as close as she dared to the edge of the grandstand. She drew in a sharp breath and shivered. They were so high up and what a view! Epsom Downs was filled with thousands of people waiting for the great race to begin, and she would witness it from the uppermost covered grandstand. They had planned on attending for weeks, but only had tickets for ground level. JG had learned of it yesterday and made arrangement for them to be here.

She wanted to remember everything about today. The weather was pleasant, a mild breeze blowing, but it had been raining for days and the track was muddy. She could see the shine of puddles below.

"Hello," JG said behind her.

She smiled and turned to him. "Hello."

"What do you think?"

"It is exhilarating to be so high up. Thank you for that."

"It was nothing. But you and I have important business to attend to."

"Do we?"

"Indeed. Bets have to be in soon."

"Bets," she repeated. "Of which I know nothing."

"It's all a guess, anyway. Ah, look," he said as something caught his eye below. "They are bringing them out."

Indeed, the noise of the crowd had escalated. She turned to watch the parade of jockeys on magnificent horses. The horses had blankets on their backs, and each jockey's shirt and cap matched the color. There was bright yellow, fuchsia, white, blue, dark green and light green and many more.

"Some tracks are in a straight line," JG said, leaning closer to her. "This one is orbicular. Actually, it's in the shape of a large C. You see? They will start there and end there."

"The track is so muddy," she remarked.

"Yes, but not as muddy as it will be once they take off. It will impact the race, too."

She looked at him. "Do you follow the sport closely?"

"I enjoy it. They are such splendid animals."

"Yes, they are." She looked back out at the parade of men and horses.

"So which of them looks lucky?" he asked.

"I have no idea. There are a lot of them, aren't there?"

"There are fourteen of them. That one there," he said pointing, "is Abjer. A lot of chaps are betting on him. Same with Pindarrie. That one."

A tall, sleek chestnut stallion caught her eye. "What about that one with the long legs?"

"That is Sailor. A strong contender. The odds are, uh, four to one," he said, consulting the data sheet in his hand.

"Sailor," she decided. "I like the way he holds his head. That's my pick."

JG assessed Jocelyn thoughtfully. "She looked up from the chestnut horse with her chestnut-colored hair and eyes, although they had gold centers." He grinned. "I don't suppose I'm as good with words as your sister."

"Few are, in my opinion," she replied with a shy smile.

"I'm going to go place our bet on Sailor," he said, taking a step back. "I ordered champagne punch so it will be here soon. I'll be right back."

As he walked away, Jocelyn caught Ada's eye. Standing across the grandstand, Ada looked happy between Mr. Bower and Hugh Pritchett. Ada gave her a knowing smile and Jocelyn returned it before turning back to the spectacle below. *High and light.* That's how she felt. She felt high in every sense of the word and as light as a feather.

~~~

Alice stood several yards away peering at the crowd below. It was said that a hundred thousand people were typically in attendance for the race. Could there really be that many? Most were celebrating boisterously. It was strange to be above it all. Nigel stood next to her, except he was facing the room. His expression seemed troubled. "What is it?" she asked, glancing in the direction of his gaze.

"My father," he replied.

She looked at Lord Merton who was jauntily conversing with two other men and having a fine time. "What about him?"

Nigel turned and looked over the track. "There are times, he gets a look," he replied quietly. He linked gazes with her. "He has sworn not to wager ever again, but he admits he can't be trusted to hold to his own edicts."

She was glad he was confiding in her. It felt right. A server appeared with a tray of glasses filled with an effervescent, orange-tinted concoction with raspberries floating atop. "Compliments of Lord Blairwood," the server said.

"Thank you," Nigel and Alice said. They each took one and sipped. It was refreshing with an orange and pineapple flavor. "That is delicious," she said.

He agreed, but he was still distracted by his thoughts. "I didn't tell you this before, but when everything was first suggested to me, meaning you, *us,* my father said that his plan was to turn the running of the estate over to me sooner rather than later. He said when everything was settled—"

"Meaning me? Or rather us?"

"Yes. When that was all settled, he was going to go live in France."

She blinked in surprise. For one thing, Nigel had just said *he.* Not they? Not Lady Merton? "France," she repeated.

He nodded again. "My mother had a more passionate reaction than that, I can tell you. But he seemed firm in the resolve. He said he could not be trusted not to gamble, and he wants to protect his reputation. Not that it hasn't been damaged, because it has, but it's not beyond redemption."

"But leaving the country," Alice mused.

"He has a cousin there and they are partners in a vineyard. I say partners. I know that father is part owner. I really don't know the details."

"Is that still his plan?" she asked curiously.

"I haven't heard otherwise."

She sipped again. "What about your mother?"

"I suppose she would go between here and there. I don't see them being separated for any length of time, no matter how much he exasperates her."

She waited for him to continue.

"To be honest, I didn't know what to think when the idea was proposed, but the more I think on it, I do see the merit. Especially when I sense the fever starting in him."

"The fever to gamble," she said softly.

Their gazes connected again and he nodded.

She looked below to the fillies and colts being paraded around the track. "I'm glad you told me."

"So am I. Our friendship has grown, but it's nothing in comparison to what it would be in marriage. I know we are not at the point of engagement, but secrets should not be kept between us. Especially not secrets that impact our lives."

She looked at him. "I agree."

"I admire your candor. I want it for myself. I want it between us."

There was such magnetism between them that her nipples had stiffened painfully and her cheeks heated. She glanced at Lord Merton to break the spell. He was having a fine time. "I hope you're wrong about him."

"So do I."

She gave him a smile and turned back to the sights below.

"I'm good with finances, Alice," he said quietly. "I can get the estate in good health and keep it that way. But he cannot be a continual detriment."

She discreetly touched his arm for comfort and nodded.

~~~

The race went by incredibly fast, it seemed like mere seconds, and Sailor won. Jocelyn cried out and jumped for joy. The whole place was so noisy and rambunctious that hopefully her breach of etiquette hadn't been noticed. JG was also laughing in delight.

"We won," he cried. "You did it!"

She felt giddy and bursting with happiness. JG picked her up, which took her by surprise, but not an unpleasant one. He quickly set her down, but she left her hands on his shoulders for a moment longer. She glanced around to see if anyone had noticed, and her gaze connected with Lord Morguston a few yards behind them. His face was so dark with dislike, she felt as if she'd been hit with a bucket of cold water.

"What's wrong?" JG asked before he saw for himself.

His grandfather's answering look was no less stony toward him before he limped away.

JG looked back at her apologetically. "I'm sorry. I would have spared you that if I could."

"It's all right."

"It's not, but he will never change." He looked at her searchingly, his expression vulnerable. "Will you wait for me?" he asked just above a whisper.

She found herself nodding before she realized she was doing it. But it was true. She would wait. If it took ten years for them to be together, she would wait.

~~~

Lakely noticed Lord Morguston's scowl and looked to find the recipient of the look. JG and Jocelyn had just embraced. Her jaw nearly dropped. When had that connection been made? She looked back at Lord Morguston and knew he would never allow it to progress further. She felt terrible for Jocelyn. They had failed her.

~~~

Lakely knocked and then entered her sister's room that evening. It smelled of floral-scented powder.

"Do come in," Ada said sardonically. "Don't wait to be invited."

Beatrice, one of their upstairs maids was fastening the buttons on the back of Ada's gown. "Is Mr. Bower staying for dinner?" Lakely asked with irritation apparent in her tone.

"Yes, he is."

"Does he not have a home and people of his own to return to? They must think he fell off the face of the earth."

Ada flicked a cool glance at her sister to make abundantly clear that she was not going to be drawn into an argument. "I wish you would try harder to be accepting of the man who will be your brother-in-law. If you would only try, you would like him."

Lakely rolled her eyes. "I do like him, but the two of you are always together. It is annoying when I want a word alone with you."

"Well, here I am and right there you are. Do you want a word?"

"Yes, I do."

"Then have it. Good Gracious. You have a face like a thundercloud and the demeanor to match. Did you not have a delightful day? I did."

"If I have the demeanor of a thundercloud, it is because I am concerned for someone we care about. By the way, I loathe it when you act mature and superior." She walked over to look at her sister's gown more closely. "That's pretty. I hadn't seen it."

"Thank you."

Beatrice stepped to the dresser to get the necklace that lay on top. "I'll do that, Beatrice," Lakely said reaching out for it.

"Yes, Miss," Beatrice said. She handed it over. "Will there be anything else?" she asked Ada.

"No, thank you," Ada replied.

Beatrice looked at Lakely. "Will you be dressing soon?"

Lakely thought about it with a frown. "I don't feel like changing. I'll ring if I change my mind."

As Beatrice left the room, Lakely placed the necklace around her sister's neck. "It feels as if you've grown up overnight."

"Does it? I've been at it for quite a while."

"There," Lakely said, fastening the clip. "Done."

Ada turned to her. "How do I look?"

"You look beautiful and as if you've grown up overnight."

"Thank you."

"I am sorry if I've been difficult. I do like Harrison. Very much. You needn't worry on that account."

"I know you do. Or rather I've known that you will. He's caring and amusing and he adores me."

Lakely nodded. "He and I have those things in common."

Ada took hold of her sister's hands. "I think you are just a little jealous of the time he and I spend together. Although you know no one could replace you."

Lakely sulked. "I hate it when you're right."

"You don't hate when I'm right. You hate it when you're wrong. Now, was there something you wanted to talk to me about?"

Lakely's expression grew troubled in earnest. "I saw something today. Jocelyn. And JG."

"Ah."

Lakely jerked her hands away. "You knew? You knew that they have formed some sort of attachment!"

"Yes."

"How did I not know? When did it happen?"

"They met at Buckley's, the same night we met Harrison. And you didn't know because you stormed off after Father and you've been occupied with your own life."

"Why didn't you tell me?"

Ada shrugged as she shook her head. "I'm not sure what there is to tell. They struck up a friendship and, yes, there is a spark there. But they are not eloping. They like one another a great deal and they are having a wonderful time together."

"I think it's more than that," Lakely rejoined.

"All right. So do I." Ada turned to look at herself in the mirror. "But Jaus is my friend and I'm happy for her." Ada turned back to her sister. "And JG is our friend. I'm happy for both of them. Don't you think it's wonderful to see love and affection blossoming all around?"

"Oh, yes," Lakely retorted. "For everyone but me. But you are missing a vital point."

"What's that?"

"Lord Morguston."

Ada didn't react for a moment. "He is a stodgy old thing," she conceded. "Do you think he enjoys being disliked? Papa says they are terrified of him in the House of Lords."

"I have no idea, but I saw him today and the look he gave Jocelyn—"

"Oh, dear. I hope she didn't see."

"She did. Ada, we should have protected her. Warned her."

"She is no more a child than I am," Ada stated. "Think about it. If you cared for someone, would you be warned off because his grandfather thought you weren't good enough?" She paused. "You know you wouldn't."

"He will not allow a connection between them," Lakely said. "He's never even approved of JG associating with Nigel and the others."

"And has that stopped JG?"

"Friends are one thing. Marriage is different."

"We do not know what JG and Jocelyn are feeling or hoping for," Ada replied. "If it turns out to be marriage, JG will simply have to be brave. He will have to stand up to his grandfather. 'Faint heart never won the lady fair, so it's been often told. But if one mite for me you care, for once you will be bold.'"

Lakely pointedly folded her arms and lifted a brow. Her younger sister's new-found confidence was wearing on her nerves. "Faint heart should take care indeed, not to get kicked by Grandfather's knee."

Ada thrust her hand on her hips. "If Grandfather kicks, then my friend JG should move away swiftly or lift his own knee."

"It's easy for us to make light of it," Lakely said.

"I'm not making light of it. I don't want anyone to get hurt. But we are none of us children. Now, come downstairs and join us in a game." Ada started for the door. "But bathe and dress first. Mamma will insist on it, anyway."

Ada walked on and Lakely sullenly returned to her own room recalling the Buckley gala when she, Ada, Jocelyn and Alice had lifted a glass to … what was it? An eventful evening? Apparently, it had been. Nigel and Alice's bond had been secured, Ada had not only met but toppled head over heels for Harrison and he for her, and JG and Jocelyn had struck up a friendship with sparks. "Everyone, but me," Lakely muttered.

~~~

"I don't know what you are playing at, JG," his grandfather said ominously.

JG had arrived home only to be summoned to appear before his grandfather in his study. "Playing at?"

"I can tell you this much," Lord Morguston stated in a determined tone. "You will marry in the next year to a lady of an appropriate station of whom I approve."

"I love Miss Jocelyn Weatherly," JG stated.

Lord Morguston upper lip curled in a smirk. "Infatuations come and go."

"It is not an infatuation, sir."

"She is not of your station!"

"I don't care."

"You will care. You will do as I say, or I will disown you."

JG blinked. His grandfather was talking nonsense. He was the heir, the only heir.

"I do not want to do that, but the legacy must be protected."

The legacy? Wasn't the legacy his by birthright?

"There are distant cousins," his grandfather stated.

JG could only gawk. "You would see everything go to some distant cousin? Rather than me? Rather than your own grandson? Because you do not approve of the woman I love? Someone you don't even know yet?"

"Dukedom comes with privilege *and* responsibility," the old man thundered as he slapped the desk. "You will marry correctly. Carry on a dalliance with this American if you must," he added, throwing a hand in the air. "But only after you sire a legitimate heir."

JG shook his head and stepped back. He turned and started for the door.

"We are not finished yet," his grandfather exclaimed.

JG turned back from the door. "Oh, we are." He opened the door and walked out, leaving it wide open.

Chapter Eighteen

Jocelyn was surprised when Julia hailed a cab during a longer than usual morning walk. "I want to show you something," was the only explanation. The day had grown overcast, there was a strong scent of rain in the air, and they had not brought umbrellas, but the cab had a hood, sides and even a curtain that could be drawn to cover them from rain if needed.

"Park Lane, please," Julia said to the driver. "Drive the length of it and then take us to number fourteen Bryanston Square."

Julia and Jocelyn enjoyed the ride, chatting amiably. When they reached Mayfair, Jocelyn was agog as she observed the palatial homes. "Can you imagine?"

"Imagine living like kings and queens? That is rather what they are in society, unroyal kings and queens and princes and princesses untouched by the realities that govern most of us." The cab turned onto Park Lane.

"They're so splendid," Jocelyn said.

"Yes, they are. I think it is that one," Julia said, pointing to a mansion on a corner. It was stone with a pillared portico and a row of ornate windows on the second level.

"What about it?" Jocelyn asked curiously.

"I believe that is the residence of the Duke of Morguston."

Jocelyn looked at her aunt. "I don't know who that is."

"JG's grandfather," her aunt returned. "And one day, it will belong to JG when he is the duke."

The words had such gravity. Jocelyn's heart felt heavy as she looked back at the mansion. "JG lives there?"

"Yes."

Jocelyn released a shaky breath. "It's just he and his grandfather."

"And at least a dozen servants."

The cab reached the end of the street and doubled back to return the way it had come. Jocelyn could not tear her eyes from the place. "Why did you show me?"

Julia looked burdened. "To prepare you, my love. Life is not a fairy tale. Not very often, anyway."

Tears tormented the backs of Jocelyn's eyes. "I thought you liked him."

"I do like him! Very much. He is kind and amusing. Somehow, he has escaped the stifling arrogance of most of his kind."

Most of his kind. JG had told her his grandfather was not the nicest of men. A terrible snob. And why not when they lived in a palace with at least a dozen servants? His grandfather did not think she was good enough for him. That was what the hateful scowl had been about at the derby. He would never accept her even though JG did.

"I do not want to discourage your friendship with JG, but you must be prepared for resistance," she said apologetically. "I hear Morguston is rather formidable."

Rain fell suddenly and hard. Julia yanked the curtain closed. Ordinarily, Jocelyn would have enjoyed the thrill of a rainstorm and the feeling of intimacy it created in the cab. She loved rain, the sound of it, the smell of it. But the joy had drained from the day.

Julia reached over to lay a hand atop hers. "You know him better than I do, but please guard your heart."

Too late for that, Jocelyn thought. It was far, far too late.

~~~

The moment Lakely walked into the dining room for breakfast, Ada held up a letter. "You're in," she cried. "You're invited to dance at the Toomey's ball."

"How do you know?" Lakely asked crossly as she walked over. She snatched the letter from her sister's hand and looked at Ada accusingly.

"The seal was loose," Ada said innocently. "It practically fell out."

Nigel chuckled and Lakely glared at him before noticing her parent's amused expressions, although her mother's gaze was on her cup of tea and her father's on the newspaper in his hand. She sat in her place and reached for a muffin before she pulled out the letter and perused the contents. "What about you?" she asked Nigel.

He nodded. "Us, too."

Lakely reached for the jam and spread it on her muffin. "Lady Toomey is allowing an American to dance at her gala? The whole point of it, besides creating a spectacle, is to demonstrate the vibrancy of young English aristocracy."

"How do you know that?" Ada asked.

"The invitation alluded to it and then Monty stayed for tea after the audition. Apparently, something was said in Vienna about British aristocracy having seen its best days. The world changing and all that."

"Well," Nigel said, "I didn't care if we got chosen or not, but now there will be at least three rehearsals and maybe more."

"And you're looking forward to it," Ada observed.

The corners of his mouth twitched. "I'm not dreading it."

"It doesn't say who I'll dance with," Lakely said, having gone back to the letter.

"You have jam," Ada said, pointing to the side of her own mouth.

"I hope it won't be Francis Beckman." Lakely dabbed her lips with her napkin. "He is so boring. He wouldn't recognize a moment of levity if it sidled up and nibbled on his ear lobe."

Ada burst out in laugher, covering her mouth after the fact.

~~~

Fisher summoned Alice from her writing because Nigel had come calling. Alice blinked in surprise, but quickly stood saying she would be right down. Her dress was a well-worn one, a shade of pale moss green she liked, but there was a smudge of ink on it. Oh, well. She had not been expecting him or she would have dressed better. She went down and found him in the foyer. "Hello," she greeted.

"My apologies for just showing up, but—" he paused and held up a letter. "We're in. We have been invited to take part in Lady Toomey's performance. I had to come tell you."

"Oh!" Alice came closer. She had not expected to be chosen.

"Do you want to?" he asked hopefully.

She realized she did. "I think it would be fun. Do you want to?"

"Yes."

She smiled. "Did Lakely get asked?"

He nodded. "She is in, as well."

"I'm so glad. And Dab?"

"I'm sure he did. I haven't heard, but he will have been asked. The Adonis darling of the ton? I can't imagine him not being chosen."

"Would you like to come into the parlour?"

"I'd be interested in a stroll if you would. It's such a pleasant day."

"Yes, I would." She put on a bonnet and grabbed her parasol on the way out. It felt good to get outdoors. Jocelyn had been in a strange mood all day, almost avoiding her or so it felt. "Is Lakely excited by the invitation?"

"She would have been displeased not to be asked. I'm trying to think the last time I saw her truly excited about something. I hope one day she can settle down and choose to be happy."

Alice pondered the statement. "Given the right circumstances, I feel certain she will be happy. Falling in love—"

He blew out a breath. "I can't picture that man," he admitted. "I can feel for him, but I can't quite picture him. My sister is not a docile lady."

"Nor will he want one," Alice rejoined. "Not every gentleman wants a docile lady."

"That is true," he replied with a devilish grin. They walked in silence for a bit. "Tell me something I don't know about you."

She drew a blank. He knew about her family, her background, her writing.

"Shall I tell you one?" he offered.

"Yes."

"I had an elder brother."

She stopped and faced him, surprised.

"He died many years ago. He was only twelve. I was eight."

"I'm sorry."

"It was a lung condition brought on by a fever. It devastated my parents, of course. All of us."

She murmured sympathetically.

"I've found myself thinking of him more these last months."

"Why?"

"He would have been the heir. The estate would have gone to him. The title, the responsibility."

There was that word again.

"As the second son, I would have been free to pursue a profession of my choice."

The statement was disturbing. It made him seemed trapped. "What would have you chosen?"

"I don't know," he admitted. "Not politics. Not medicine. Not the clergy. Business, I suppose. Commerce of some sort. That's what comes most naturally."

"Instead, you are the heir," she said. *With the estate, title and responsibilities.* She recalled Lakely saying he had done nothing but try to live up to his responsibilities. Alice was getting a bad feeling again. She started in motion again and Nigel stayed by her side. She put up the parasol.

"I'm sorry if I made you sad," he said.

"You didn't," she said, although it wasn't perfectly true. Conflicted was probably a better word. "What was his name?"

"James. After my father. It's also my middle name. We called him Jamie. Now, it's your turn."

"My middle name is Emmanuel. I was named after Granny." He nodded.

"And what else?" she murmured. "We have a dog at home."

His answering smile was bright. "Do you?"

"Yes. A lovable old mutt named Tildy. Matilda, but we call her Tildy. She showed up one day in the backyard when I was seven or eight. Sophia and Jaus and I were playing and here she came. Poor darling. She was half starved and had everything wrong with her, but we took her in and she got better. She's an old thing now. She doesn't do much but nap." Nigel looked amused and happy. Was he? Was it an act? "Are you sorry you're the heir?" she blurted.

"No! Oh, no." He stopped and faced her. "Did I give that impression? I'm not sorry at all. I have had most of my life to prepare for it. It's the other notion, that things would have been different had Jamie lived, that's what's odd. I'm not sure why I've dwelt on it of late. It's just that I don't really know who or what I would have been."

She nodded slowly. He seemed sincere. She believed he was. "You can't know what you would have done as a profession, but as to who you are, I don't know why you would be so different."

"Is that a good thing?"

"In my opinion, it's a very good thing." He smiled, she returned it and felt better. She had to stop letting her imagination run away with her.

~~~

As the clock struck four in the morning, Alice's eyes fluttered open. *Go back to sleep,* she ordered herself. She turned onto her side and discovered Jocelyn looking at her. It gave her a start. "What are you doing awake?" she asked softly.

"Thinking," Jocelyn replied. "I haven't been awake long."

"Are you all right? You were preoccupied today."

"I was, but I'm fine." She paused before adding, "I don't care if he's rich."

"Who?"

"JG. He's rich. His family is very rich."

Alice gave a light shrug. "They all are."

"You realize they think that about us."

"What? That we are rich?"

"Yes. The first night I met JG, he thought I was you. He said, 'Oh, you're the heiress from America.'"

Alice scoffed. "Heiress."

Jocelyn nodded. "Ada corrected him and then he apologized for offending me. I said I wasn't offended, but we were *not* heiresses."

"That damned dowry," Alice complained.

"I wonder how much it is," Jocelyn murmured.

"So do I. Do you think Papa would tell me if I asked?"

"Probably not. He'd say it was gentlemen's business."

"Now, *that* is offensive," Alice declared.

It grew quiet. There was only the sound of the mantle clock ticking. "Perhaps it is best to think of it as business," Jocelyn reasoned. "As long as there is love, what does it matter if there is also a business transaction in the beginning?"

"Because it muddies the water," Alice retorted. "Turns it all dark and slimy. You can't see what's under the surface. In my opinion, business does not belong anywhere near love."

Jocelyn thought about it. "I imagine our sisters both had a dowry and look at them. At least Clara and Ross. They couldn't be happier or more in love."

Maybe it would help to consider that. "Now I really want to know," Alice admitted. "Did they have a dowry? How much was it? How much is mine? And yours?"

"I want to know, too. But I know who JG is. And you know who Nigel is." She took a deep breath and closed her eyes, ready to go back to sleep.

Alice wished she felt the same peace of mind, but she could not shake the disquieting notion that she and Nigel would not be courting except for the dowry. That fact muddied everything.

Chapter Nineteen

lice looked around the Toomey's ballroom at the others who had gathered for the first dance rehearsal. Twelve couples would dance, twenty-four ladies and gentlemen, twenty-three of whom were either noble or connected to nobility. And then there was her. She was glad to have come with Nigel and Lakely and to be standing between them. Standing on Lakely's other side was Franklin Hopewell, the gentleman she had been paired with. Dab stood on Nigel's far side with his partner, Lady Cora Greenwood.

Phineas Skeffington stood before them all with a middle-aged lady and a younger man who both resembled him. "May I introduce my assistants?" he said in a loud, clear voice. "My sister, Miss Honoraria Skeffington."

Miss Skeffington curtsied with the graceful flourish of an experienced dancer.

"And my nephew, Mr. Bartholomew Hammersley."

The young man bowed in such an effeminate manner that Alice wondered if he wouldn't rather have curtsied. It's possible he could have outcurtsied his aunt. She suspected he would have given her a run for the money.

"Before we begin," Phineas continued, "I must establish the requirement of secrecy. The dance will take the ton by storm, but only if it remains *non dévoilé* until the night of the ball. Do not speak of it outside this room, not even to your mammas. Should we learn of a breach of our confidence, the breacher will be summarily dismissed, uninvited and disenfranchised."

"What about beheaded?" Lakely whispered to Alice.

Alice struggled not to smile. She could not afford to get tickled. Laugher might lead to being summarily dismissed, uninvited and disenfranchised.

"If you will, ladies and gentlemen," Mr. Skeffington said, "come and make two lines, gents standing across from your partners." When everyone had complied, Mr. Skeffington continued. "Everyone should be able see me and my fellow instructors. The music you are about to hear is original and the dance has been choreographed for it." Mr. Skeffington motioned for the musicians to begin playing. "There will, of course, be a full orchestra playing, but these gentlemen will provide both tune and tempo to learn by."

"During this prelude, you will all be making your way to the floor, each gentleman with his lady on his arm. You will walk around the floor to your place, which will be decided later. For now, we shall concentrate on the beginning steps. Facing each other," he paused as Miss Skeffington and Mr. Hammersley faced one another. "Hands at your sides. You can stop the music," he called to the musicians who complied.

"We will learn the steps and then put the music to it. To begin, gentlemen, your right hand goes to her waist while the left goes behind your back. Like so." He demonstrated at the same time his nephew did. "Now you."

Nigel reached out as demonstrated and Alice's breath caught at the feeling of his hand on her waist. She felt her cheeks heat. *Please go on*, she silently begged the instructor. The longer they stood like that, the warmer her face would grow.

"Ladies, your arms remain at your sides, hands ever so slightly turned out. What is the story, you may ask? I put it to you that only you can decide. Perhaps the man before you is your intended who has blundered. Quite by accident. Now he is trying to win your affection back and you are deciding how long you will stay miffed, although, deep in your heart, you want to forgive him. Or perhaps the story is that you have never danced with a man before. You have learned your steps but have no idea how your steps fit with his. He, being more worldly and experienced, is showing you. You make up your own story, but the dance must demonstrate it."

"I've got the steps so far," Nigel teased.

It was difficult for Alice to focus on anything other than his hand on her waist and their closeness.

"The dance begins with the gentlemen directing all movement. For twelve counts, with the music, you flow. It is back and forth, back and forth, normal waltz step, normal waltz step and repeat." Mr. Skeffington did the motion as he said the steps as did his assistants who obviously had the entire dance memorized.

"In this way, you make a circle, ending where you began. Now you try. Ready? Back and forth, back and forth, normal waltz step, normal waltz step. Back and forth, back and forth, normal waltz step, normal waltz step. Good. Again."

The dancers then did the step several times.

"Now, gentlemen, take your left hand from behind your back and lift her hand up in the air insisting that she participate in the dance and not simply be led around. Ladies, your arm is lifted by him. Allow him to take it up. Follow it with your gaze, point gracefully toward the ceiling. Finally, you will give in and enjoy the dance. Assume a normal waltz position, left hand on his arm near the shoulder, your right slips into his hand. And we shall waltz around the floor. Let us try it from the beginning with the music."

The steps felt sensuous. The story being told seemed to be that she was shy and reticent while he was taking charge. Touching her, controlling her. Moving her about, coaxing her into joining the dance. Each couple circled the dance floor in tandem and yet locked in their own pairing.

The dance master signaled for the music to stop. "Next. Separating again. Gents, reach out with your right hand, dramatically, like so. Ladies, your hand accepts his, softly. He takes your hands up, up, now the left hands connect low and he turns you under his arm."

It took several attempts to get the move right. Alice wondered if everyone one else was as breathless as she. It wasn't the exertion as much as it was that the movements of the dance were so very intimate. She could tell Nigel felt the same. His gaze was intense, his eyes blazing with passion.

"Next. Gentlemen, if you please, place your right hand upon her waist, your left pointing upwards, like at a diagonal, just so. Ladies, right hand on his shoulder and left hand pointing diagonally downward. You see the line that is made from ceiling to floor with your arms. In this position, you will waltz. The step gets quicker here, but we will take it at the normal pace in order for you to get the feeling. And one-two-three, one-two three."

Rehearsal continued for another hour before they broke for refreshments. By then, the atmosphere was one of relief and joviality. They'd gotten comfortable with their partners and made a good start on learning the steps. Phineas Skeffington had no doubt that the performance would be a crowning achievement for him, and they were all beginning to sense it might be true.

During refreshments, and after being warned not to eat to excess, the ladies were informed they would be measured and fitted for a gown to be paid for by Lord and Lady Toomey. Without question, Alice had become more sensitive and responsive to Nigel. Cognizant of his physicality. The strength and yet gentleness of his hands, the line of his jaw. There were the moments their bodies had contact. Her breast brushing against his arm. His hand on her waist. His warm breath on her neck. She feared she was looking at him with arousal. Could everyone tell? Could he? Even sitting with him during the break and endeavoring to be perfectly proper, it was as if a barrier had been crossed and they were undeniably a couple. It was thrilling.

When the rehearsal concluded and Alice, Nigel and Lakely had taken their seats in the carriage for the return home, Lakely realized she'd left her wrap behind. She went after it, leaving Nigel and Alice facing one another across the carriage.

Nigel's eyes danced with merriment. "What would Robina Rathke have to say about a man and a woman seated in such a fashion as this? Especially when the man was thinking of stealing a kiss."

"But an unmarried lady and gentleman are *never* alone," Alice replied innocently. "She is always chaperoned."

"Ah. That's right. I forgot." He leaned slightly forward, took hold of her gloved hand and pressed a kiss to it. Looking up at her, he said, "I enjoyed being your partner today."

In an impulsive move, Alice leaned forward until their faces were mere inches apart. "So did I." He closed the distance and softly kissed her lips. When they separated, her lips were tingling, and her blood was surging. The timing was fortuitous since the door was opened for Lakely who climbed in and sat beside Alice.

"I thought that went well," Lakely said.

"So did I," Nigel said. "I can't wait for the next."

Alice's heart hammered. She could hardly wait either.

Chapter Twenty

O n the days designated to paying social calls, it had become routine for Lakely and Ada to breakfast while discussing whom they might visit. A typical conversation might be, "We should see Cecelia Markham today," one would comment. "Yes," the other would agree. "And we should not forget to pay a visit to the Sloan sisters."

Naturally, Lady Merton inconspicuously listened. She was, after all, a careful mistress of her household and its occupants. The girls then readied themselves, bid their mother goodbye, since she had her own friends to visit, and set off for the Weatherly home in Bryanston Square. They were always mindful not to actually say they were going to any particular home, only that they should and might and ought.

In the upstairs parlour of the Weatherly home, Alice, Jocelyn, Lakely and Ada discussed all manner of things. Alice's work was frequently a topic. Lakely had uncovered a possible storyline through a friend of her aunt, and Ada was delving into the story of Harrison's ancestor who had perished aboard a troop ship in route home from the war.

The second chapter of Alice's manuscript was the story of Horace Madsen and Catherine Kerr, a couple who had been on the brink of marriage when the rebellion began. Alice had only two of Horace's letters, one written before he left home, and another brief letter written shortly before he fell in battle. Catherine had written to him frequently, but she had rarely known where to send the letters, so she still had most of them when Alice approached her. Catherine had gladly loaned them with her blessing to tell their story.

This afternoon, the girls had been discussing the chapter over tea and crumpets served with a choice of clotted cream or lemon curd. "The question in my mind," Alice mused, "is whether I end the chapter with his final letter, followed by the date, place and manor of his death. That may be too abrupt, but it serves to … shock the reader in the same way Catherine must have been shocked. It's fitting that it should be devastating, don't you think? It *was* devastating."

"Yes," Lakely agreed. "Through everything that has been revealed in her letters, her feelings are clear."

Ada nodded. "I feel as if I know her. May I see the miniatures again?"

Alice passed over the painted portrait miniatures, one of Horace and one of Catherine. Horace had never seen the one of her. It would have been sent to him if only she had known where to send it. His whiskered face had a poetic quality and dark brown eyes. Catherine was more plain than pretty except for lovely, very blue eyes.

"I don't know, Ali," Jocelyn replied. "The scene you wrote when Catherine finds out he's gone was beautifully done. It was heart wrenching."

"I fear it's maudlin," Alice said.

"Read his final letter again," she suggested.

Alice picked it up. "It's dated the eighth of September. 'Dearest Catherine. I am sitting in an inn on the first afternoon I have had off in over three weeks. It is good to leave camp behind for a spell and enjoy a pint, but I cannot get you off of my mind. Nor can I shake a foreboding in regard to the upcoming battle. Howe is trying to take Philadelphia, and we have to stop him. We march at first light.

My sweet Cat, you know how I longed to be married, but upon reflection, I believe it is for the best that we did not. If we had and if you had gotten with child, you would have suffered that much more in the event of my death. If I survive this war, we shall begin afresh. God willing, before too much longer. Each day is long here. Nights, even moreso. That said, you know how greatly I believe in our cause. My life is wholeheartedly pledged to the achievement of freedom for us and the generations to come.

I pray this dark feeling that has taken root in my breast is mistaken and that I will make it home to you. I have visions of that day. I will sweep you up into my arms and kiss you as you have never been kissed. If bruises are left upon your skin from my too-zealous embrace, I will gratefully press soft, wet kisses to them until they fade.

If, however, this premonition of mine is not wrong, but a sort of gift, a warning for readiness, I beg you to know that, above all, I want happiness for you. Have no further concern for me as I will be beyond all hurt. I believe my spirit will linger in the dappled sunlight of our orchard grateful for the love we have known. This life is not the end. I grow more certain of it by the hour." Alice paused before adding, "'Yours Eternally,'" in a voice choked with emotion.

Jocelyn sobbed and Ada did the same a split second later. Even Lakely was wiping her eyes and breathing raggedly.

"The last line of the chapter will read, 'Horace L. Madsen, born January 6, 1754, died September 11, 1777. Battle of Brandywine.'"

"Three days after he wrote her," Lakely said thickly.

Alice nodded.

"I think you should end it that way," Lakely said. "It's heartbreaking, but it damn well should be."

"I agree," Ada said from behind her handkerchief. She blew her nose.

Dinah appeared in the doorway, opened her mouth to speak, but shut it again in alarm at seeing them all in tears.

"It's all right, Dinah," Jocelyn said as she dried her face. "We just heard a sad story, but we're fine."

"Do you need anything?" the girl asked sheepishly.

Ada looked at the girl. "Will you tell cook that was the best lemon curd I've had in ages? Maybe ever."

"Yes, Miss."

"You know," Lakely said to Alice. "Life is short. Just ask Catherine. Is there any wine?"

"We're fine, Dinah," Alice said with a smile. "Thank you." When the girl had walked on, Alice cocked a brow at Lakely. "I've learned from you." She rose and fetched a bottle of homemade orange wine she'd stashed in a decorative side cabinet.

"You are a bad influence," Ada said to her sister with mock severity.

"Thank you," Lakely rejoined. "I do try."

~~~

"JG," Sir George James greeted as he rose and walked around his desk to meet him. They shook hands exuberantly. "Good to see you!"

"It's good to see you, Uncle George."

"Sit. Sit. Or would you rather go to the club now? Are you hungry?"

"May we chat first?" JG asked with a certain gravity.

"Of course." George studied him a moment and then went back around his desk and sat. JG was his godson. Henry Baillie, JG's father, had been his closest friend. "Is anything wrong?"

"How like you to get right to the point."

"I'm a barrister. That's what we do."

"That is precisely what I wanted to speak to you about. I would like to learn the law and become a barrister."

George leaned back in his chair. "Did something happen to the dictate that gentlemen do not work?"

"You're a gentleman. The finest I've ever known."

"Thank you for that, but allow me to rephrase. Gentlemen of the peerage do not work. Beyond managing their wealth and sitting in the House of Lords and so on and so forth. So, something has brought this on. What is it?"

JG sighed. "I don't know how much he means it," he began reluctantly, "although I fear he might. Granddad has threatened to disown and, even worse, disinherit me."

George sat up straight in alarm. "Why?"

"Because I've fallen in love."

George blinked. "Normally I would say congratulations without a moment's hesitation," he said warily. "But please continue. Obviously, your grandfather does not approve of your choice."

"That would be correct. He has only ever clapped eyes on her from across a very crowded grandstand, glared at her, in fact. But he has not deigned to meet her. Nor will he."

"Oh, dear. Who is she? The maid?"

JG laughed. "No! Nothing of the sort. She is Miss Jocelyn Weatherly from America, an angel on earth who is visiting family here. Her father is a native."

"Not Richard Weatherly?" George asked curiously.

"Yes!"

"I knew him as a lad. We were at Eton together."

"Really?"

"Yes, indeed. He was a good chap, as I recall. He was younger than me."

"I don't know him yet, but his daughter –"

George waited as JG searched for the right words. It seemed to him that his godson had matured greatly these last months.

"Jocelyn is the kindest, most gentle lady in the entire world. We fell in love the night we met. Perhaps even the first minute. At least the first minute I looked into her eyes. You see, her elder sister, Alice, has two different colored eyes. One blue and one green."

"How unusual."

"Yes. Very. Anyway, I noticed it and then turned to see Jocelyn's. She shook her head and said her eyes were both the same color, boring brown. Oh, but they are not boring. They are beautiful with golden centers. They are life itself."

"Oh my," George said under his breath. "So, your grandfather," he said with a subtle wave of his hand.

"Says we have ten thousand years of noble blood, and I will not be the first to corrupt the line."

"*Hmm.* Well, I can't say I'm terribly surprised."

"I knew he would resist, at first, but I thought he would meet her. Eventually. If he did, she *would* win him over. She would win anyone over. But he is adamant. He says I will marry someone he approves of in the next year or he will disown me. Apparently, there is a distant cousin the estate could go to."

George's hands were folded on the desk, but his index finger repeatedly tapped an opposite knuckle. "My questions are these," he said calmly. "How long have you known Miss Weatherly? Do you truly know her well enough to have made this decision? And does she know your feelings? That is the first round of questions."

"And the second?"

"JG! To give up your birthright! Wealth, connections, the title—"

"I do mind giving up the money. I have never had to think about finances. As for the rest of it?" He shook his head resolutely. "If there is a bottom line to this situation, it is this. I will not give Jocelyn up. Not if she'll have me."

"Does she have similar feelings?" George asked carefully.

"Yes."

"She's said so?"

"Not in so many words, but we know one other's heart. I'm not certain I can explain it, but we each know the other and did from the very beginning. I realize it was not that long ago, but I also know that I have never felt so allied with any other human being so completely. I never expected it to happen, but we each know what the other is thinking and feeling. I haven't told her I love her, but she knows it anyway. And she believes in me. Not my title, me. She doesn't care about the title. Her father does not have one. She's American. They think about things all differently. And the way she looks at me? She sees me, Uncle

175

George. Me. She is helping me to find and believe in myself. Does that make any sense?"

"Of course, it does."

"I have wonderful friends, but I am always on the outside, even if only slightly. I always have been. Early on at school, later at school. I can be a bit of buffoon."

"Don't say that," George scolded. "You are too hard on yourself."

"I'm being honest. But with Jocelyn, I'm not an outsider. I'm right where I should be and who I should be. If I can go through life with her at my side, I will. So I must prepare to make my own way in the world."

"I see."

"Truthfully, I rather look forward to it. Making my own way, my own path." He paused. "Will you take me on as an apprentice?"

"It's not that simple. To become a barrister, you have to join one of the Inns of Court and go through the schooling."

JG nodded slowly. "I think I knew that."

"I will help you through any path you choose to go if it's in my power to do so, but I strongly urge you to speak to Jocelyn first. Tell her what you are planning. Tell her the truth."

JG nodded. "Agreed."

"And then speak with your grandfather. He is stubborn, but he is your grandfather. He loves you."

"I don't know that he does," JG replied earnestly.

"He does," George said emphatically. "He is not an easy or demonstrative man, I know. He was the same way with your father."

"Was he really?"

"Yes."

"I hate that I don't remember my father more than I do. I remember nothing of his relationship with Granddad. In fact, most of what I know has come from you. But, Uncle George, if I tell Granddad what I am thinking and planning, he may show me the door."

"If he does, you'll come to us."

"You know I appreciate that. It's just that I assumed I'd have a year to plan and adjust."

"Honesty is the best policy," George counseled. "Honesty with yourself, Miss Weatherly and your grandfather. Before proceeding, be very certain you are serious in the matter, because doing what you have suggested will not be easy."

"I know that, and I have never been more serious in my life."

George nodded. "All right, then. Let's go to lunch. I'd want to hear more about your Jocelyn."

"Thank you for listening, Uncle George."

"I will always listen and try to advise and help. You are the only godson I have." He rose, as did JG, and they left.

Chapter Twenty-One

B y midway through the third rehearsal, the dancers had learned all the moves. The song was just over eight minutes in length. It was a powerful musical number that started sedately and then built in volume, passion and tempo. As Phineas Skeffington observed them, he swayed and waved his hands with each move while counting in his head. Lady Toomey also watched. The dance master had warned that it was not yet polished, but she found it enthralling. When the men lifted their partner in the air, she gasped. It was just what she'd hoped for. No one would be able to take their eyes from it.

"Good," Skeffington called when the dance concluded. "Let us take a short break and then go again. Drinks and nibbles are on the refreshment table."

As the dancers vacated the floor, Nigel dallied. Alice was slightly out of breath and flushed from the dance, but she felt happy. She was so glad they were taking part in the exhibition. It was great fun.

"May I?" Nigel asked quietly, reaching for her right hand. He was facing her, his back to the others.

She complied with a confused smile. He quickly lifted it, twisting it slightly so that her wrist was exposed. He pressed a kiss to the inside of her wrist, stopping her breath. The sensation of his warm lips against her skin sent a tremor through her. And then he lightly bit a pinch of skin. With a smile on his lips. He released her hand, and she was left frozen, staring into his eyes and the fathomless desire there. She looked away to break the spell and saw that, fortunately, the deed had not been witnessed. She was trembling all over.

"Shall we?" he asked calmly, offering his arm.

She hesitated and then took it numbly; the world around her had slowed again, and they started toward the refreshment table. What had he just done to her? It was as if he had melted and remade her into something lascivious.

"He said something about nibbles," Nigel said, barely able to keep from smiling.

Rather than reply, she pinched his arm, which had no effect through her gloves and his jacket.

He chuckled. "One question," he said. He stopped before they reached the others. "One possibly inappropriate question."

"One possible inappropriate question to follow one possibly inappropriate action?" she said lightly.

"I hope I didn't upset you."

He did not appear to be worried. "Do I look upset?"

His grin vanished. "You look glorious. You are glorious. I couldn't help myself."

She was melting. She was absolutely melting. Again, she glanced at the others, who were chatting amongst themselves. "The question?"

"If we lived in a world of no restraint and we were alone, what would you like to do right now?"

Numerous thoughts and visions flooded her mind, plus the retort, *I'll show you nibbles*, but she lifted her chin slightly, feigning offence. "I am a lady, sir." She paused long enough to watch him sober. "I cannot possibly answer that," she added mischievously. She walked on but glanced back to see what she had expected to see, him smiling with delight and ardor. Oh Lord! What was he doing to her?

When rehearsal commenced again, Lady Toomey continued to watch with her bejeweled hands clutched beneath her chin. She observed one couple and then the next. There was something about Nigel Walston and the pretty American she noticed, an undercurrent of barely restrained passion that was arresting. Watching them made one feel like a *voyeur*. When Skeffington circled close to her, never looking away from the dancers, she pulled out her fan and used it, having grown warm. "Mr. Walston," she said quietly to him. "And his partner."

"Miss Weatherly," he said, still not looking away from the floor.

"They look as if they might whirl off and—" She stilled her fan in front of her lips, "make love in the corner."

He chuckled and then looked at her with a grin. "If I could make every couple look the same, I would."

"I think not," she laughed. "That would take the performance from *almost* scandalously sensuous to … purely scandalous."

He laughed at the wickedly delightful thought.

Chapter Twenty-Two

*A*lice and Jocelyn strolled in the park on a Thursday morning wearing light day gowns and carrying parasols to shield their faces. "We've been here six weeks tomorrow," Jocelyn commented. "Can you believe it?"

Alice nodded. "I know. It has flown by."

"It has and yet it feels longer than that."

"I agree," Alice laughed.

The original plan had been for them to return home the first week of July, but they had been invited to go Merton Park, the Walston's country estate in late July. The city was hot and smelly in the heat of summer so everyone who could escape did. Alice and Jocelyn both wanted to go to Merton Park and experience the country dances and long walks in cooler weather and cleaner air, but they had not received their parent's permission yet.

"Have you and Nigel talked any more about things?" Jocelyn asked casually.

"We talk about most things." Alice gave her sister a sideways look. "We have not discussed an engagement, if that's what you mean."

"You know it's what I meant."

"We haven't wanted to rush the matter when things are going so well."

"Ah."

"Does that make sense? Things are going so well. They are so nice between us. Perfect, really. I don't want it spoiled. I've never thought of myself as a pessimistic person, but it does sometimes feel that I'm waiting for it to go to pot."

"But why would it?"

"I don't know. There are so many beautiful ladies here, so elegant. Many of them, most of them have to have substantial dowries."

Jocelyn nodded. "Yes."

So why me, Alice wondered. Why had she been sought out as the solution to Lord Merton's gambling debt? "Jaus, do you think I've changed?" Alice asked curiously. "I feel so changed."

"How so?"

"In so many ways. I feel …more. And I felt a lot before."

Jocelyn smiled. "That's to be expected when you fall in love," she replied wistfully.

Alice stopped abruptly. "I have not declared that," she said carefully.

"Which does not mean it's not so. Oh, Ali, what are you afraid of?"

Alice began walking again. "I want to remain myself."

"Who else would you be, silly?"

"It's different to be a wife. I've always felt so independent. I suppose that's silly when our parents have taken care of everything."

"It's not silly. You are more independently minded than most young ladies. And it's true that when you love someone, there is dependence there, but it's a dependence on one another. It doesn't make you weak any more than it makes him weak. In fact, together, the two of you are stronger."

"That's very well put."

"Thank you."

"It would be difficult to live away from everyone. Our family is in Boston."

"And also here."

They walked in silence for a few minutes before Alice said, "You've changed, too."

"I know," Jocelyn agreed. She smiled jubilantly. "Do you not sometimes want to shout out to the world that you love him?"

Alice stopped and studied her sister. Jocelyn's eyes were gleaming and her color was high. "Is there something you want to shout to the world?"

"I will if you will," Jocelyn challenged.

Alice nearly laughed. "I have no desire to shout."

"No?"

"No. One of the ways I've changed is becoming very mindful of how others see me." Alice knew Jocelyn was unsatisfied with her response. "All right," she relented. "Obviously, I won't shout it, but—" Alice leaned closer and whispered. "I love him."

"I know," Jocelyn whispered back.

"Is it noticeable?" Alice asked worriedly.

"To me, it is, but I know you."

Alice sighed. "I don't want it to be apparent. I'm not ready for that yet. If this was all happening in Boston, it would be different."

"But it wouldn't be happening there. It's only come about because we're here where society is different."

"If I do agree to marry him, would you really live here part of the time?"

"Yes. I may, anyway. I love it here."

Alice smiled with relief. "I would miss everyone at home, but I cannot imagine being without you."

"Nor I you."

"Now your turn," Alice said eagerly. "What would you like to shout?"

Jocelyn leaned in and whispered in her sister's ear. When she pulled away, Alice was stunned. "What is it?" Jocelyn asked in alarm. "You like him!"

"Yes, I do. I like him very much. And I knew that you liked him." She paused. "You *love* him?"

Jocelyn nodded. "I do. With all my heart."

Alice looked worried. "I should have known it that night you said you didn't mind that he was rich."

"Why do you look that way?" Jocelyn fretted.

"Lakely is concerned," Alice admitted. "She's afraid you'll be hurt. You see, Lord Morguston—"

"Oh, I know. He is a pompous old snob who seems to loathe me without having bothered to meet me."

"Jaus, if he forbids the match—"

"Then we will wait until he dies."

Alice gasped.

"I'm sorry I shocked you, but it's true. JG asked me if I would wait."

"Why didn't you tell me your feelings were so advanced?"

"I suppose I've been all caught up in it. The same as you've been with Nigel. We've been so busy and happy and distracted. It was never my intention to conceal it. Actually, I assumed you knew."

Alice felt terrible she had failed to comprehend something of such major significance to the person she was closest to in the world. "I am so sorry I didn't—"

"No," Jocelyn exclaimed. "Do not be sorry. Not for one instant. Think of it, Ali. We came here for a summer excursion and to visit our family, and we have both fallen in love. We should be nothing but exultant and grateful."

"But what if Lord Morguston lives to be ninety? I don't want you to give up a normal life with a husband and a family."

"I don't want to give those things up either. And I have never wished anyone ill. But I rather do wish that—" she leaned in to whisper the rest in Alice's ear. To which, Alice's eyes grew wide. A guilty grin struggled for containment as she grabbed her sister's arm and started them moving forward again glancing around to make certain no one was observing them too closely.

The girls arrived home to great excitement. Jeremy had received correspondence from JG asking when he could visit again and take a few paintings with him. He had found a gallery owner interested in seeing them.

Jeremy had been at the selection process for the last two hours.

Mr. and Mrs. Weatherly were wondering who JG Baillie was and how he had come to be a friend of Jeremy through Jocelyn.

Julia was pacing, equally thrilled by the idea of her son's paintings selling in a gallery and worried he would end up hurt if rejected.

The girls gleaned all of this within two minutes of being home.

"He's asked permission to meet us," Richard Weatherly said to his youngest daughter.

"Why the worried expression?" she returned lightly. "He is a very nice person whom you will like a great deal, just as we do," she added, glancing at Alice who nodded in agreement.

"He's very nice," Alice echoed. "Very likeable."

"With reddish hair?" Mrs. Weatherly asked Jocelyn suspiciously. "I've seen you dance with him."

"Yes, that's right," Jocelyn replied. "Did anyone reply to him?"

"Yes," her father replied. "Your very nice, very likeable friend has been invited here tomorrow at eleven."

Jocelyn managed to contain her smile and her excitement, but her parents sensed it anyway. *Oh dear*, her mother inwardly groaned.

"Did Aunt Julia mention that she'd met him?" Jocelyn asked.

"She did," her father replied. "She said I should ask you for particulars."

"Well," Alice said with nonchalance. "Now you have them." She looked at her sister. "Let's go help Jeremy choose which paintings he'll send." And out the two went in a whirl that left their parents bemused.

Chapter Twenty-Three

JG arrived ten minutes before the appointed hour and began to pace on the sidewalk in order to present himself on the dot, but Jocelyn had been watching for him, and she opened the door and invited him in.

"I'm early," he apologized as he stepped in.

"I'm glad you are," she replied.

"I'm hoping to speak with you, if I might," he said. "While I'm here, I mean. It doesn't have to be first thing."

She was nodding. "All right. Come meet my family," she urged.

"I'm nervous," he whispered.

"You needn't be," she whispered back. "I promise." She led the way into the parlour where the adults were gathered. Her father stood when they entered. "Mama, Papa, this is our friend, JG Baillie." She looked back at him with a bolstering expression. "Of course, you already met Aunt Julia and Granny."

"Yes, indeed. Hello, again, ladies."

"Hello, JG," Granny said cheerfully.

"It's a pleasure to see you again," Julia said. "We were delighted to receive the news."

He blinked and his smile dimmed. "News?"

"About the gallery?"

"Oh! Yes."

"And, of course, you know Alice," Jocelyn said as Alice entered the room.

"Yes, hello," he said to her.

"Hello, Lord Blairwood," she said in a formal tone with a teasing bow of her head.

"Oh, none of that," he laughed.

Alice looked at her parents. "JG is modest, but he is the heir apparent of the Dukedom of Morguston and he currently has the title of Marquess of Blairwood, thus Lord Blairwood." She looked at him. "Did I say it all correctly?"

"You did." He looked at Mr. Weatherly. "But JG is preferable."

"In that case, it's a pleasure, JG," Mr. Weatherly said.

"The pleasure is mine, sir." He looked at Mrs. Weatherly. "Thank you for allowing me to visit."

"We are pleased to meet you," Mrs. Weatherly said. "Will you sit?"

"Yes. Thank you."

They all took seats. "So the gallery," Jocelyn said to JG.

"It's called The Bast Gallery and it's owned by a man named Thomas I. Bast," he said looking around the room at each occupant. "And he goes by Thomas I," he added to a general chuckle. "He is an affable fellow, but serious about art and artists. The gallery is on Bond Street."

"Yes," Mr. Weatherly said. "I've passed it. Nice place."

"It is," JG agreed. "He's been in business for twelve or thirteen years in that location. Before that he was a partner in an establishment on Pall Mall. Apparently, the partners had different visions, so they parted ways. Bast's vision is more progressive, I suppose you'd say, which is good for us," he said, directing the last of it to Jocelyn with a smile that she instantly returned.

Eliza Weatherly saw it and cringed internally. For the first time, she was seriously regretting the trip.

"He frequently exhibits the work of newer artists, most of them British. Also good for us. He represents Zoffany, Swaine, Bonington, who is still alive. Artaud, still alive. Now, personally speaking, I'm not terribly impressed with the chap's imagination, but he can capture a face. He always seems to use the same colors though. Let's see, there is Ingalton and his landscapes. Still alive. Knox, still alive." He paused before adding, "I can see Jeremy's work fitting right in."

Julia shook her head in amazement that they were having this discussion. "I never imagined his paintings would sell."

"Oh, they will," JG rejoined. "They are marvelous." He looked at Mr. Weatherly. "Have you seen them, sir?"

"No. Not yet. He's been quite protective, even secretive about it and I never wanted to push."

"That is true," Julia concurred. "I've only had glimpses these last years. It's the girls who broke through his reserve. For which I'm so thankful."

"At the moment," Alice spoke up. "He is still choosing which paintings to send. But he is enjoying it," she said tenderly to her aunt, who nodded back.

"I can't wait to see what the choices are," JG replied.

"So," Jocelyn said. "You will take the paintings to Mr. Bast?"

"Yes. He sent me with sturdy boxes, and I brought both a driver and footman, so we'll have it well in hand. And anyone who wishes to go can join me. I'm going there when I leave here."

Jocelyn looked hopefully at her father. "I'd like to go. If it's all right?"

"So would I," Alice spoke up.

"Perhaps we'll all go," Mr. Weatherly said cheerfully. He looked at Julia. "Including Jeremy."

"I would love to see it," Julia replied. "I don't know if he'll want to go or not."

Jocelyn looked at JG. "Would we overwhelm Mr. Bast? All of us converging on his gallery?"

"Not at all. That's what the place is for."

Jocelyn gazed at him adoringly, sending her mother's heart plummeting.

"If Jeremy does not wish to go," JG said. "I've been thinking we could create a brochure about him. He could do a miniature self-portrait that would go on the brochure, and Alice, being masterful with words, can write a biography of sorts."

Jocelyn beamed. "That is brilliant."

JG basked in her praise. "That way, the buyer feels connected to the artist. Perhaps even invested. We also create a bit of mystique about him. He's so handsome, so why does he not make personal appearances?"

"I think it is a wonderful idea," Alice agreed. "I hope Mr. Bast will be interested."

"He will," JG replied. "I know he will."

"Shall we go up now?" Jocelyn asked JG. She looked at her father. "Is that all right?"

"Yes," he replied graciously.

"Will you stay to lunch, JG?" Granny asked.

"I'd be delighted, Mrs. Weatherly. Thank you."

Jocelyn stood and JG and Alice did as well. "Would you like to come with us, Aunt Julia?" Jocelyn asked.

"I think it may be better with just you three," she replied.

They started from the room, but JG turned back. "Oh. Mr. Weatherly. I wanted to tell you that I know someone who knows you. My Uncle George. He's not really my uncle, not by blood; he's my godfather. He was my father's closest friend, and I am proud to say he is one of mine. George James? You went to Eton together."

Mr. Weatherly sat up taller. "Yes! Most everyone knew him. He was a member of Sixth Form Select and Pop. A good man."

"He said the same of you, sir."

"I'm surprised he remembered me. Do give him my regards."

"I will, sir."

When they reached the third floor, Jeremy was nervous. JG offered his hand, and the younger man hesitantly shook it. "Good to see you again, Jeremy. So, what are you thinking? These?" He gestured to the three paintings on easels, although three more were lined up against the table. "They're wonderful."

"Which do you think?" Jeremy asked his cousins.

"You can't go wrong with any that you choose," Alice said, "but I think this one is an excellent choice," she pointed to a

189

picture of a couple stretched out on a blanket by the side of a lake in late summer. The man was propped on his elbow, looking out at the water with his body turned from the viewer. The woman was lying flat, peering up at the cloudy sky. There was a basket, a bottle of wine and two glasses. It was intriguing because of her expression and because Jeremy had captured the essence of flowing water.

"And this one, too," Jocelyn said, pointing to the carriage picture she had first seen. "The Invitation. It fascinates me."

Alice agreed. "I want to go into the carriage and find out everything about both of them."

"It has that effect," JG concurred. "And the spilled vase. That one fascinates me. But it is your choice," he said to Jeremy. "Which are your favorites ...that you'd be willing to part with?"

Jeremy shrugged. "Those are fine."

"All right," JG said. "Done. Now, I have a question for you. When I leave here, I'm going to bring the paintings to the gallery. Would you care to go along?"

Jeremy frowned. "I—"

"You don't have to decide this moment," JG said. "I've been invited to stay for lunch."

"I don't want to be judged," Jeremy said. "It should be the work. The paintings should be judged. Not me."

It was such a lucid, straightforward thought and so full of vulnerability that it affected them all.

"Oh, Jeremy," Jocelyn breathed.

"I agree with you," JG replied in all earnestness. "And I am confident it will be so. Bast will see to it. He is so passionate about art. You know, all artists are a bit of a different breed from the rest of us. Probably because you are attuned to a world us mere mortals can only experience through you." He glanced at Alice. "I include Alice in that, as well." He looked back at Jeremy. "I think you would enjoy seeing the gallery, but you can do that any time, so there is no pressure today if you'd rather not. I will proudly act as your proxy if you like."

Jeremy nodded. "Yes. Please."

"All right. Now, in regard to setting a price and all that, I think we should leave it to Bast. He receives a commission, thirty-five percent, I believe, so it's in his best interest to get top price for everything he sells. It is what he does and what he knows, so, in my opinion, we should leave it to him."

"Yes," Jeremy agreed. "James I. Bast. Formerly with Solomon Quigley at The Seymour Gallery."

"Uh, yes," JG said. "I believe that's right."

"Jeremy," Alice said. "What would you think of doing an illustration of yourself, a mini-portrait for a brochure? JG had the idea of creating one to let Mr. Bast's customers know about you."

Jeremy held his thumb and forefinger apart and moved his hand to create a circle. "Like so?"

"That would be ideal," JG replied. "If you did a matching full-size portrait, I'll bet it would sell from the brochure."

Jocelyn smiled at her cousin. "I have an idea. Why don't we carry these down and show the others?"

Jeremy smiled back at her and nodded. "All right."

"Just out of curiosity," JG said. "Which is your favorite?"

Jeremy hesitated a moment and then went to a large cabinet in the back of the room, opened it and pulled out a painting. It was turned around so they could not see the image yet.

"Let me move this one," JG said, going to an easel. He picked up *The Invitation*, walked over and carefully set it against the wall. "Then we'll close our eyes until your favorite is in place." He closed his eyes and the girls happily complied.

"Now," Jeremy said when he had placed it.

They opened their eyes to see a painting of a woman of twenty years of age or so in a filmy gown on a breezy, moonlit evening. They drew in closer, looking at the lady's serene face, the wisps of hair that had blown free of a loose chignon, and the way her gown rippled in the breeze.

"It's Aunt Julia," Alice realized. She looked at Jeremy. "It's your mother when she's young, isn't it?"

"Yes."

"It's so beautiful," Jocelyn marveled. "Has she seen it?"

He shook his head. "Will she like it?"

"She will love it," they all replied at the same time, followed by laugher by all.

"The Breezes Of Providence," Jocelyn read the brass plate on the frame. "Oh, Jeremy. It should hang where everyone in the family can see and enjoy it. I love it."

Alice reached over to touch her cousin's arm. "It is perfect," she said to him.

Alice popped into the parlour, disrupting the conversation. "Ladies and gentleman, we are about to present the paintings that will be taken to the gallery. If you will please close your eyes."

The elder adults did as asked, each with a smile.

"Don't let me fall asleep," Granny said.

"We won't be that long, Granny," Alice replied. She ducked back into the hall and then she, JG, and Jocelyn came into the room, each with a painting in hand while Jeremy remained in the doorway to watch the reactions of the family. Alice and Jocelyn turned their backs to their elders so that only JG's picture was seen.

"Ready," JG said. "You can open."

The family opened their eyes. Their reactions – from the sharp intake of breath, to the exclamations of surprise and delight filled Jeremy with pride. Everyone rose and drew in closer, even Granny although it took her a few moments longer.

"Oh, Jeremy," Mrs. Weatherly exclaimed.

"It's magnificent," Mr. Weatherly said. He was clearly stunned.

JG nodded. "I do believe that was my first comment, as well."

Julia put an arm around her mother, who had tears shining in her eyes.

"Next," JG said as he turned away with the painting.

Jocelyn turned around with the carriage painting and the reaction was just as enthusiastic. Alice went third and the adults were enraptured.

"Darling," Julia said, looking at her son. "They are wonderful."

"There is one more to show you," Jocelyn said when the excitement died down. "Although it is not for the gallery." The three filed from the room and set their paintings against the wall in the hallway. "You want to take it in?" Jocelyn asked Jeremy.

Jeremy shook his head and glanced at JG. "My proxy."

JG grinned. "Glad to."

Alice stepped into the room. "Close your eyes again. This picture you are about to see is Jeremy's personal favorite. And mine too now that I've seen it."

"Mine, too," Jocelyn said, coming into the room to see it again.

JG entered with the painting while Jeremy remained where he was, focused on his mother. "Open," JG said.

The painting moved everyone, but Julia most of all. After several moments of staring, she turned to Jeremy with eyes full of tears.

He nodded.

Tears spilled down her cheeks and Eliza handed her a handkerchief before smiling at Jeremy, too moved to speak for the moment.

"Behold the power of art," JG said.

"You have a rare gift, Jeremy," Mr. Weatherly stated.

"I've known it," Granny said. "And I am still overcome. I love this one so much it hurts my heart." She fumbled for her own hanky and blew her nose.

Jeremy went to his mother and she embraced him. It was not a common occurrence which made it all the sweeter. "Thank you, my love," she said. She drew back and looked at the painting again. "Thank you for seeing me that way."

There was not a dry eye in the room.

~~~

Before leaving for the gallery, JG and Jocelyn went for a stroll around the block. "So," he began. "As I mentioned to your father, I went to see my Uncle George the other day. Not just because a visit was overdue, but because I am interested in learning the law."

She looked at him curiously. "Oh?"

He nodded. "Justice and all that. It's interesting and I think I might be good at it. Do you think I'd be any good at it?"

"Yes, of course. If it's what you want to do. One of my brothers-in-law is an attorney."

"Really?"

She nodded. "He is very successful. He has an outgoing personality which helps, and so do you. But how will your grandfather feel about it?"

"That's just it, you see." He stopped and turned to her looking pained. "The crux of the matter is that Granddad thinks I can be forced to marry."

It felt as if she had been struck. "What do you mean? Who? Whom would you marry?"

"There is no specific lady in mind. You see, it does not matter who she is, only that—"

"That she is from a noble family," she said haltingly when he paused.

He sighed and then nodded. "My grandfather is from a different generation. Sometimes I think he is of an entirely different world. One where love is not important. Nor is affection. Nor is even like. And you can definitely forget fun and friendship. Only lineage and duty are important."

She looked away thinking about the loneliness of such an existence, but then she looked back at him. "What does that have to do with your Uncle George?"

"I'm afraid there is no gentle way to say this. My grandfather has threatened to disown me."

She gawked.

"Unless I marry someone of his approval in the next year."

She let out a shaky breath, shaken to her core.

He took hold of her hands. "Jaus, listen. Please. I went to Uncle George to ask if he would take me on as an apprentice because I have to prepare in case Granddad does what he threatened. Of course, I didn't fully understand the process. Turns out I have to go to a school of law first. But he'll help with all that."

"Are you saying you won't marry—"

"I am declaring that I will not live without you if it's my choice."

She shook her head slowly, the truth dawning slowly. "Oh, JG."

"Please don't look so stricken."

"But disown you," she repeated. Her eyes filled. "It's so terrible."

He shrugged and shook his head. "It would mean I would live like most people. I'd have to make my way in the world. I have given it a good deal of thought and I think I could do a good job of it as a barrister or a solicitor. Uncle George has done well and he's happy. You said your brother-in-law has done well."

"But to give up everything. For me."

"For us," he corrected. "For the life we would have together. It's a selfish decision, really, based on what I need and want. I know this is a lot to take in. I have had time to think it over. Not that there was any doubt in my mind as to what it had to be. The truth is that it is merely a change of circumstances. I'll no longer have a fortune and a large house and a title."

She swallowed.

"I promised my uncle that I would speak to you and be honest about my feelings."

"Your Uncle George sounds like a wonderful man."

"He is. He asked if …we had spoken of our feelings. I said we had not, not in words, and yet I believed with all my heart that we both knew how the other felt. I have not proclaimed aloud that I love you and that I don't want to live without you, but it is true. Nor have you said it. That you love me. That you want a life with me as badly as I want one with you. But I believe it is true. If I am wrong, please tell me."

She shook her head slowly. "You are not wrong, but—"

"No buts. What was just said is all that is important."

She was reeling with the information he had shared. *For me,* kept whispering in her mind. *He will give up everything for me.* He'd claimed the decision was made for *them,* and she understood that, but had it not been for her—

"I also assured Uncle George I would speak with my grandfather and be honest with him."

"Yes, you must," she agreed.

"It won't make a difference. My grandfather cares more about the title than me."

She shook her head emphatically. "That cannot be true."

"My mother died when I was two from complications during a second childbirth. I have no memory of her. My father died from an illness when I was seven. I've lived with my grandfather a long time. I know him very well." He looked down at her hands and then lifted one higher. "May I?" he asked as he slowly began tugging off one of her gloves.

She did not stop him. She did not even look around to see who might be watching. It was a most sensual feel. When the glove was off, he raised her hand to his lips and kissed it. Once, twice, three times. Slowly, lingering over it. Her breathing had become labored and she felt flushed all over.

"Will you love me without the wealth and title and trappings?"

"You already know the answer to that," she said just above a whisper. "I love you and I will love you no matter what. I do not care about the wealth and the title and the trappings."

"Then I am without fear. The future will be what we make it."

"What we make it," she echoed.

"I don't mind giving up anything …except for you."

They came together in a kiss, neither of them knowing who had initiated it. What did it matter? They were together now. They were one.

The Earl and Countess of Goffston

Request the Distinct Pleasure of your Company

M. Alice Weatherly and M. Jocelyn Weatherly

At their annual

Ball and Midnight Supper

Ditton Place, No. Six St. James Square,

Westminster

Saturday, May 27, eight o'clock

"Dum vivimus vivamus!"   *"While we are alive, let us live!"*

Chapter Twenty-Four

*A*lice stood next to Nigel in the middle of a line of couples waiting in a particular vestibule outside the ballroom. Between dance sets, people of 'distinction' were being announced before making an entrance. Her parents and sister were already inside, as were Lord and Lady Merton, the latter having chosen to skip an introduction. She, too, would have chosen to skip it and to slip inside without a fuss. She was somewhere between tense and terrified.

When the orchestra stopped playing and introductions began again, they would walk up a short set of steps to reach a landing with a doorway. Once the couple in front of them vacated the stage that the doorway represented, it would be their turn to face the crowd in the ballroom below. Their names would be called and then they would descend the staircase. Not so terribly difficult unless she tripped or fainted or froze.

Nigel leaned closer. "You know what would make this whole thing even worse?"

She prepared herself for the jest he was about to make.

"Right before we are announced, the music starts again. Only it's a funeral march." He said it darkly, but then smiled and nearly laughed.

She shook her head. A mere joke was not going to make her forget her nerves.

"Would you rather us leave and go to a different ball?" he asked.

"Yes, please. Or we could simply step out of the line and sneak into the ballroom."

"The problem with that is they already have us in the queue. I don't think it would be better to have our names announced with us nowhere around."

"I suppose you're right. Think of the rumors that would fly. I just wish it were not so nerve wracking."

"Why is it?"

"Because everyone will be looking."

"That's rather the point."

"What if I turn all red?"

"You never turn all red. You blush in a most appealing manner. I like it when you blush. It usually means you've gotten my point."

"Nigel," she complained under her breath.

"Alice," he returned. "Tell you what. If you do turn red, I'll hold my breath and do the same." He sucked in and held his breath, puffing out his cheeks with it.

"That would not help since everyone would wonder what we'd been up to that had us both blushing."

He made a face. "True."

The teasing had, in fact, helped allay her anxiety. "Why is this introduction so important to your mother?"

"Appearances. Speaking of which, and I say this with all honesty, you are the most beautiful lady here. You should not worry about a thing. You will be perfect."

It was a ludicrous statement, but he seemed to mean it. "I shudder to think how beautiful I'll be if I trip and fall down the stairs."

"I won't let you fall," he said in earnest. "I promise."

She inhaled and blew out a quiet breath, determined to calm herself. "All right."

"Better?"

She nodded. "Thank you."

"Did you choose the colors of your gown or did the dressmaker?"

"She suggested them and showed me how the fabrics would work."

"The colors of your eyes," he said with an affectionate smile. "It may be my favorite yet."

She smiled, but then the music stopped, and she stiffened again.

He patted her hand that was wrapped around his arm. "It will be fine," he whispered.

"His Grace, the Duke of Gramhurst," a deep voice intoned. "And Her Grace. Philippa, Dowager Duchess of Gramhurst."

Alice bit on her lip. She would be the only one without a title. What was she doing here?

"The Most Honorable, the Marquess and Marchioness of Quellinshire."

Nigel and Alice reached the base of the stairs. Only two couples were in front of them.

"The Master of Banbridge and Miss Dorsett."

Miss Dorsett? Another commoner? Alice felt a surge of relief. She lifted her skirt and they began ascending the stairs. Only one couple was left.

"Sir Augustus Fulton and Lady Fulton."

Oh, Lord. It was their turn.

"I will place a glass of champagne in your hands within the next five minutes," Nigel said under his breath.

Another deep breath. In and out. This was not that difficult. They stepped through the door and the scene before her was just as she'd imagined. A thousand people were watching her.

"Mr. Walston and Miss Weatherly."

It was said and they were moving on. The steps were wide and shallow and she had an excellent grip on Nigel's arm. He might end up bruised from her clutch, but they were nearly to the bottom.

"The Right Honorable Lord Kenner and Miss Cleaves."

The couple behind them had been announced, the attention shifted to them. It was over and she hadn't fallen on her face. "I believe you said something about champagne," she said shakily.

"So I did," he replied proudly. "Would you care for a glass or a bottle? I'd say my mother owes you that."

~~~

"Oh, Alice," Jocelyn said to her a quarter of an hour later. "You looked like royalty up there. So beautiful and regal. I was bursting with pride."

"I was so certain I would trip."

Jocelyn shook her head. "Nigel wouldn't have let you."

The words caused a sharp thrill. "He said the same thing," Alice confided.

Two gentlemen approached and asked the sisters to dance, and they consented. It was expected for a lady to dance when asked, especially this early in the evening. Nigel would have to do the same. Until they were engaged, they had to keep appearances in mind. Alice felt a jolt as she realized she'd thought of their engagement as a certainty.

When she came off the floor from her fourth dance of the evening, she did not see any of her party, but Dabney Adams was there.

"Hello," he said as she joined him.

"Hello," she returned. "Did you just arrive?"

"Yes. I was delayed because—" He shook his head. "Well, it doesn't matter."

She looked at him quizzically.

"It's my father. Apparently, he is ill."

"Oh, I'm sorry."

"We're not close," he said quickly. "In fact, it's rare when we see one another." He paused. "I suppose I should go to him, though." When she refrained from comment, he gave her a curious look. "At least nine people out of ten people would have said, 'Yes, you should go to him. He is your father, after all.'"

She gave a small shrug. "I have the mind of a writer. I always imagine all sides of any given situation. Even when a crime has been committed and guilt seems evident, I always wonder ... but what if he didn't do it. Or if he did, then why did he? There are two sides to every story."

"Yes, Miss Weatherly. There are."

~~~

Nigel had been detained by Lady Pearson and her entourage who had an insatiable curiosity about Alice. As they babbled on, he noticed Alice speaking to Dab. The two seemed engaged in a curiously serious discussion. They looked striking together. *If you don't want her,* Dab had kidded.

Nigel experienced an urge to tug at his collar. Was this jealousy he was experiencing? When he was able to politely extract himself, he went to stand by Alice. Asserting his place? Ada, Harrison Bower and Hugh had also joined the circle. "Hello," Nigel said to Dab. "You missed our big entrance," he added, glancing at Alice with a smile. He looked back at Dab. "Everything all right?"

"Yes," Dab replied with an easy smile. "I'm sorry I missed it. I'm sure it was spectacular."

Nigel looked at Alice. "Spectacular. Would you go that far?"

"Well," she prevaricated. "Nigel was nervous, but—"

There was general amusement in the group, but a few moments later, Nigel caught a significant looking glimpse pass between Dab and Alice. *What in the world?* "Shall we dance?" he asked Alice. It was foolish, he knew, but he wanted to get her away from Dab.

Chapter Twenty-Five

The final dance rehearsal had begun at ten o'clock in the morning on the twelfth of June in order to perfect moves. It was followed by a final fitting and luncheon for ladies only. At lunch Alice was seated between Lakely on her right and an amiable Miss Benson on her left. The ladies across from were also pleasant. Fortunately, Diana Fletcher was seated on the same side of the table as Alice, so they were not in one another's line of sight. That was a good thing since either Miss Fletcher did not like her or did not care for the idea of an American taking part in the dance.

Many of the discussions around the table were about the king and queen. Queen Caroline, who had been in virtual exile for years, had returned to London a week earlier to claim her rightful place in the monarchy, but the king despised his wife. Theirs had been an arranged marriage that he had never wanted and he had been trying to divorce her for years. Public sentiment was largely in favor of the queen since the king was generally loathed for his excesses, vanity and loose living, and his reign was seen as corrupt.

"I have a question for you," Lakely said. So far, they had enjoyed a delicate white wine, crab bisque, and oysters that had been wrapped with bacon and seared.

"I have one for you, too," Alice returned lightly.

"Me first," Lakely said. "Are you going to Merton Park with us? Nigel is dying to know. It's not that I will tell him, if you don't wish, but it's always good to know something he doesn't."

Alice smiled. "I want to. So does Jocelyn. It's just that we'd planned on leaving by then."

"I know. Your sister is having her baby. But the baby won't know you for ever so long."

"That is not the point," Alice rejoined.

"Oh, I know."

A plate of salad topped with delicately sliced vegetables was placed in front of her. "I still have to get permission," Alice said.

Lakely pouted. "You must come."

"I want to." She took a bite. She particularly liked the vinaigrette. "I'll speak with Mama again later today."

"So what is your question?" Lakely asked.

"You don't have to answer, of course, but I'm wondering about your heart's desire."

"Besides desert?"

"I have a suspicion."

"I can hardly wait to hear."

Alice glanced around to make sure of sufficient privacy and then lifted her napkin to her lips to discreetly mouth one word.

Lakely's smile vanished. She looked away and then picked up her wine. She sipped and set the glass back down before speaking again. "Why do you say that?" she asked quietly. Only then did she look at Alice.

"It was just a feeling. Should I not have guessed?"

"You are the only one who has. You won't say anything?"

"No," Alice replied with a shake of her head. "Of course, I won't."

"You see people quite clearly," Lakely observed.

"Most of the time, but not usually myself. Isn't that strange?"

"I see myself quite clearly," Lakely said. "Although I frequently don't care for what I see."

"You should look harder then. I see someone who is beautiful, intelligent and fearless."

"Not fearless," Lakely replied quietly. "Not at all."

~~~

At the same time, Nigel looked over the contents of each glass display case in a jewelry store on Hatton Garden seeking the perfect gift for Alice. He wanted to show his regard without being ostentatious. He'd recently sold some stock at a good profit and Alice's gift would be purchased with some of the proceeds. Hopefully, it would be the first gift of many.

He had never expected to feel so definite a desire to marry a particular lady, but he did. Unfortunately, he sensed that something or someone was holding her back. He wanted to marry Alice, but only if his feelings were reciprocated. Good Lord! Loving someone who did not love you back would be wretched. It would be intolerable.

Was he being a hypocrite? Many marriages were like that. Before Alice came into his life, he'd never given it a moment's thought. Nor would he have thought the idea of unreciprocated love would trouble him as greatly as it did.

"Does anything grab your eye, sir?" one of the clerks asked. It was the fourth time he'd been offered assistance.

"I like that one," Nigel replied, pointing at a necklace with a pink teardrop-shaped pendant. He had seen Alice in that same shade of pink.

"Ah, yes," the man said, reaching for the necklace. He extracted it and handed it over. "Both striking and delicate."

"What is the gem?"

"Pink topaz."

"Interesting. I didn't know there was such a thing. You can probably tell I haven't shopped for ladies jewelry a great deal."

"Apparently, now there is a need?" the man said lightly.

"I hope so."

"It will certainly make an impression, if I may say so. It has matching earrings, as well."

Nigel handed the necklace back with a smile. "I'll take them. Can you wrap it?"

"Oh, yes sir. With pleasure."

~~~

The dinner party at Larkspur House consisted of the Walston family, the Weatherly family, including Julia and Jeremy, Harrison Bower and JG. After the meal, they convened in the salon, but Lord Merton and Mr. Weatherly excused themselves to smoke and sample a new cache of cognac, and Harrison went with them, which pleased Ada. The mothers, Lydia, Eliza and Julia had enjoyed a bit too much wine and were now sipping ratafia while playing The Royal Game of Goose to their great amusement.

Lakely and Jeremy, who had struck up an odd camaraderie, had begun a puzzle, which he was amazingly good at. The others, Nigel, Alice, Ada, Jocelyn and JG had been playing five card loo, but a game had just ended with JG as the winner.

"May we step outside?" Nigel asked Alice, gesturing the open French doors. "In plain view," he directed to his mother, who glanced over.

"Did I say anything?" Lady Merton asked lightly.

"Of course," Alice replied to Nigel.

"In that case, we'll play Euchre," Ada suggested. JG and Jocelyn were more than agreeable, although the two of them could have twiddled their thumbs while peering at one another and been content.

Nigel led Alice to a particular spot, positioning himself so that he was only partially in view to the occupants of the room. Alice was facing him, not in view of anyone other than him. "I've planned this," he whispered.

He was up to something, but she had no idea what. "Planned what?"

"Sunday will be two months since we met," Nigel said. "And knowing you has changed me."

Was this going to be the proposal? Her heart began hammering. "It's changed me, too," she admitted.

"I have something for you. Stay right there."

She watched as he went to a tall urn of flowers with overflowing greenery and extracted something he'd obviously placed there. Since he had stepped away from the window, she could now be seen from the room, but no one was paying attention to them. He came back with a long jewelry box, not a ring box, placing himself precisely where he had been, essentially blocking her from view. He handed her the gift. "I hope you like it. It made me think of you."

She opened the gift, murmuring how prettily it was wrapped. Inside the box was a necklace and earrings with dangling pink pendants. "It's beautiful." She looked up at him. "Thank you."

"You're welcome. I believe you have something that color."

She nodded. "I do."

"It's pink topaz."

She released a breathy utterance. She was going to say that she loved it, but the words were stuck in her throat. She felt ridiculously emotional. For a moment, she'd thought it was the proposal. It's not that she was disappointed. Was she? The gift was lovely.

"I wanted to show my regard."

She wiped away a tear that slipped her grasp and nodded.

He reached out and stroked her ear lobe. "The earrings will look exquisite on you."

The teasing touch of his finger sent desire pulsating through her. A shaky breath escaped her as the backs of his fingers traveled caressingly down her jaw and the side of her neck. He was doing it again. Melting her.

"The necklace," he whispered. He lightly placed his hand over her throat and she quivered. With one finger, he traced a path past the well of her throat and down. It stopped at the swell of her cleavage. He seemed to remember himself and withdrew his hand. He glanced down at himself. "I thought I planned this out, but—"

She was shaken in the most deliciously sensual way. When he turned, she saw the significant bulge in his trousers. Her breath caught from the realization that she was hot *down there.* Her body was throbbing with need. How warm her face was. Her face and everything else. It was possible she was glowing with heat.

"Why don't we sit over there," he said, gesturing to a bench. "And perhaps you can tell me a joke. A joke would be good."

She laughed. It was sheer release, but also the situation was comical. At least, one day they would find it comical. At the moment, he was in some discomfort, and she was flushed and trembling from head to toe. "I love the gift, Nigel. Thank you."

"You're welcome."

By Invitation of the Duke and Duchess of Toomey
Your Attendance

Mr. and Mrs. R. Weatherly the Miss Weatherlys
& Mrs. J. Alward

Is Cordially Requested
At their
The 8ᵗʰ Annual Ball
'An Evening of Splendor'
June 17   Half past eight o'clock

<u>*Chapter Twenty-Six*</u>

ocelyn came into the kitchen to find Fisher seated at the
table shelling peas, and Mrs. Halley hard at work on
dough, putting her heft into the kneading before slapping it
over and doing it again. Dinah sat the table hemming while Ethan
worked on a page of arithmetic and looking none too pleased
about it. "What's the matter, Ethan?" Jocelyn asked. "You don't
care for mathematics?"

"Not a bit," he replied glumly. "Don't see why it's important
neither."

"Either, dear," his aunt said. "I do not see why it's important
either."

He smirked. "If you agree, then why do I have to do it?"

Mrs. Halley barked a laugh. "He got you there."

Fisher gave her nephew a patient smile and gestured for him to
continue.

"It is important," Jocelyn said to him although she looked
empathetic. She looked at Fisher. "Is it all right if Dinah helps
with Alice's gown in a little while?"

"Of course," Fisher said.

"In about an hour?" Jocelyn said to Dinah who nodded.

"There's such bustle in the house this afternoon," Fisher
commented.

"Yes, there is," Jocelyn agreed. Tonight was the Toomey ball.
Alice was fretful over it, fearful she would slip up on the dance
moves, but she knew them by heart. Her gown had been
delivered earlier, compliments of Lady Toomey, and it was
gorgeous, but strangely constructed and complicated.

Eveningwear had also arrived for Jeremy. He hadn't been
included on tonight's invitation, but it hadn't proved to be a

problem. Nor had dressing in the unfamiliar clothing since JG and Hugh had come to assist.

"Are the gentlemen staying for dinner?" Halley asked, pausing to give her a stern look.

"No. They're going to their club. We wouldn't just spring that on you."

Halley grunted and went back to her work. The poor dough did not stand a chance of reprieve.

"You seem as happy as a clam at high tide, Miss Jocelyn," Fisher commented with a twinkle in her eye.

"I am," Jocelyn admitted. "I'm excited for the ball, especially to see the dance they've worked so hard on."

"We want to hear all about it tomorrow," Fisher said.

"We'll tell you all about it," Jocelyn promised.

~~~

"The skirt is so heavy," Jocelyn complained when she and Dinah had managed to maneuver Alice's gown in place. "There must be ten yards of fabric in it."

"For good reason," Alice said teasingly.

"Indeed. The big secret. I can hardly wait."

Dinah began fastening the buttons and ties on the back of the dress, and Jocelyn stepped back and admired it. It was pale periwinkle with an open, square neck revealing a good deal of cleavage and half her sister's shoulders, although a short matching capelet had been sent, as well. The sleeves were short and puffed, the bodice tightly fitted with a long waist. "It is an Italian design?"

"I don't know. They never said. It is pretty, isn't it?"

"It's exquisite. Are all the ladies gowns different or the same?"

"They're similar, but different colors. Lakely is wearing indigo. She has the darkest."

"That will be good on her. Did you get to choose the color?"

"No. They held up bolt after bolt of fabric against each of us until they decided what was best."

There was a knock at the door and Alice called to come in. Jeremy stepped in looking dapper in his suit. The girls all praised him at once. Grinning, he walked over and held out an invitation he had forged based on the one that had been sent to them. The actual invitation had included every member of the family except for himself and Granny who was too old to go or care or so she maintained. Alice and Jocelyn had seen the forgery in progress; now it was a spot-on match. "It looks perfect," Alice said.

"It does," Jocelyn agreed.

"I'm going with them," Jeremy said.

"JG and Hugh?" Jocelyn asked. "To their club?"

He nodded.

"Enjoy yourself," Alice said calmly although she was thrilled enough to dance an undignified jig. When he'd gone, Alice and Jocelyn looked at one another, moved by how much confidence he'd gained.

"JG will take care of him," Jocelyn said quietly.

"I know he will," Alice replied.

~~~

At ten fifteen, Alice left the ballroom and went to a designated drawing room where attendants were waiting to assist. Four others dancers were being helped. They looked at her with friendly, nervous smiles, which she returned.

"Use the pot first, if you need to," said an older lady sitting in the corner.

Alice wondered if the lady's job was to inquire after their bodily functions. The use-the-pot lady. Alice smiled politely in acknowledgement of the counsel. "I don't," she replied a moment later at the lady's continued scrutiny.

"Here you go, dear," an attendant beckoned to her.

Alice stepped up to her and slipped off her capelet, which she handed over. "I'm nervous," she admitted.

"You'll be fine," the lady said as she perched on a low stool to begin undoing the elaborate hooks and eyes that held the folds of fabric within the skirt. "You'll be brilliant. I've seen you dance."

"Thank you."

The attendant worked quickly and competently, saying "turn" when she was ready for the next section. There were six hidden folds down the length of the skirt. The dancers had been instructed that, from now until the dance began, they were to move carefully without lifting or fluffing the skirt. Thus the importance of the use-the-pot lady. Each dancer knew precisely where to go from this point on. *Just don't let me be the one to mess it up,* Alice prayed.

~~~

"I am so anxious for her," Jocelyn said to JG when the clock was about to strike eleven. An announcement for the performance had been made and the crowd had packed in to witness the much talked about entertainment.

"You," JG said, "are so—" He leaned closer and whispered, "adorable," in her ear.

"I believe you are biased, sir."

"I am," he happily agreed. "And I always will be. To be honest, I am a little anxious for her, too. I know how much it means to her. I was nervous for Jeremy, but he's doing well."

"I know. I don't believe he's spoken to anyone other than the family and you, but I know he is having a wonderful time. I am so proud of him. It's been challenging for him to leave the house, but he is doing it now."

JG nodded. "He knows he's different, but the more he gets out, the more he will see that most people are only concerned about themselves. Besides, anyone who judges others harshly for the sheer sport of doing it isn't worth worrying about."

She murmured her agreement. "Why don't we find the family and watch together? Do you know where they are?"

"No, but we'll find them." He offered his arm, which she took. "I love having family to belong to," he confided.

Her heart swelled.

~~~

Susan Moorcraft watched JG and Jocelyn with fascination. She dutifully stood next to Therese, but she had grown weary of trying to cheer her up. Therese's downheartedness was not a ploy for pity, but the fact that she was feeling so very melancholy made no sense. Therese was beautiful and erudite. She would have her choice of gentlemen, save one or two who were already spoken for. One in particular. And, yes, Nigel Walston was the root of her sadness. Susan wasn't thinking of Nigel at the moment or even the connection between him and the lady she had been watching. "They don't seem to realize anyone else is in the room," she commented.

Therese looked at Susan and then at Lord Blairwood and Miss Jocelyn Weatherly. The way they conversed. The way they looked at one another. It seemed so effortless and wonderfully, perfectly comfortable. "Are all Americans so at ease?"

"I don't know," Susan replied. "He is looking much better these days, don't you think?"

"Yes."

"Not so fat," Susan added.

Therese gave her a disapproving glance.

"All right, fat is an exaggeration," Susan conceded. "But he's looking better. That was my point."

"That's what love will do for a person," Therese said wistfully. "When it's returned."

"I suppose. Do you think Dab Adams will ever fall in love? He couldn't possibly look any better." Apparently, Therese didn't deem the question worthy of answering.

~~~

"It's time," a lady said.

Alice, standing in back of the room, clasped her hands together. One by one, the dancers slipped from the room to go meet their partners, moving carefully. For the most part, their gowns were blues and purples of various shades. There was one peachy-pink and one deeper pink. Alice wore her mother's diamonds and she had paired it with a small, matching tiara. She filed out and went to join Nigel.

He was waiting, as expected, and with a proud smile. Guests had crowded into the ballroom and Phineas Skeffington had the floor and was talking about the Toomey's and Venice and inspiration.

"May I kiss your cheek for luck?" Nigel asked.

She nodded and he leaned in to press a soft kiss to her cheek. His breath tickled her ear and made her body react. He pulled back and she realized how in love she was with him. It made it hard to breathe. "Oh," she said, as if disappointed. "I thought you meant the other cheek."

"I do beg your pardon," he played along. "Allow me to correct that?"

She turned her head to offer the other cheek, but turned it back just before his lips reached it, causing their lips to meet. When they pulled apart, she looked impish. "I know what you must be thinking. Those brash Americans."

"Close. I was thinking … *my* brash American."

Ask me, she thought. *Ask me to marry you right this instant and I will say yes.* Instead, the music started, the cue to move in and take their place. They entered the ballroom and started down one of the paths that had been kept clear for them.

It was time.

~~~

Wide tiers had been built around the outer perimeter of the ballroom with tables and chairs in the front of each. The ballroom was packed, every table, chair and the floor behind. Jocelyn stood near the front of the dancefloor with her family and friends. JG was next to her and her mother was on her other side. As the dancers moved in and took their place, she reached over and grabbed JG's hand out of nerves.

"I like the dance, already," he said, squeezing her hand.

The dancers all looked so smart as they took their places in a circle around the floor. The ladies were lovely and elegant, the gentlemen handsome and confident. The ladies were not smiling and they were not looking at their partners. The music changed to a slightly faster tempo, and each man reached out and wrapped his hand around his partner's waist. Jocelyn sucked in a breath. Each man's other hand was held behind his back in what stuck her as a military pose.

The couples began to dance, but the ladies were not holding onto their partner. Both her hands were at her sides. He was leading and directing, she was merely going with the steps. She was still not looking at him or smiling, but he did not seem bothered by it. It almost seemed as if he found it a welcome challenge. Why the dance felt so seductive, she wasn't sure, but it was. When the man took his hand from behind his back and lifted her arm, the lady watched it, almost surprised it was happening, and then she relaxed, smiled and assumed the normal position, one hand in his, the other on his arm near his shoulder.

The tempo picked up as did the pace of the dance. When each man turned his partner under his arm in a fast, almost violent thrust, the ladies skirts opened in volume, sweeping out about her. A general gasp came from the audience. Dancers spun about the room in a glorious array of colors, like exotic flowers opening. Swirls and swirls of blues and pinks and purples.

The dancers went around the dancefloor and then crossed through it, passing one another with such agility and at such close proximity, it made one's breath catch to watch.

"It's fantastic," JG said.

The dancers began circling again, but now one of his arms was pointed upward while hers was pointed downward. A whirling dervish. Jocelyn had never actually seen the spectacle, only heard it described, but that was what she was reminded of. It seemed somehow ethereal. The dance had been startlingly physical and sensual, very much about a man and woman's enmeshment, but now there was almost a spiritual quality to it. As there should be, Jocelyn thought.

One move seamlessly flowed into another. Some of the audience in the back of the room stood on chairs to better witness it. When the dance ended in a deep bow and curtsy, the applause was thunderous. Anyone who had been sitting rose to their feet. Jocelyn looked at Jeremy, who was smiling and clapping along with everyone else. He looked over at her and they laughed in amazement.

Phineas Skeffington joined the dancers and took his due acclaim, bowing multiple times and enjoying every second of it. Jocelyn still felt enraptured as another waltz began and people crowded onto the floor. Alice and Nigel finally made their way to them after being repeatedly stopped by countless compliments and questions.

"It was spectacular," Jocelyn cried. "You were fabulous! Both of you. It was extraordinary."

"Thank you," Nigel laughingly replied. "We had fun."

"I thought it would just be a dance," Jocelyn said to Alice. "But it was a true performance. I've never seen the like."

"Oh, darling," Mrs. Weatherly said, stepping up to embrace her daughter. "It was wonderful!"

"We're proud of both of you," Mr. Weatherly said, clapping Nigel on the shoulder and then kissing his daughter's cheek.

"Thank you, Papa," Alice said.

"We might as well dance," JG said cheerfully to Jocelyn.

Jocelyn nodded. She felt giddy with happiness as they made their way to the floor.

"If they do it again next year," he said. "Perhaps we'll try."

She beamed. "I would love that."

~~~

Alice and Jocelyn lay in bed and listened to the clock strike three. It was Alice's usual wakeful hour but, this time, she was awake because they had not yet slept. They were tipsy, exhausted, and yet still invigorated from the excitement of the evening.

"I'm so glad they chose you for the dance," Jocelyn said. "It would have been thrilling to watch, no matter what, but it was even more so because you were in it."

"Oh, Jaus. I think it was the most wonderful night of my life."

"And think of all the wonderful nights to come."

"I'm going to marry Nigel," Alice confided. "If he would have asked tonight, I would have said yes."

"I'm going to marry JG," Jocelyn returned. "Had he asked tonight, I would have said yes."

Alice laughed. "That's the best thing really. We'll have each other."

"I will miss the family," Jocelyn said. "Wouldn't it be perfect if they moved here? All of them?"

"Yes, but they won't." Alice yawned.

"You were splendid tonight, Ali," Jocelyn said, closing her eyes.

"So were you," Alice whispered.

Chapter Twenty-Seven

*L*akely looked up at the ivy covered arbor that blocked the sun's punishing brightness and heat, mesmerized by the shades of green and specks of gold from the sunlight that filtered through. The ladies were in the Weatherly's back yard having partaken of lemonade and cucumber sandwiches. "I love this," she murmured. "I feel so relaxed here."

The late June weather was too warm, but at least there was breeze enough to stir wind chimes to life. Julia's garden was rambling, but Lakely preferred it to theirs which was highly structured. This one boasted a myriad of sporadic colors. The scent of strawberries and honeysuckle, peonies and sweet peas comingled into a heady perfume. "Can we fit three in your bed?" Lakely asked. "I'm thinking of moving in."

"We could simply trade you for Alice," Ada teased. "You move in here and she moves in with us."

Ada and Jocelyn sat next to one another, thumbing through issues of The Lady's Magazine, and Granny dozed in a chair, snoring lightly. Alice was making notes for the book. "I love it, too," Alice said without looking up.

"What?" Jocelyn asked.

Alice looked at her. "The backyard, of course."

The delayed reaction made the others laugh, which woke Granny.

"Remember when I said she goes into her own world?" Jocelyn asked.

"I was not in my own world," Alice objected.

"Sometimes she won't hear a question at all," Jocelyn added.

219

"Is Julia still gone?" Granny asked.

"Yes," Jocelyn replied. "Still shopping with Mama. Do you want to go back inside?"

"No. I'll take some more lemonade, though."

Lakely leaned forward for the pitcher and filled Granny's glass.

"Thank you, dear. Are there more sandwiches?"

Lakely rose to get the plate and pass it to her. "A few left just for you," she said. "Does anyone else want lemonade?"

"Please," Ada said. As her sister filled her glass, she said, "What an excellent maid you would make."

"It's a thought," Lakely replied.

There was a pleasant lethargy to the day. The warmth had slowed everything down.

Alice said, "I never thought I would get tired of going to balls."

Lakely groaned. "I'm bored stiff of it."

"She's actually counting them down," Ada said.

"Yes, I am," Lakely agreed. "I'll be ready for them again by Christmas, but it's so hot now. Besides, there's a—"

"What?" Jocelyn asked.

"A sad desperation, I suppose. For those who had high hopes for a match and haven't been pierced by Cupid's arrow. Even if you don't feel it, people expect you to. They think you do."

Granny shook her head. "You mustn't worry about what others expect," she said. "If you do, you'll do nothing but worry. Bugger that."

The younger ladies burst out laughing.

M. Weatherly (s) and M. Alward

Please join an evening of celebration

Thursday, June 22 at Seven o'clock

-L. Foster, Esq.,   No. 38 Stanhope Street

Acceptance Required by the 14th

Chapter Twenty-Eight

*A*lice availed herself of the chamber pot in one of the upstairs retiring rooms. It was well after midnight and the Foster soiree was going strong. Before their third dance of the evening, Nigel had leaned closer to say, "You know we really shouldn't dance again. People might talk."

"I know," she'd agreed. He'd happily offered his arm, and she had just as happily accepted. Now she checked her appearance in the mirror and then headed to the door. She'd just pulled it open when she heard her name spoken by another female. She froze.

"Miss Weatherly?" a second female asked in a hushed voice.

"The American. Don't tell me you haven't heard."

Alice opened the door wider and saw the back of one of the two ladies that had just passed by. They were walking slowly while gossiping. She strained to listen.

"She's to marry Nigel Walston in exchange for an enormous dowry."

Alice felt as if she had been punched in her stomach.

"Because of Lord Merton's debt," the voice continued. The last of this was whispered, which made it all the more cutting somehow.

"Poor Nigel hates it, but he doesn't have a choice. Of course, it is Therese my heart breaks for. She and Nigel were ready to announce their engagement you know. She is shattered."

Alice stepped into the corridor, gawking, a hand pressed to her stomach. One of the gossipers was petite, the other was Diana Fletcher. No wonder Miss Fletcher detested her. She was Therese St. Clair's friend. *Poor Nigel hates it, but he doesn't have a choice.* How had Miss Fletcher known the information unless someone had said so? Had it been Nigel? To Therese? *Oh, dear God.* Had they truly been planning their engagement?

~~~

Diana Fletcher could not keep the smile from her lips. She could barely restrain herself from looking back to see Alice Weatherly's face. She'd known from the instant she saw the American leave Nigel's side and head upstairs what she was going to do. She'd grabbed Susan and instructed her exactly what to say and when. It had gone perfectly, too.

She would keep doing it, too, spreading word that Nigel Walston had been bought and paid for because of his father's gambling debts. She wasn't daft; that had to be the explanation. Nothing else made sense. Cursed Americans thought they could barge into the ton with sweaty wads of cash and get exactly what they wanted. They all needed to be cold-shouldered out. There should be no place for them in polite society.

~~~

Alice returned to the ballroom feeling ill and conspicuous. Every glance from every stranger seemed to confirm what she'd overheard. It was humiliating. She joined Jocelyn who introduced her to Miss Hubbert. Alice tried to keep her mind on their conversation, but she could not help looking around for Nigel. She spotted him standing by himself looking pensive. Early on in their relationship, he had claimed that she had not been foisted upon him, but what if she had? When he loved Therese St. Clair?

"Alice?" Jocelyn said. "Are you all right? You seem a million miles away. Are you tired?"

Alice nodded. "I am." She gave Miss Hubert an apologetic smile. "It seems to have hit all at once."

"I've had that happen," Miss Hubbert said. "You're fine one moment and feel like collapsing the next."

Jocelyn nodded in polite agreement. "We can leave now, if you want. Mama and Papa left the carriage for us and went with Lady Merton. She was ready to go and Lord Merton had something else to do. Although I think he is still here. I saw him a bit ago and he asked if we were having a good time. He was as gracious as always."

"If you don't mind," Alice said. "I am ready to go."

"I don't mind at all."

Alice knew it was true, since JG had been obligated elsewhere. "I'll go let Mr. Walston know," Alice said.

Jocelyn started to laugh at the formal way Alice had phrased it, but then she sobered and frowned with concern.

Alice walked off, trying not to look at anyone else. They were anonymous faces. She did not know these people and they did not know her. Did they all think she was a monster who thought only of herself? An engagement breaker?

Nigel smiled to see her. Was he nothing but an actor? He'd seemed happy when she left him and then brooding when she was gone and now instantly happy again? "Jaus and I are leaving," she said. "I'm suddenly very tired."

"I'll go, too," he replied without hesitation.

"Please don't on our behalf," she said stiffly.

"I'm ready to go." His gaze flicked to a corner of the room. "There are individuals I would rather not see," he confided.

As she started back to her sister, she could not stop herself from looking in the same direction he had, seeking out auburn hair. She didn't see it, but had Miss St. Clair just been there? Alice glanced at Nigel walking beside her. For as lighthearted as he had been earlier, he seemed taciturn now. Because of having seen Miss St. Clair? From guilt and remorse? He saw them to their carriage and they bid one another goodnight.

"What's wrong?" Jocelyn asked when the carriage door was shut.

Alice shook her head and stared out the window. The carriage started in motion.

"Ali! Tell me."

Alice leaned forward and watched Nigel turn and start back toward the house. He was going back in. She sat back and looked at her sister who was watching her with concern. "I heard someone talking about me and Nigel and the dowry and the debt."

Jocelyn's jaw dropped. "Who?"

"We don't know her and she doesn't know us," she replied in a flat voice. "Although she thinks she does." Alice shook her head. She felt so emotional. "Oh, Jaus, what if we are the ones who don't know? I didn't know before. I can be so blind to what is right in front of me."

"What are you talking about? What don't we know?"

"That I have been forced on Nigel."

Jocelyn looked pained. "You cannot be serious. That is like saying he has been forced on you. No one can force anything on you, and no one has forced him. He told you as much."

"I know he did. But now I wonder if he is an actor."

"Alice!"

"How does everyone know about the arrangement? The supposedly *secret* arrangement our fathers cooked up?"

Jocelyn shook her head. "You're being silly. Everyone does not *know*. Unfortunately, it is not the secret of the world that Lord Merton has a problem with … you know what. People talk and people see that our families are friends when we are not of their station. They see that you and Nigel are frequently together. Anyone with eyes can see there is a spark between you. I am purposely stating that mildly."

Alice looked back out the window.

"What exactly was said?" Jocelyn pushed.

"Have you noticed a beautiful, auburn-haired lady by the name of Therese St. Clair?"

"No. Who is she?"

"She and Nigel were—"

"What?"

"Courting. They may have even been close to an engagement."

Jocelyn thought about it. "Well, maybe they were and maybe they weren't. This is before we arrived, correct?"

"Yes."

"Well, there you have it."

Alice huffed. "What do you mean …there you have it? So, I show up with my dowry and—"

"That is not what I meant. I do not believe for one minute that Nigel has fallen for you because of your dowry. Alice, he is in love with you."

Alice chewed on her lip. Was he? Or was he simply a talented actor who had responsibility to his family?

"Some busybody spouts some ugly words," Jocelyn said.

Alice sighed. "I don't want to talk about it anymore. I really am so tired all the sudden."

"I hate to see you miserable. Please don't allow it. Do not let the gossiper win. Anyone can see that Nigel is in love with you."

Alice shook her head in befuddlement. She had thought so, but now nothing was clear.

"You should admit you're in love with him too. By that, I mean you should let him know."

Alice found herself shaking her head before she realized she was doing it. "No. Not now. I have to be sure of him first."

"Promise me you won't overreact."

"I'm not. I have no wish to." How ironic it was that Nigel had gone on and on about honesty and not having secrets. Had he said all the right things for no other reason than to win her trust and her heart? And her money? Who was the individual he had wanted to avoid? And why had he headed back inside when he had claimed he was going home?

~~~

Nigel knocked on the door of his mother's room. When she called to enter, he opened the door to find her reclined on a chaise lounge in a dressing robe with an unopened book on her lap. "Is Father gambling again?" he asked without preamble.

She sighed. "I don't know. I hope not."

"Where is he?"

"He said he was going to the card room to watch. Only to watch."

"Well, I looked in before I left." He shook his head. "He was not there."

"What makes you think he's gambling again?" she asked warily.

"I imagine it's the same reason you have for fearing it. It's a feeling. It's a certain look he gets."

She looked away. "Oh, Nigel," she said dejectedly.

He walked over and perched on the side of the chaise lounge realizing that he hadn't really considered how hard this had been on her. "I'm sorry, Mother."

"So am I. And so is he. But what good is that?"

"I'll go look for him."

"You could go out and search every club and not find him. Or you could find him, and it would be too late." She shook her head. "I'm afraid he has to live this nightmarish compulsion out. Either blunder again or pull himself back from the void."

She was probably right, but it was frustrating to do nothing. He kissed her cheek and left the room. It seemed the fate of the estate was in his father's hands. *Please, let there not be a pair of dice there, too!*

Chapter Twenty-Nine

The late morning was humid as Alice stepped out of the house. She looked up and down the street but did not see her aunt and her sister. She had declined a walk with them not ten minutes ago, but changed her mind. Perhaps it was just as well. A walk by herself might be precisely what she needed.

She had already decided a few things. Chiefly, that she was not going to let Miss Fletcher's gossip undermine her feelings for Nigel. If it turned out that he had been dishonest with her, that was a different matter. This evening, she would find a way to the truth. She needed to know if he was in love with Miss St. Clair. She needed to know, if not for her dowry, would he have an interest in her? Most importantly, *are you in love with me?* Obviously, she would not be so blunt about it, but she had to determine his true feelings.

"Alice," her mother called.

Alice turned and started back to meet her mother who had just left the house and was hurrying toward her.

"Fisher wants to know which gown tonight," her mother said. "If it's the cream—"

"No, I'm wearing the pink again. It's ready."

"Of course. Your new jewelry." Her mother turned to go.

"Mama," Alice called.

Eliza Weatherly turned back. "Is something wrong?" she asked when Alice seemed at a loss for words.

Alice took a breath. If today was Truth Day, it was time to begin. She stepped close and lifted her chin. "I will only marry when I am in love and that may not be by the day I turn twenty-two."

Mrs. Weatherly looked puzzled.

"I may be twenty-three. Or twenty-five."

Her mother waited. "And?"

Alice drew back. "What do you mean *and*? You exacted a promise that—"

"Oh, Alice. Don't be silly. What difference does it make?"

Alice felt her jaw go lax. "But you—"

Her mother waved a hand in the air. "I vaguely remember some meaningless conversation after you'd rejected the Mickelson boy. Goodness, that was years ago."

"Yes, I know," Alice said accusingly. "I was eighteen."

"I was frustrated at the time. He was so nice and well established and he had those lovely dark curls." She paused. "Water under the bridge," she said with a one-shoulder shrug. She turned and started off. "Enjoy your walk."

Alice could only stare in disbelief. Meaningless? Water under the bridge? *What?*

~~~

That night, Alice stepped out on one of the second-floor verandas, which was cooler than the cramped ballroom and reception rooms inside Sandon Hall. This particular veranda, chosen because it was empty at the moment, faced the side of the house and looked out on a street, or as much as one could see of it due to a giant oak. Alice placed her gloved hand on the balustrade and wondered if she could lean forward far enough to touch its branches. If she leapt out, she could certainly catch hold of it, but would it hold her?

"Here you are," Nigel said, having followed her.

She turned to face him. They'd had a fine time this evening, but it felt as if something unsaid lurked between them. Was it her imagination? Looking at him now, he seemed unbothered and he had been nothing but amiable. It would be easy to let the matter go. *Do not get cowardly*, she chided herself. "You spoke of honesty between us," she began.

He stepped closer. "Yes."

She looked at his top button since it was easier than meeting his gaze. "Have you ever been in love?" At his sharp intake of breath, she looked up in alarm. "Not with me," she added quickly. "I ... didn't mean that."

He cocked his head in confusion. "Oh."

"I meant before. Let's say in March. On the last day of March, had someone asked, and if you were being perfectly honest—"

"On the last day of March of this year," he repeated.

"Yes."

He looked bemused. "On the last day of March of this year, some rather nosy person is asking if I have ever been in love."

She nodded.

"Is this a game?"

"No."

"Because if it is a game, I should know the rules. I like to win, you know."

"Doesn't everyone?"

He considered her for a moment. "No," he replied.

She gave him a look. "I do not know a single person who does not like to win."

"I meant no to your first question. In March, someone is asking me if I have ever been in love. The answer is no."

She felt a release of tension. In fact, it was a heady rush. "Oh."

"What about you?"

She blinked. "If I am being asked the same question?"

"Yes."

"No," she replied. "The answer is no." Inside, music began again, musicians having returned from a break. "So, as of ... say March, you had never planned to become engaged to anyone?"

"I have always assumed I would become engaged at some point in time."

She felt herself becoming flustered. She had asked it all wrong. "Did you ever ask anyone to marry you?" she blurted.

He barked a short laugh.

She cringed. "I didn't mean that to come out so abruptly."

"Well, it did. But no. I have never asked anyone to marry me."
He looked perfectly at ease, as if he were enjoying himself.
"What about you?"

"I, too, have never asked anyone to marry me."

"Very funny. You know what I meant. Has anyone asked for
your hand?"

She shrugged and shook her head noncommittally before she
gave in and nodded. This is not where she had wanted to
conversation to lead, but she would not lie to him.

He sobered. "Yes?"

"A time or two," she added weakly.

He looked offended. "Well, was it a time or two?"

"I said no, of course. I did not love them."

"Them. Plural. So there were two," he said sticking up two
fingers and looked more and more bothered.

"Three if you must know, but what does it matter?"

He huffed. "Who were they?"

"You don't know them. They're in Boston." Clearly, she had
botched this thing. "That is not what I wanted to talk about."

"What did you want to talk about?"

"Your feelings."

"Well, maybe I want to know your feelings," he countered
defensively.

She suddenly recognized his vulnerability. "I have them," she
said softly.

His gaze turned tender. "I have them, too. I have them now. I
did not have them in March."

It was what she had wanted to hear.

"Alice, if you … if you did not want to go further in our
relationship," he said haltingly. "You would say so? You would
tell me?"

"Of course," she exclaimed. Oh, Lord! Surely, he didn't think
she was someone who collected proposals for the fun of it. As a
point in fact, it was not fun to refuse a gentleman. It was
miserable to hurt anyone.

"In less than a month, we'll be leaving for Merton. I so want to show you the place."

"I want to see it. I want to go."

"Have you spoken to your mother again?"

"Yes, but she hasn't spoken much back. The truth is, she detests the idea. She wants us to return home as planned. But I'll bring it up again."

"Good." He paused. "Why the questions earlier? Did you think I had asked someone to marry me?"

She did not want to convey what she had overheard or admit how greatly it had bothered her, and she definitely did not want to conjure Therese St. Clair between them. "I have seen a lady or two looking your way with interest," she hedged.

"Have you? Oh, please tell me you experienced a moment of jealousy. No one ever has before."

"I doubt that's true."

"I have experienced moments of jealousy when a gentleman paid too much attention to you," he admitted. "It calls up all sorts of insecurities."

"You don't need to feel them," she said tenderly. He glanced around, found the coast clear, and leaned in to kiss her. She knew it was coming and she wanted it. The feel of his lips on hers and his body close to hers did something volatile to her. She gripped his arms as he pulled her closer. She felt his hands close around her back, and her hands slipped around his shoulders, urging him closer.

She had been kissed before, but not like this. A fever had loosened inside her that threatened to consume her, possibly consume them both. His hands tightened possessively. Hers cupped the back of his neck and felt the tickle of his hair on her fingers. Her lips parted at his urging and his tongue teased her lips before comingling with hers. She felt such heat! As if they were melding together.

They jerked apart at the sound of a throat clearing. She looked over Nigel's shoulder and saw the throat clearer had moved on.

She looked back at Nigel. His gaze was wary, wondering her reaction, but also full of hunger. "Oh, dear," she whispered.

He nodded. "Was that everything you wanted to discuss?"

It was so casually asked that she laughed, and he did the same. She turned and gripped the iron railing. They could not walk back inside right now; both of them were far too flushed and flustered. Anyone who saw them would think they had been up to no good. Oh, but it had been good. So, so good. "I have one last question," she said.

"Yes?"

"Do you think it's possible to scamper down the tree and come back around to the front door looking innocent?"

He looked thoughtful and then began to take off his jacket. "I'll go first. Throw me my coat if I reach the ground."

She laughed with delight. "Put it back on. We'll take our lumps from the gossips rather than a fall."

He grinned as he tugged his jacket back in place and offered his arm. "Let them talk."

Lord and Lady Roxon

Of Roxon Hall in Berkley Square

Request Your Presence At

Le Grand Ball

On Saturday, July 1 / Nine O'Clock

'Joy, gentle friends!'

The Courtesy of an RSVP is Requested

Chapter Thirty

JG walked into the dining room and sat at the place that had been laid for him cattycorner from his grandfather. JG had come at his request. It would be the first meal they had shared in five days and it would be a light one since JG was going to the Roxon Ball. "I do not like the strain between us, JG," Lord Morguston began in a conciliatory tone. "We are family. All the family there is."

"I believe there are distant cousins, are there not?"

Lord Morguston picked up a small silver bell and rang it. A consommé was promptly served. "The Roxon's will serve a hearty banquet, so cook has prepared a light meal."

"Are you going?" JG asked.

"I don't think so. Too tired."

They ate the soup in silence and sipped at an intriguing wine. "What is this?" JG asked as he swirled the liquid to enjoy the scent.

"A madeira that was recommended. There's a Bordeaux open, if you prefer."

"No, this is fine. I don't want much, anyway."

"George James wrote to me."

JG looked at him with an inscrutable expression. "Did he?"

"He advised that I should take care to not alienate you." He paused. "Do you believe that is my wish?"

"To alienate me? No. I think you would like to control my life."

"I want the best life for your life," Lord Morguston stated.

"So do I."

"But I have lived longer and seen far more. I want what is in your best interest."

"We have different ideas on that," JG said. "And shouldn't mine count more? It is my life."

This firm resolve was not like JG. As the next course was served, a tantalizing meat with onions and carrots, Lord Morguston studied his grandson. Something had changed in him. He was being unreachable and unreasonable.

"This looks fabulous," JG said to Ensley, the butler. "What is it?"

"Rabbit, sir," the butler replied. "Marinated in red wine and beef broth."

JG tasted it. "Delicious. What's the sweetness in the sauce?"

Lord Morguston inwardly smiled. "Cranberries I believe."

"Begging your pardon, my lord," the butler said. "It is juniper berries."

"Ah," Lord Morguston said. He watched Ensley go to the sideboard for the carafe. The butler returned and filled JG's glass. He stepped closer to refill Lord Morguston's but was waved away. "I want to move beyond this disagreement between us," Lord Morguston said when Ensley had gone. JG did not reply. "Is that not what you want?" he snapped.

"I wish it could be so."

Lord Morguston picked up his fork and took a bite. Everything about this discussion had to be timed right. "Losing your father," he said.

JG looked at him, surprised by the words.

"May you never know the torment of losing a child. Six weeks. He was ill for six weeks. But I was no more prepared for his death at the end—" His voice cracked and he broke off.

"Don't distress yourself," JG said quietly.

"The thought of losing you is distressing. I want to make it right between us."

JG was silent a moment. "So do I," he finally replied.

Lord Morguston sighed with relief. He smiled wanly and reached for his wine, which he lifted in the air. JG did the same and they drank. "Perhaps it's time I hear about your American friend."

JG studied him. "Do you mean that?"

"I do."

JG smiled in amazement. "I'm so glad."

"Miss Jocelyn Weatherly, you said. What intrigues you about her?"

"Everything. But I'm not just intrigued. I love her."

"I can see the depth of feeling you have," he admitted.

"You'll see, Granddad. You will like her. She's kind and good."

"I saw her, so I know she is attractive."

"She is more than attractive. She is beautiful."

"Where is she from?"

JG reached for his wine. "Boston."

"Oh, that's right. You said she's here visiting family."

"Yes."

~~~

In the hallway, Ensley paced with a dark frown. At what seemed the appropriate time, he went to fetch two of the footmen.

~~~

"It's quite a coincidence that your godfather knew this Weatherly chap at school," Lord Morguston commented. The conversation was flowing well. Exactly what he needed.

"Yes. I was surprised when Uncle—" JG broke off and cleared his throat. It suddenly felt tight. He had been having difficulty articulating and now the room seemed to be tilting. He grabbed hold of the table aware his grandfather was ringing the bell insistently. What was happening? He hadn't had much wine. He heard echoing footsteps and felt hands on his arms. The footmen.

"Here you go, sir," one of them said. "We'll get you up to your bed."

Bed? Why? What was happening? Everything was moving and tilted and strange and distorted. JG realized he was going to be sick. He was going to faint. What was happening?

~~~

As the footmen took an incapacitated JG away, Ensley picked up the carafe. "I'll get rid of this," he said quietly.

"Yes," Lord Morguston said under his breath. "He made it easy to say cranberry. I wish he hadn't." He pushed back from the table and rose. He patted one side of his chest to make certain of the packet of banknotes in the inside pocket. It was time to take care of this American friend business once and for all. "Call for the carriage."

"Yes, my lord."

~~~

The Stratford Club was a place for gentlemen to play cards. Unbeknownst to most people, even some of its members, there was a room on the second floor where an occasional high-stakes game of hazard was played. James Walston, the esteemed Lord Merton, although the esteem had tarnished of late, had been playing in the room for six straight hours.

Initially, he had won, but then luck turned her fickle back on him and he'd repeatedly lost to the tune of eight thousand pounds. At this point, he was panicked and feeling sick to his stomach. He had to get it back. If he could just win his losses back, he would never pick up a card or a pair of dice again. *I swear it,* he prayed to providence. Of course, he had sworn before.

"In or out, Merton?" Lord Kronwall asked with a sly smile.

Everyone was looking at him, but James Walston kept his gaze on Kronwall. He hated the man and his damned smugness. If he slunk away now, a loser, he would never be able to get this evening or that sneer out of his mind. He had to win again. He had to at least break even. "In."

"Merton," Lord Kelly chastised under his breath. "You will lose it all."

"Anyone else?" Kronwell asked the other men in the room. Four of them, including Kronwell, were acting in collaboration as the bank and they would either split the profits or losses. "No?" He shrugged and looked back at Merton. "Just you and I then. It is winner's choice to roll or defer, and I defer." He slid the dice to Merton. "What is your bet?"

"Eight thousand," Merton said, causing a stir in the room.

"A possible doubling of your loss," Kronwell said with mock sympathy. "Are you quite sure you want to go that big?"

God help him. He had to get it back. "Yes."

Kronwell shrugged and said, "Roll."

Lord Merton closed his eyes for a moment, hoping for inspiration. For some reason, Alice came to his mind, smiling, amused at something. "Five," he said. He opened his eyes and rolled. His muscles were tense, his breath held. One die landed on a six, the other a four. Ten. He had rolled a ten, meaning he had neither won nor lost. Now, he *had* to roll a ten, called the chance, before he rolled a five, the main.

He rolled again and got a total of seven. Animated side bets began about whether he would roll the main or the chance first. No other number counted. If he won, he would keep going. It would take three consecutive losses before he had to pass the dice on, but all that really counted was this roll. If he won, he would not bet so much again. He picked up and gently tossed the dice in his hand. *Come one, come on*, he silently chanted. He rolled. A double three.

He swallowed and retrieved the dice again. Side bets had picked up fervor. The men were like sharks who smelled blood in the water. He rolled. A four and a six. He drew in a sharp breath and exhaled hard, listening to the room erupt in exclamations of delight or dismay, depending on how each man had wagered. But he had won. He had negated his earlier losses. At least from tonight.

He considered his next move. Then he took a drink of his whiskey and picked up the dice. "Betting two thousand," he said. He jiggled the dice in his hand. "Nine. The main is nine." He rolled.

~~~

Alice was fastening the last of Jocelyn's buttons when there was a knock on the door. "Come in," she called.

Their mother stepped in with a letter in hand. "You both look wonderful."

"Thank you," they said in unison. Alice wore white with a violet sash and white netting over the skirt embedded with tiny pearls and bits of silver. Jocelyn's gown fell between rust and red. It was a new design, slightly off the shoulder and draping in back. They had gone to extra effort with their appearance because tonight was said to be the zenith of all balls. The season was mere weeks from its conclusion, the marriage mart in full frenzy.

"Your father and I are not going tonight."

"Why not?" Jocelyn asked.

"Clara wrote and—"

There was something in her tone. "Is everything all right?" Alice asked worriedly.

"Sophia's labor began."

"But it's too early," Alice said in alarm as both girls hurried to their mother.

"Sometimes nature decides these things," Mrs. Weatherly replied.

"Is she all right?" Jocelyn asked. "Did she have the baby?"

"Yes to both questions. Your sister is weak," Mrs. Weatherly stated calmly. "And the baby is small." She smiled. "It's another girl." ·

"A girl," Jocelyn repeated. Tears flooded her eyes.

"How small?" Alice asked. "And how weak is Sophia?"

Mrs. Weatherly handed over the letter. "The doctor believes Sophia will be fine and hopefully the baby will be, as well. She was exceedingly small." Mrs. Weatherly held her cupped hands open and palm up with five or six inches between them. "And she's having difficulty feeding."

"You're going home," Alice realized aloud.

"Yes. Your father and I will leave in the morning."

"Should we go, too?" Jocelyn asked.

"That is entirely your choice, but I don't know what you can do at home that Clara and I cannot. If you want to stay, you may. Julia will chaperon you when the need arises."

"We discussed going to the country with the Walstons," Alice said sheepishly.

Eliza sighed. "How important is it?"

"We want to go," Alice replied. "I do."

Mrs. Weatherly looked at her youngest who nodded.

"It is a family trip," Alice said. "Lord and Lady Merton will be there. And Lady Merton's sister, Lady Vinson. She escorted me once before. There will be plenty of chaperones if Aunt Julia would rather not go. "

"All right," Mrs. Weatherly relented. "Since your hearts seem set on it."

"Thank you," Alice said expressively.

"You're welcome." She studied Alice. "You're in love with him, aren't you?"

"Yes," Alice replied. She paused before adding, "I hope that doesn't disappoint you."

"Only the distance," her mother admitted.

"What's the baby's name?" Jocelyn asked.

Mrs. Weatherly smiled. "Eliza."

Her daughters reacted with "oh" and "ah" as they hugged her. "Little Eliza will be all right, Mama," Jocelyn added. "They both will."

Mrs. Weatherly could only nod. She was too close to sobbing if she uttered another word.

Chapter Thirty-One

*Q*lice asked her aunt if she was having fun as they left the dance floor after taking part in the cotillion. It was an old-fashioned dance, a product of the previous century and rarely danced anymore, but it was quaint and such fun.

"I am," Julia replied. "I'm having a marvelous time. But now I am going back to the ladies closer to my age now, to catch my breath and watch people your age."

"Do you think we'll ever get Jeremy on the floor?" Alice asked.

Julia smiled longingly. "Wouldn't that be wonderful? Why don't we make it our mission?"

Alice smiled and nodded. As Julia walked on, Alice looked around but didn't see Jocelyn or Nigel. She carefully made her way through the crowd until she saw Lakely coming toward her looking exceedingly anxious.

"There you are," Lakely said breathlessly as she reached her. "Where is Nigel?"

"I've just come off the floor. I don't know."

"I wanted to tell you both together, but I have news." She clutched Alice's hands. "My father—"

There was an almost feverish look on Lakely's face. Alice couldn't tell if the news was good or bad, only momentous.

Lakely leaned forward to whisper. "He gambled again."

Alice's breath caught. *Oh, no.*

"And he won," Lakely added. She pulled back and tears shone in her eyes. "He won it all back!"

Alice could not help gawking.

Lakely nodded. "All of it. He has cleared the debt. Oh, don't you see? Ada doesn't need to marry Mr. Bower now. I have to find her." She squeezed and released Alice's hands and hurried away.

Alice stared after her, stunned by the statement. Ada loved Harrison Bower and he loved her. Did Lakely truly not realize it? *But what about Nigel?* Alice looked around frantically until she spotted him across the way talking to his father. Nigel's back was to her, but he was being told the news at this very instant. Alice held her breath. Were things slowing down? Of course, it was just her imagination, her mind, but things seemed to be moving unrealistically slowly.

Lord Merton clapped his son's arms looking joyous and then he motioned for glasses of champagne. An attendant complied. Lord Merton handed his son one. No, two. He had handed Nigel two glasses of champagne and then taken one for himself. Nigel turned in her direction and his expression was astonished and utterly joyful. She smiled to see it. He was looking around ... for her? *Oh, God, please let it be for her!* She willed him to look her way and catch her gaze as they had done so many times before, but people got in her way.

She stepped closer to where he had been, but people kept getting in her way. She finally saw him. Lifting a glass with Therese St. Clair. Alice stopped short, suffering a sharp pain in her stomach. She turned away, but she was too lightheaded to move. She was shaking all over. From stupidity. And betrayal. *You stupid girl!* Hadn't she known the truth in her mind? But she had let her heart get in the way of common sense. When she was steady enough, she put one foot in front of the other, desperate to get away.

~~~

On the balcony above, Ada saw events unfolding. It was akin to watching two carriages collide in slow motion when there was nothing she could do to stop it. There was pure devastation on Alice's face. Why? Why in the world was Nigel standing with Miss St. Clair? He needed to be going to Alice. He had no idea how close she had been. Now she was leaving. *Go to her. Go after her*, she willed.

"Ada?" Harrison said, touching her elbow. "Darling. What is it?"

She shook her head because she did not know what had just happened, but she had a terrible feeling about it. The last ten minutes had been some of the strangest of her life. First, her mother had informed her that her father had won a high-stakes game of hazard that very day, and their debts were now cleared. Naturally, that was cause for great celebration, but also concern because he had promised never to gamble again and again, but he continued to do it.

"It changes nothing between us," Harrison uttered weakly.

His face was full of such trepidation that it made her heart ache. "No," she said with a fervent shake of her head. "You know it doesn't. I love you."

He bent to kiss her hands. "I live for the day you're my wife."

~~~

No more debt. Nigel heard the words, but they were almost too earth-shaking to accept. It was a miracle of sorts. He and Alice would begin their lives without a shortfall. Glasses of champagne were pressed into his hands and went to find her. Unfortunately, he nearly collided with Therese St. Clair.

"Nigel," she said. "Mr. Weatherly," she corrected herself, lowering her head in embarrassment.

He felt for her. He realized she had feelings for him. If he hadn't fallen in love with Alice, they might have considered an attachment. "Hello," he said.

"I wanted to tell you," she stammered miserably. She suddenly noticed the two glasses in his hand. "Oh! I beg your pardon. You were—"

"No. It's all right. They are plentiful. Here," he said, handing her a glass. "To good fortune," he said. She looked as though she might burst into tears. *Please don't*, he silently begged. He wanted to be celebrating with Alice. "I wish you the best of fortune," he said.

"I wish the same for you," she returned. "That's what I wanted to say. I have learned that some unkind things have been said—"

He shook his head because the last things he wanted to hear were harsh remarks about his father's recklessness. As if he didn't already know and as if they were not true, but he didn't need or wish to hear them now. "Never mind that," he said gently. "It's in the past. Truly. Thank you for the thought, but …will you excuse me? There is someone I must speak with."

"Of course."

He pushed on to find Alice. First, he needed another glass of champagne for her.

~~~

Dab stepped back inside after smoking and saw Alice going toward the front doors. She looked peculiar, almost as if sleepwalking. "Alice?" She stopped and looked at him but didn't seem to recognize him for a moment. She was pale and visibly trembling. He closed the distance between them. "What's wrong? Are you ill?"

She looked away. "It wasn't real," she uttered under her breath.

"What wasn't real?"

She shook her head slowly. "I was never real. It was n-never love."

"What are you talking about?" He realized he had asked it more sharply than he had intended. "Has something happened?"

She sighed and looked at him. "Yes," she replied dispassionately. "And it is over."

"What is over? You cannot mean it's over with Nigel."

She shuddered. She looked stricken.

He was tempted to shake her. "Alice!"

"There was someone before," she uttered. Her eyes filled and spilled over, but she quickly wiped the tears away.

He drew back, dumbfounded. Her relationship with Nigel was over because there was someone from before that she'd cared for? Why in the world hadn't she let Nigel know? He would be devastated. Nigel was in love with her. And now she had the audacity to say it wasn't real and it wasn't love? Only a moment ago, he had been worried for her, but now he felt angry.

"Dab?" Nigel said as he closed in on them, looking from one to the other.

Dab felt terrible about what was to come, but it wasn't his place to be in the middle of it. Later, yes. After Alice had shattered his heart into a thousand pieces with her revelation. All he would be able to do at that point was commiserate over how deceitful women were and get his friend drunk, but he could damn well do that much. He walked toward Nigel and clapped his shoulder. "I'm sorry," he said and then walked on.

~~~

Nigel's heart pounded. What the hell had he just walked up on? He went to Alice and offered her the glass of champagne he had just gotten. She had just been in tears; her face was not completely dry of them. What had he just stumbled upon? Except he knew. He had feared it for a while. Dab and Alice. "I suppose we need to talk," he said almost tonelessly.

She looked at the glass of champagne. "Champagne," she said. She huffed and shook her head. "Why not?" She took it.

"Is there something you want to tell me?" he asked, dreading the answer.

Her eyes flashed at him. "Isn't there something you want to tell me?"

He couldn't make out her expression or demeanor. She seemed shaken. In fact, she was shaking. He couldn't make out the emotions seething in her and it was making him feel wildly off balance. He needed to stay calm, but that was not easy. "As a matter of fact, I do. My father won a good deal of money today."

"So I heard. Congratulations. There is no more debt."

He blinked. What should have been a joyful proclamation had been uttered dispassionately. He needed to steel himself because she was about to tell him what he had secretly dreaded for weeks.

"No more need for me," she added.

The full and obvious truth dawned on him. Alice had been drawn in by his family's sorry situation and felt compelled to help. She had been determined to make the best of the situation, but she didn't love him. There were times, so many times, he had convinced himself she did, that she loved him as he loved her, but then there was Dab. Impossibly handsome, irresistible Dab. Once again, Nigel Walston was second best. Had he ever been anything but second best in his entire life? "There's someone else," he heard himself say. The words were painful to get out.

"Yes," she replied shakily. "And you are sorry, and I am sorry. I must say I d-don't know what the champagne is f-for." Tears ran down her face again. "I mean … *really*? Champagne?" She shook her head and handed the glass back to him and then turned and walked out the door.

He felt so nauseated, he feared moving.

~~~

"Finally," Lakely said to Ada. "I have been looking all over for you."

"Not now. I have to find Alice," Ada said, trying to push by her sister.

"Wait! I have news."

Ada turned back to her impatiently.

"Papa—" Lakely began.

"I know," Ada interrupted. "He won today. And, of course, that's good news, but it's only good news for this moment in time. Don't you see? He broke his promise and gambled yet again. He won this time, but he won't win the next. So what difference does it really make?"

"Ada! You don't have to marry Harrison."

Ada ducked her head sighing audibly. Then she looked at her sister again and took hold of her hands. "I was never marrying for the money," Ada said emphatically. "I love him. I am still going to marry him."

Lakely drew back.

"Lakely. Do you not know me as well as I know you? How can you not see that I love him?"

Lakely looked crestfallen. "I—"

"No, I know the answer," Ada rejoined gently. "You have been so worried about protecting me, it's all you could think about. And I understand that. I do. I want to protect you, too. And Nigel and Alice. And something is happening on that account. Come on." She walked on, taking Lakely by her arm. "We have to find them."

"What are you talking about?"

"Just look for either of them. Jaus, too. She can help."

"Ada!"

"I'll explain as we go," Ada said, pulling her sister along.

For a quarter of an hour, Ada and Lakely worked their way through the ballroom, but guests were continually shifting place to place. Besides the vast ballroom, there were salons and parlours, the dining room and wide corridors filled with people. They'd had no luck and Ada was so tense that Lakely also felt the urgency. "We didn't look on the verandas," Lakely said as they glanced in a smoking room in full use.

Ada nodded. "Let's look on the portico first and then we'll separate and work our way around again."

They found Nigel sitting on a bench in the foyer with two empty champagne flutes in both hands. He was staring out blankly. "Nigel?" Ada said as they came closer.

His sisters closed in and sat on either side of him. "What's wrong with you?" Lakely asked.

He didn't reply. Nor did he look at them.

"Where is Alice?" Ada asked worriedly.

"Gone."

"Gone?" Lakely repeated. "Gone where?"

"I don't know." His voice was devoid of emotion. "She felt badly, and she left."

Ada stiffened. "What do you mean?"

He handed Ada one glass and Lakely the other. He got to his feet and started for the door.

"Nigel," Lakely called, rising to her feet.

He ignored them and kept going.

Lakely looked at Ada. "Has everyone gone mad tonight? Why does he look like that? Should we go after him?"

Dab walked up from behind. "Where is Nigel?"

"He just left," Lakely said. "Acting very strangely."

"That is because Alice ended things between them," Dab said bitterly. "Apparently, there was someone else from before."

"What?" both girls exclaimed in disbelief.

"That is nonsense," Lakely said.

Dab shook his head. "I'm telling you what she told me."

"No," Ada denied with a shake of her head.

"When was this?" Lakely snapped. "Exactly what did she say?"

"It was a bit earlier. I had a smoke, came back inside, right here, and saw her walking toward the doors. I thought she was ill, so I went to see what the matter was. That's when she said it was over. That there was someone from before."

Ada groaned. "I know what happened. At least half of it."

Lakely and Dab turned to her.

"Alice wasn't talking about herself," Ada said to Dab. "She believes Nigel loved someone before her. That he still loves this other lady."

Lakely's eyes widened. "Therese St. Clair?"

Ada nodded. "I even know why she thought it. I saw it all from the balcony."

"Nigel doesn't love Therese St. Clair," Dab objected. "He never did."

"But Alice thinks he does," Lakely realized. "She asked me once if they would have been together had she not shown up." She brought her fist to her lips as she thought about it. "I'm not altogether certain what I said, but there is something about Alice's candor that prompts you to be truthful, and … well, truthfully, I always thought it was a possibility. I mean before Alice, of course. Never afterwards." Lakely shook her head. "But I'm still confused. Nigel and Alice must have spoken."

"Yes," Dab said. "They did. They must have. I had just spoken to Alice when he walked up with glasses of champagne. I detested what I thought she was going to tell him, but it wasn't my place to be in the middle of it, so I left and got a drink. I just now came back to check on him."

"You thought *she* loved someone from before?" Ada asked Dab.

"Yes. I thought that's what she was saying," he admitted.

Lakely looked at her. "Could Nigel have thought that as well? Is that what you're thinking?"

"I don't know," Ada replied, "but we should find him. You saw him. He looked terrible. He looked … betrayed. I know he loves her."

"And we know she loves him," Lakely said.

"Could you be mistaken?" Dab asked searchingly. "Might there be someone from before who she loves more?"

"No," both girls said at once.

"But what I don't know," Ada said, "is why he was having champagne with Miss St. Clair after father told him."

Lakely looked at her sharply.

"Told him what?" Dab asked.

"Father won a game," Ada replied. "Or several, I suppose. The debt has been cleared."

Dab blinked in surprise. "Well, that is something. But Nigel didn't seem excited or cheerful when I saw him. Just the opposite, really."

Lakely looked at Dab. "Can you try and catch him?"

"Of course."

"Convince him to come home," Ada said. "Please. I think this is all an appalling misunderstanding, but it needs to be corrected."

Dab nodded and left.

"I'm going to find Harrison and tell him we're leaving," Ada said. "Why don't you walk though one more time and try to find Jocelyn? And we should tell Mamma we're going."

Lakely agreed and the girls went in different directions.

~~~

Since clapping eyes on Lord Morguston an hour previous, Jocelyn had not been able to keep her gaze off the man for long. She had been discreet about it. She did not think he had noticed her. It was strange that JG had not shown up this evening. Or was he here and had simply not found her yet? Either way, the fact that he was not with her yet made this an opportunity.

JG was not only willing but planning on giving up his title and fortune for her, but if she could meet his grandfather and he could see she was a good person who loved his grandson, perhaps his heart would soften. Not toward her, so much, but toward JG. Surely, if he went so far as to disinherit his own grandson, he would hate himself for it one day. How could he not? If she could prevent it from happening, she had to try.

When Lord Morguston finally left the ballroom, she followed. In the corridor, she looked one way and did not see him. She looked the other way, and he was there. His hands were clasped behind his back, and he was looking at her. He was not glaring at her, as before. In fact, he was strangely expressionless. So, the time was now.

She started toward him, as nervous as she had ever been. She stopped a few yards away from him. "Lord Morguston." In the thick silence that followed, she wondered if she should curtsy, but a young lady did not introduce herself to a gentleman. This was all highly improper. "May I speak with you?"

"You are speaking to me," he replied coldly.

"I am—"

"I know who you are," he interrupted. "You are the American who would see my grandson ruined."

The words were shocking. "No," she exclaimed with a shake of her head. "I would never."

"Then prove it. Go back to where you came from. Leave him to his proper destiny."

His animosity so stymied her, she could neither find the breath nor words to respond. She had made a mistake. There was no reaching him. JG had been right. Lord Morguston would never change his mind or his attitude.

"I will pay you to go," he added in a low voice. "Tell my grandson you are not interested in a life with him and then go."

She shook her head slowly, fighting back tears. She stepped back, poised to turn and go, but froze when he started toward her.

"Name your price," he said unfeelingly.

"I do not want your money!"

"Make no mistake," he uttered. "If—" He jerked to a halt, grabbed his hip and cried out as he fell to the floor.

She rushed toward him, but before she reached him, he looked up at her with such loathing that it stopped her in her tracks. She heard footsteps and shouting. Others were coming. They were all around, some bending to help and others standing back. Jocelyn felt dizzy and strange, her legs almost too weak to stand.

"She tripped me," she heard from a distance.

Oh, God in Heaven! It had not been from a distance. It had been uttered by Lord Morguston. He was glaring at her, declaring that she had purposely tripped him.

"That's the American," a woman said.

It was as if time had slowed. Alice had explained the phenomena, but Jocelyn had never before experienced it. She glanced around and saw the confused expressions on some faces, accusing expression on others, and pure disgust on a few. More people were rushing into the fracas.

"That is preposterous, Morguston," a gentleman exclaimed. He was a balding man of fifty or so with a gray mustache. "I saw you walking toward her when you collapsed. I was coming to speak with you and saw the whole thing."

"Reilly," Lord Morguston seethed. "You were probably in on it with her."

"Someone fetch a physician," Reilly ordered. "Lord Morguston has fallen again. Probably cracked his head as well as his hip," he muttered under his breath.

"Is there a physician in the house?" someone shouted.

"We need a doctor," someone else called.

Jocelyn turned unsteadily. She had to leave before she vomited.

"He displayed abominable behavior, Miss," Reilly said as he fell into step beside her. "Try not to let it upset you."

She stopped and looked at him. He had compassionate looking gray eyes.

"We serve in Parliament together," he explained. "I've known the old goat for years. All I can think is that he must have been talking out of his head from the pain. He is insufferable, but not usually insane. It's that hip of his. He refuses to use a cane as he's been told to." He paused. "Are you all right, my dear?"

"Yes," she lied. "Thank you, Lord Reilly." She turned and walked on concentrating on one placing one foot in front of the other. *Ignore the looks people are giving you. They don't know you. You don't know them. Walk! Just walk.* The front doors were a welcome sight. She stepped out into the night. Thank God! She took blind steps. She was shivering, she was so cold. Had it turned cold? On the first of July? She looked around for a bench. She needed to sit before she collapsed.

"Jocelyn?"

She turned toward the dark-haired man with a mustache who had spoken. Joel Stewart.

"Are you all right?" he asked.

"N-no. I need to … to leave."

"Are your parents here?"

She shook her head. "My Aunt Julia."

"Are you ill?"

She nodded and looked away from him.

"Why don't we get you inside and you can have a lie-down?"

She drew back in horror of the thought. She was not going back inside to face those people again. "No!"

"All right, then," Joel soothed. "How can I find your aunt?"

The questioned perplexed Jocelyn for a moment. "Nigel or Alice," she stammered. "Or Lady Merton. The Walstons know her."

"I'll find her," he said reassuringly. "If not, I'll take you home and then come back and find her. All right?"

Her eyes were full to the brim with tears and then they spilled over. Fortunately, Joel had already rushed inside.

"Is she all right?" a man asked Joel as he stepped back inside.

Joel stopped short. The man was none other than Robert Reilly, Earl of Greenwich.

"I'm afraid not, Lord Greenwich. I believe she is ill. I'm going to fetch her aunt."

"Who is she?" gesturing toward Jocelyn.

"Miss Jocelyn Weatherly."

"An American," Reilly said.

"Yes. Her sister Alice is courting Nigel Walston."

"I heard something about that. Lovely girl with two different colored eyes, they say."

"Yes." Joel looked back at the chaos at the end of the hall. "Do you know what's happening there?"

"Morguston fell again." He huffed in disgust. "If he hasn't broken his hip this time, it's only a matter of time. That was the third fall that I know of."

"Does JG know that he's hurt?"

"His grandson? I haven't seen him this evening."

"If you'll excuse me," Joel said. "I need to find her aunt."

"Of course."

Joel entered the ballroom and looked around. It felt as if the evening had gone horribly askew. Jocelyn ill. Lord Morguston hurt. After minutes of fruitless searching, the strange feeling increased. Nigel seemed to be missing. Alice seemed to be missing. Lakely, Ada, even Mr. Bower were no longer anywhere he could see them. They had all been present not a half hour ago. Come to think of it, Dab was nowhere to be seen.

Hugh was on the dancefloor, seemingly unaware of any fiasco. So was Jonathan. Joel finally spotted Lady Merton standing with two other ladies and hurried to her. "Lady Merton, forgive the interruption, but I'm looking for Jocelyn's aunt."

"I am her aunt," another lady said.

"She's not well," he explained. "I said I'd fetch you."

"Oh! Yes." She excused herself and the two of them hurried away.

~~~

"Darling," Julia said to Jocelyn as their carriage drove away. "What's wrong?"

Jocelyn shook her head and burst into tears. All Julia could do was to hold her. They had not found Alice and it felt wrong to leave her behind, but Mr. Stewart had assured her he would find her and relay what had happened. Undoubtedly, Alice was with Nigel having a wonderful time and there was no reason that should change.

~~~

Joel, Jonathan and Hugh stood in a bewildered huddle. It felt as though there had been a splitting open of the earth and their friends had been swallowed by the chasm while they had not felt so much as a tremor. It was exceedingly strange that JG had not shown as planned. JG always did as planned. If he said he was going to do something, he did it.

It was also peculiar that Nigel, Dab, Alice, Lakely, Ada and Mr. Bower had left without a word to anyone. Apparently, Jocelyn had been rendered ill by Lord Morguston's rudeness to her. They had learned that from Henry Gaines who had heard it from Diana Fletcher. Miss Fletcher was busily circulating that

Jocelyn had purposely tripped Lord Morguson and caused his fall.

"Someone should lock that viperous woman in a closet," Jonathan said. "Where no one would discover her for a few days."

Joel nodded. "Everyone knows she's a harpy."

"I think I'll go see about JG," Hugh said worriedly.

"Lord and Lady Merton are still here," Joel noticed. "As happy as I've seen them in ages."

"Word is, he won big at hazard earlier today," Jonathan replied.

"Would the others have gone off to celebrate?" Joel asked.

"I doubt it," Hugh replied. "Not without telling us. Besides—"

"Yes," Jonathan said darkly. "Besides. Something feels off."

Joel nodded in grim agreement.

A half hour later, Hugh employed the heavy door knocker of Lord Morguston's Park Lane home with Jonathan by his side. The door was opened by a maid who inquired whether she could help them. "We're here to see JG," Hugh replied.

An uncomfortable expression crossed her face. "I'm sorry, sir. He is indisposed." Footsteps were approaching and she quickly stepped back as the butler appeared.

"May I help you gentlemen?"

"We are here to collect JG," Jonathan spoke up. "We're late, but—"

"I'm sorry, sir," the butler said coolly. "He's not available. Perhaps he went on without you."

"He's not at home or he is indisposed?" Hugh asked, glancing back at the maid who looked cowed.

"If you'd care to leave your card or a message," the butler said, ignoring the question.

Hugh did not normally overreact, but he was twitchy with nerves. "I will humbly beg your pardon if I am wrong." He suddenly pushed inside past the butler.

"Sir," the butler snapped, incensed by the intrusion.

Jonathan followed. "He is our friend, and we are checking his room," he stated.

"You will do no such thing!"

Jonathan and Hugh picked up their pace. The butler was following, ordering them to stop. Already, footmen had been sent for to physically remove them.

"Do you know which room it is?" Jonathan asked Hugh.

"Yes."

"You have no right," the butler harangued.

"It's this one," Hugh said, zeroing in on a door. They opened it and went inside. The room was dark, but someone was in the bed. Jonathan went to the windows and opened the curtains and shutters.

"JG," Hugh said, going closer to him.

Between the light in the hallway and the illumination from the moon and gas lamps on the street, they could see JG was dead asleep. He was still and pale. If he had taken ill, why hadn't the servants said so?

"JG," Hugh said again, shaking him lightly. JG didn't stir. Hugh turned on the bedside lamp.

"What the hell," Jonathan muttered, coming closer.

The butler lurked in the doorway, suddenly silent. Footsteps were heard, probably the footmen hurrying to the butler's aid. The butler held up a hand to stop them from advancing.

"JG," Jonathan called, shaking him harder.

JG didn't stir or wake.

"What's happened here?" Jonathan demanded of the butler.

Hugh bent closer to JG to feel for his breath with the backs of his fingers. Not feeling it, he picked up a limp wrist and took his pulse.

The butler stepped closer looking worried.

"He needs a doctor," Hugh snapped at the man. "Get a doctor!"

"I'm certain he's fine," the butler said, but he did not sound it.

"I can barely make out breath or a pulse," Hugh retorted furiously. "Get a damned doctor here now! Or I swear to God I will see you hang!"

The butler nodded to one of the footmen, who hurried off.

"What is this?" Jonathan asked the butler. "What happened to him?"

"He had some of his grandfather's medicine …to help him sleep," the man said. He was suddenly sweating.

"What medicine?" Hugh demanded.

"It's from laudanum."

"JG hates laudanum," Hugh stated. "When he broke his wrist, he could hardly get it down. You are lying."

"I said it was *from* laudanum. It is a powder version. Given to him by orders of his grandfather, my employer."

"You drugged him," Hugh accused. When the man didn't deny it, he huffed in disgust. "Powder form? What? Snuck into his tea or wine?"

The butler turned and left the room and the remaining footman and maid followed.

"Let's sit him up," Jonathan suggested.

"JG," Hugh called as they pulled him to a sitting position.

"He is lifeless," Jonathan said worriedly.

"Do not say that. JG!"

"I'm going to make sure a doctor has been called," Jonathan said. "Or I will get one myself."

"I've got him," Hugh said. "I'll keep him upright."

Chapter Thirty-Two

ocelyn heard her name being called as she was jostled from sleep. She struggled to open her eyes. When she managed it, she saw it was morning. She was so disoriented; it took several moments for the memory of the previous night to come back to her along with an avalanche of humiliation and misery. Alice was beside her wearing her traveling gown.

"I'm sorry to wake you," Alice said. "But I'm going home with our parents. I couldn't leave without telling you."

Jocelyn made herself sit up. She felt woozy. *Oh, yes.* She'd had a dose of Aunt Julia's powder. It had rendered her senseless which was what she had wanted at the time. "What?" she asked, wondering if she had misunderstood.

"I'm going home," Alice repeated. "We're leaving in an hour."

Jocelyn shook her head. The statement made no sense.

"Are you all right?" Alice asked.

"I'm going, too."

"You don't have to," Alice replied.

Jocelyn rubbed her face and swung her legs out of bed. Then she shook her head in confusion. "Wait. Why are you going? What about Nigel?"

"It is over between us. I've already packed. I couldn't sleep."

Jocelyn stared. "What do you mean it's over?" she stammered

"Just what I said," Alice stated sadly. She stood. "Did something happen with you last night? Or were you upset because you heard about—"

"Wait. I am not thinking clearly at all," Jocelyn complained. "How can it be over between you and Nigel?

"He loves someone else."

Jocelyn huffed. "Alice," she scolded. "That is not true."

"It is true. I saw them. And he admitted it. So I am going home."

He admitted it? Jocelyn stared in disbelief.

"You needn't go with us," Alice repeated tenderly. "But if you are going, you'll need to get ready. Mama will not miss the departure."

"What has happened," Jocelyn wailed softly. She felt two steps behind.

"Jaus, are you quite awake? How much did you have to drink last night? I am too dull-witted to think for both of us today. I didn't sleep at all. Or did I already say that?"

Jocelyn rose.

"I'll help you," Alice said. "I would have woken you sooner, but I didn't think you would want to go."

Jocelyn clumsily readied herself and, together, they managed to do her packing. "I have to write JG," she said quietly.

"He'll hate you going," Alice said.

"Yes," Jocelyn said under her breath.

Alice started for the door. "I'll bring you some tea and biscuits. We're nearly out of time."

Jocelyn stood stock still for several seconds after Alice left. She hadn't said goodbye to anyone yet. Nothing felt real. She sat, pulled out a piece of parchment and readied her pen.

Dear JG,

I fear this will come as a blow and I beg your forgiveness for that, but I cannot be the one to come between you and your grandfather. I wish things were different. I am returning home with my family. Pursue the life you were meant to have and be happy. I will never forget you.

Warmest regards,

Jocelyn

A choked sob escaped her and she cried bitterly.

~~~

"I do not understand it," Julia said to her brother and sister-in-law as they stood together in the parlour. "I have to be the worst chaperone who ever lived. The girls seemed fine. They were having a wonderful time. And then—"

"It's not your fault," Eliza replied. "Alice saw Nigel with a lady and later he confirmed he'd always had feelings for this other lady. Lord Merton won a large sum of money yesterday and so the need for Alice's dowry is no longer there."

Julia shook her head. It did not feel true.

"Jocelyn must have learned of it," Eliza continued. "That's why she was so upset. She didn't explain because …perhaps because she didn't feel it was her place. At least, that's my guess."

"It feels as if the rug has been whipped out from beneath me," Julia said.

"We all do," Granny spoke up from her chair.

"Especially Alice," Richard said. "I feel horrible for having introduced her to the Walstons in the first place." Eliza drew breath to speak, but he glowered. "Do not say I told you so," he snapped. "Please."

~~~

"Yes?" Jocelyn called in response to the knock on the door. She had managed to stop crying and bathed her face in cool water, but it had not erased the evidence. She looked terrible.

Dinah came in with a tray. She set it down and gave Jocelyn a sympathetic look. "Did you hear another sad story?"

Jocelyn grabbed a towel and pressed her face into it, sobbing. It felt as if her heart was being torn into bits.

~~~

"I don't want you to go," Jeremy said to Alice.

She nodded, unable to speak for the moment. The last eight hours had been the hardest of her life and saying her goodbyes was the brutal conclusion. "I know," she whispered. She cleared her aching throat. "But we'll see you again."

"When?"

She blew out a breath and tried to steady herself. "I don't know. But I know that we will. You can come visit us."

"In America. I would like to see Indians with feathers."

"I was teasing about that."

"Will there be a place for me to paint?"

She reached out and took hold of his hands. "Of course."

"I wish you weren't going."

~~~

"Compose yourself," Jocelyn whispered to her mirror image. She was packed and ready and it was time to go. She'd consumed a cup of tea and forced two bites down her throat. Anyone could see she had been crying, but no one would say anything. She looked down at the envelope on the table, pressed a kiss to her fingers and touched the envelope.

She squeezed her eyes shut and drew in a deep breath willing the tears to stay in check, and then she started for the door. Someone knocked just as she reached it. She opened it to find Jeremy standing there. They looked at one another a moment and then he did the almost unthinkable. He stepped up and pulled her into a brotherly embrace and held her while she sobbed again. She feared there were not enough handkerchiefs in the world to get her through this day.

~~~

Alice and Jocelyn stood with their hands on the railing watching people on shore waving farewell to other passengers as their ship left port. No one they knew waved. They felt disconnected and utterly spent as the coastline grew farther and farther away. Loosened strands of their hair blew, and their skirts billowed in the salty wind. The end of their stay had come about so abruptly, it did not feel real.

Their parents had gone to their stateroom. Alice and Jocelyn had their own cabin, a cramped area of eight feet by eight feet. Mr. and Mrs. Weatherly's room had a narrow double bed, a small set of drawers, a short bench and a cabinet with a washbasin, a bucket for wastewater, a pitcher and a chamber pot. Alice and Jocelyn's cabin had two narrow berths, one over the other. One trunk per girl had been shoved under the lower bed and the others had been stowed.

"I wonder if anyone has ever slept for six weeks straight," Alice said.

"I don't know, but it's worth a try," Jocelyn returned. Still, they stood watching seagulls soar and hover. "We didn't say goodbye to Lakely and Ada."

"I wrote a note to them," Alice said.

"Good," Jocelyn said quietly.

"I'm so tired and my eyes sting. I have to lie down."

Jocelyn continued to stand there long after Alice had gone to their cabin. She needed time to comprehend all that had happened and what she had left behind.

~~~

When Nigel stumbled through the door of his home in the morning, he was insensible with drink. His family had been reduced to nearly hysterical worry, but there was no impressing that or anything upon him. He was helped to bed singing some obscure tune about judges and juries and wings of an eagle and an ocean journey.

"This is ridiculous," Lakely complained to her sister. "I'm going to the Weatherly's to see Alice."

"I'll go with you," Ada replied.

Unfortunately, their plan of action led to the discovery that the Weatherly family of Boston were on a voyage home. All of them. The knowledge was shocking.

"It all fell apart," Julia relayed. "In one night."

Ada and Lakely left feeling wretched. They had two letters in their possession, one Alice had written to them to say goodbye, and one that Jocelyn had written to JG that they had promised Julia to deliver.

"I'm going to write to Alice and explain," Ada said as they rode home.

"It should be Nigel who explains," Lakely replied as she put the notes inside her reticule.

Ada sighed heavily. "What a tangled mess."

Lakely shook her head. "If only we could have seen Alice before she left. And dragged poor Jocelyn with her. I should have tried to see her last night."

"I thought we'd have a chance. I still cannot believe they're gone." They rode in silence for a while. "Do you think Papa will still go to France now?"

Lakely rolled her eyes and groaned. "Who can say? Do you think Granny and Aunt Julia will let me move in with them now? Life is so much simpler there."

"Perhaps I'll elope with Harrison right away and you can move in with us."

"Perhaps I'll jump the next ship to Boston. I'll carry your letter with me."

They returned home to find Dab and Hugh waiting for them. Dab had arrived first and Hugh a few minutes later. They had come to see Nigel, but with him being indisposed, they had waited on Lakely and Ada to return.

Dab had come with questions, which they could not answer since Nigel had not provided any. Hugh had come with the information that Lord Morguston had fallen and injured himself the night before, but only after he had verbally assaulted Jocelyn. And before that, he had essentially poisoned his own grandson to keep him at home. JG had nearly died from an overdose of something called morphine.

"I cannot believe what I am hearing," Ada exclaimed. "Poor JG! Jocelyn could not have known, or she would never have left."

Lakely wondered what Lord Morguston had said to Jocelyn to so upset her. "What if Jaus didn't return home for moral support? Does anyone know what Lord Morguston said to her?"

"No," Hugh replied. "But there was an ugly rumor circulating about her having tripped him to make him fall."

"That is ridiculous," Ada exclaimed furiously.

"I know," Hugh agreed. "But he was the one who claimed it."

Ada gaped. "He ... Lord Morguston?"

He nodded grimly.

"Well, it is a lie!"

"I don't doubt it. In fact, Lord Reilly was there, he saw the whole thing and he established that it wasn't true. But you know rumors."

Lakely went to the table where she had set her reticule. She opened it and pulled out the note to JG.

"Lakely," Ada warned. "Do not!"

It wasn't sealed. It was one piece of parchment folded into an envelope. "What?" Lakely said innocently. "Break the seal? Look. There is no seal." She opened the folds of the letter.

"Stop it," Ada cried, starting for her. "That is a private—"

Lakely twisted away, hurriedly scanning the note and then turned back as Ada reached her. "You're right. I'm sorry. I won't read it."

"Give it to me," Ada insisted with an outstretched hand.

Lakely handed it over and Ada refolded it without looking at the contents and then walked over and handed it to Hugh. "Will you see JG again today?"

"Today or tomorrow. I am exhausted at the moment. We stayed until he was out of danger."

"Will you please give him this when you see him? It's a note from Jocelyn."

"Of course, I will."

"Thank you. We'll let Nigel know what happened when he wakes up."

Hugh said his goodbyes and left, and Dab followed.

When they were gone, Ada scowled at her sister.

"My curiosity is like Papa's gambling," Lakely said guiltily. "It gets the better of me from time to time."

Ada shook her head as she walked out. "I'm going to write to Alice," she said over her shoulder. "I am not waiting one more hour."

"And I'm going to write to Jocelyn," Lakely said under her breath. She waited thirty seconds and then followed.

Chapter Thirty-Three

$\mathcal{N}$igel stared in confusion. "Left?"

He had come downstairs for sustenance since the servants had apparently been instructed not to bring him anything other than water. It was vexatious as hell, but it had forced him up. It was daytime, but he didn't know the hour, nor did he care. He wasn't even altogether sure what day it was.

He had been relieved to find the dining room empty, but the sideboard was also empty. Luckily, a maid came to his rescue. She went to fetch a meal and a pot of tea and said she would bring it to the morning room. Thankfully, that room was also empty of people. He plunked down in the most comfortable chair and rested his aching head in his hand, thinking he might doze until his food arrived.

"You look like something the cat dragged in," Lakely stated coolly as she walked in. "Are you finally sober?"

He didn't so much as glance at her. "Unfortunately. I do not plan on staying that way."

"Spoken like a responsible grown up."

"Go. Away."

"Fine, I will. But allow me to let you in on a bit of news first."

He clenched his jaw. If the news was about Alice and Dab being together—

"Alice is gone."

He braced himself for it to be about the pair having run off together. The humiliation was going to be profound.

"The Weatherly's all left," she added.

He finally looked up. "Left?"

"Yes. They are sailing back to America. They left yesterday. We searched high and low for you in order to stop it."

"Why did they leave?"

She came further into the room, strolled actually, and sat. "Alice and Jocelyn's elder sister gave birth early and the baby is frail. That is why the parents left."

He already knew this. Alice had told him. Lakely was purposely trying his patience.

"As you know, Alice and Jocelyn were both going to stay and go to Merton Park with us, but the night of Le Grand Ball changed everything."

The maid entered the room with a tray for him. She set it down on the table, sensed the tension in the room, and scurried back out.

"Eat," Lakely urged sarcastically. "Please, do not let me hold you back. Eat, drink and be merry."

He glared at her and then poured a cup of tea and took a drink. "Are you being serious about them all being gone?" he finally asked. "Or are you toying with me?"

"I swear it," she said soberly. "They are gone. All four of them."

He felt a pain in his stomach. It's because it was empty. He picked up a muffin and took a bite. What did the news matter? Alice was already gone to him. He had not fully accepted it, not in his heart, but the fact was she had chosen a different man. Undoubtedly, she would see her sister and the new baby and then return, only to Dab this time. At least, in the interim, he could make himself scarce. Go to Italy or Belgium or China.

"There's something else," Lakely continued. "Lord Morguston did not approve of JG's feelings for Jocelyn. It is a long story, but he tried to incapacitate JG the night of the ball so that he, Lord Morguston, could essentially either buy Jaus off or scare her away. To accomplish the deed, keeping JG home, he had something put in his wine. It was only supposed to make him sleep, but it nearly killed him."

Nigel gawked. This had been happening while he'd been drunk? "What?" Nigel breathed.

"He's going to be fine," Lakely added, allowing compassion into her tone. "Your friends have been worried about you, too."

A surge of bitterness came sweeping back. "Have they?"

She drew back in bewilderment. "What on earth has—"

"Do not!" He rose but had to battle a moment of dizziness and nausea. He was not meant to be a drunk. He didn't have the constitution for it. "Do not say one word about Alice and …any of my so-called friends. I don't want to hear it!" He picked up the tray and left, leaving her speechless.

~~~

Lakely stood staring at the doorway her brother had passed through. Something had happened. Something had changed, had closed off within her brother. Perhaps they really did not know what had gone on between him and Alice after all. Whatever the truth was, she would not simply let the matter lie. Not when it had led to such all-around misery. She left the room. "Crichton," she said when she saw him inspecting the dining room. "Where are my parents?"

"Your father is in his study, I believe. Your mother went out."

Lakely hurried on to her father's study. The door was open and he was seated at his desk bent over a ledger. "Something is wrong with Nigel," she exclaimed, causing him to jump.

He glowered at her.

"Something is very odd. Very off. We cannot let him leave this house and disappear again, and I think he is planning to do just that."

"What do you expect, Lakely? Alice left him. Of course, he's acting oddly."

"We explained it to you. She left because she thought he loved someone else."

"That may be true. I do not know. The point is, she left. You, my dear, will simply have to give him time to get beyond it."

She thrust her hands on her hips. "I will not give him time to get beyond it. He needs to fix it. I want you to come down and wait with me until he appears. Then we will try and get through to him. We'll tell Crichton not to let him leave until he faces us."

"I know you care about your brother, but you are going to have to let him work his way through this difficult time."

"It is all a misunderstanding!"

"You do not know that. You assume that."

"I need your help," she insisted.

"Close the door on your way out. I have work to do."

She glared at him and left, slamming the door shut behind her.

"Thank you, my dear," her father said sarcastically under his breath.

Ada was reclined in the tub with her eyes closed.

"This is no time for a bath," Lakely said, barging in.

Ada opened her eyes. "I disagree. I went for a long walk with Harrison to talk about everything and I got hot. Is Nigel up yet?"

"Yes, he is up and angry. He wouldn't even let me speak. I have a terrible feeling he is going back out to drink himself into oblivion yet again and our father refuses to help. Mamma is out, so I need you." She turned and left. "Hurry up."

Ada shook her head, sighed and closed her eyes again.

~~~

Lord Merton emitted a put-out sounding sigh when a knock on the door interrupted him yet again. "What?" he called. He expected Lakely, but it was Nigel who stepped in. He was dressed and ready to leave by the looks of it.

"Is it still your plan to go to Reims?" Nigel asked with no real interest evident in his face or tone. He seemed almost blank, but unless his father was mistaken, something seethed under the surface. Damned if Lakely hadn't been right.

"How are you feeling?" Lord Merton asked.

"Is it still your plan to go to Reims?" Nigel repeated, ignoring the question.

Lord Merton stood. "Not at this time."

"Then I wish to," Nigel stated. "I don't know anything about the vineyard and the wine business, and I would like to learn. Any objection?"

Lord Merton was stymied.

"Good," Nigel said, and he turned and left.

~~~

Lakely was pacing in the drawing room when Nigel stepped in. The smile on his face was false and chilly. "I could have simply shoved Crichton aside and left," he stated. "But since I did not, since I am here, let us get one thing clear. You are not in any position to tell me what to do." He had advanced steadily and was no longer smiling.

She lifted her chin. "We need to discuss what hap—"

"Don't say it," he exploded jabbing his finger threateningly in the air. "I do not want to hear her name."

"Nigel," his father exclaimed, stepping into the room. "Calm yourself."

"I am leaving," he said to his father. He looked back at his sister. "I am going to France. Today. I will be gone for some time. I cannot say how long. For this one day, *one* bloody day, you can refrain from saying the name Alice Weatherly."

Nigel's fury was mind-boggling. It was not like him at all.

"If you do not," he continued. "If you dare mention her name to me, please believe this if you give a damn, I will never speak to you again. I swear it."

Lakely swallowed, shaken by his resolve.

Nigel glared at his stunned father. "That goes for you, as well." He started from the room but stopped short to see Ada standing in the doorway in her dressing robe. Wet tendrils fell around her shoulders. Obviously, she had just come from a bath. If that was not shocking enough, tears were streaming down her face, and she was trembling. Was she ill? Was that what Lakely had wanted to tell him? Or had JG taken a turn for the worse? Oh, God. How self-centered had he been? "Ada," he said.

She moved like a flash, reaching out and slapping his face.

He held a hand to the stinging place on his face and stared. "What—" he uttered.

Her face was wet and her nose running. She was a mess. "How dare you!"

Lakely could only gawk. Ada had never lashed out in a moment of violence in her entire life. Not a tantrum as a child, not a fit of temper as a girl, nothing. And then this.

"You broke her heart," Ada railed. "I saw it. And you do not even know it. We could have told you. We all searched for you. And now they have gone. Alice is gone because you broke her heart!"

Without question, she had shaken Nigel, but it was because of her outburst, not because he believed she knew what she was talking about.

"Alice," Ada cried. "Alice, Alice, Alice. I am saying her name. Are you going to threaten never to speak to me again? Well, do it! Alice!"

"Ada," he said with a shake of his head.

"You are not the only one who grew to love her, Nigel. Now, I will tell you what I saw," she said in a shaky voice. "We will explain what happened."

"What happened is she left me! What happened is she fell in love with Dab."

Ada's jaw dropped. And then she burst out laughing.

He jerked.

"Dab?" Lakely repeated. "You horse's ass! Dab tried to help find you. He was upset for you because he thought she was about to break your heart."

"Dab would never betray you," Ada joined in, furious again. "How could you even think it? How could you be so blind? His friends are all he cares about in life. Damn your stupidity!"

Nigel took a step backwards. He was shaken by how traumatized his youngest sister was.

"Alice believes you love Therese St. Clair," Ada said.

He frowned furiously. "That is nonsense."

"No," Lakely rejoined. "It is not. She saw you and Therese together early on and she asked if the two of you would have—"

"Would have what?" he snapped.

"I don't remember how she phrased it," Lakely snapped back. "Been together. Fallen in love. Courted. Married. You get the idea. Therese is in love with you. Any fool can see it." She shrugged. "Alice saw it."

"What did you say?" Nigel asked incredulously.

"I believe I said it was possible," she admitted. "I didn't think it mattered at the time."

He glared at her, but he was recalling the conversation on the veranda. *Have you ever asked someone to marry you?*

"At the ball when Papa told you his news," Ada continued. She was quieter now, but still trembling. Her face was blotchy and pink, her eyes red-rimmed. "I was in the balcony above. Alice had come off the dance floor and spoken with Lakely who—"

"I told her the news," Lakely interjected. "About the debt being cleared, and then I went in search of Ada."

"I was watching it all," Ada said. "As soon as Lakely walked away, Alice turned to find you. She saw you talking to Papa. It was obvious Papa was sharing the good news with you and then you were given two glasses of champagne."

Nigel's heart had begun to pound in an unpleasant way. "Yes. One of them was for Alice."

"Of course, it was. I do not doubt your heart. The point is, Alice had started toward you, but people kept getting in her way. Then the way cleared and she saw you and—"

"Oh, God," he breathed. "Therese."

Ada nodded. "Yes."

"Miss St. Clair was only being nice," Nigel explained. "She wanted to apologize or offer support for unkind things that had been said. She was only being nice and then I was only being nice, but the entire exchange didn't last a minute."

"I know," Ada sympathized. "But Alice saw you and Therese lifting a glass together. As in celebration."

"No," he exclaimed. "It was nothing of the sort." He walked over to the settee and sat. "I did hand her one of the glasses to quell her embarrassment, but I only wanted to get to Alice." He bent over and buried his face in hands. "Are you suggesting that Alice thought…"

"Alice thought," Lakely said, "that you were only ever with her because of her dowry. And since the debt was gone—"

He jerked his head up. It didn't look like he was breathing.

Lakely came and sat next to him. "Why would you ever think she'd fallen in love with Dab?"

He shook his head as tears sprang to his eyes.

"She loves you," Lakely said. She reached over and took hold of his hand and held it tightly. "Alice loves *you*."

Ada crowded in on his other side. "After you left that night, Lakely and I didn't know what to think, and then Dab came back into the foyer. He was concerned for you and angry at her because he had misunderstood."

Nigel looked at her and his gaze sharpened. "What?"

Lakely nodded. "He said that Alice looked ill when he returned from smoking. Naturally, he went to her. She muttered that it wasn't real, that had never been love. She said it was over. He asked what was over. He said, 'you're not talking about Nigel, are you?' Then she said there was someone else from before."

"She meant Therese," Ada said, "but Dab thought she was admitting that she had loved someone before. All he could think was how hurt you would be."

Nigel was recalling Dab say he was sorry. Nigel had thought he was expressing remorse. Instead, it had been concern for his feelings? "No, no, no. This could not have all been a stupid misunderstanding," Nigel uttered miserably.

"We think it was," Lakely replied.

"It was," Ada echoed. "I know it in my heart. I saw Alice's face when she turned around after seeing you and Therese. She was crushed. Nigel, you have to fix it."

Nigel stood and walked to the windows. "How? If they are gone?"

No one replied because they all knew the answer.

Chapter Thirty-Four

The ache in her bladder finally got Alice out of her bunk. She attended to her needs and then went to the shuttered door that led to the deck. She opened the louvers and got a rush of salty wind in her face. A threating-looking gray sky made the time of day impossible to judge. She turned to look on the top bunk, recalling Jocelyn leaving the cabin some time ago in what had seemed the middle of night. Where had she gone?

Alice closed the shutters, returned to her bunk and scooted back until she sat against the wall. She felt physically weak and as sore as if she had been knocked around by prizefighters for the fun of it. Why would her body be sore?

When Jocelyn came back, she bent down to peer at Alice and then handed her a mug of tea. "I brought you this and an apple."

Alice gratefully accepted the mug. "Thank you." Jocelyn pulled the apple from her pocket and sat next to her. Alice sipped the tepid brew. "Where did you go?"

"Walking. Thinking. I have traversed every single deck. Repeatedly."

"Are you all right?"

Jocelyn shook her head. "No. I have made such a mistake."

"What mistake?"

"Allowing that hateful old man to chase me away … as if I was a worthless little mouse."

Alice shook her head in confusion. "What?"

"Alice, you have slept the better part of two days."

"I have?"

"Yes. Now, get up, get dressed and come eat something. Then we'll walk and I'll tell you everything and you will tell me everything. Doesn't it feel as if you've been trapped in a nightmare? Or like the old man in…oh, what was that story that came out last year? Rip Van Winkle."

Alice did feel a nightmare-like disorientation. "I feel weak."

"Of course, you do. You need to eat. Come on."

"Wait. Tell me what you meant first."

"As you get dressed," Jocelyn insisted.

Alice worked her way out of the bunk. She did not feel well at all.

"I do not know why, but JG was not at the ball," Jocelyn began as she too got up. "His grandfather was, however."

Alice pulled off her nightgown and took her day dress from the hook, slipping it on without bothering with a corset. Already, she felt as if she needed to sit down again.

"So I decided to speak with him." Jocelyn said as she walked over to the doors. Making sure Alice was decently covered, she opened the slats for light.

Alice was staring with concern.

"He accused me of trying to ruin JG's life."

Alice shook her head. "I'm so sorry."

"And then he fell."

Alice drew back. "Fell?"

"Yes. He had begun walking toward me. He has a bad hip, and it gave for some reason and he fell. But then he practically shouted that I had tripped him."

Alice's jaw dropped. "What!"

Jocelyn shook her head in reassurance. "Someone saw everything. He had actually been coming to speak with Lord Morguston. Thank Goodness. He spoke up right away in my defense."

"Oh, Jaus," Alice said tightly. She did not feel well and she was close to tears. "How terrible for you."

"It was. I thought I was going to be sick. I made my way outside and Joel Stewart saw me. He went to find you or Aunt Julia so we could leave."

"When was this? What time?"

"Half past midnight."

"I had already gone," Alice said.

Now Jocelyn looked confused. "Gone?"

Alice turned to the tiny counter that held a wash basin. She wasn't sure he was up to the explanation after all. She reached for her brush and began working out the tangles.

"Gone where?"

"Will you brush my hair? I feel so weak."

Jocelyn came and took the brush from her and began working out the tangles. "JG was ready to give up everything for us to be together. He was going to learn the law and become a barrister in order for us to have a life together."

Alice nodded. She already knew this.

"And then I let that hateful old man chase me away. It wasn't fair to JG. I was wrong."

Alice sighed. "It never would have happened if Mama and Papa hadn't been leaving," she realized.

"True," Jocelyn replied. "So, when it comes down to it, it's Sophia's fault."

In the small, tilted mirror above the basin, Alice smiled wanly at the jest.

"Do you know," Jocelyn continued. "When I woke in what I thought was the dead of night; it was actually near dawn, I was baffled as to where I was and what had happened. As if I wasn't in control of my own faculties and actions."

Alice understood the feeling. Her head was tugged as Jocelyn formed a simple hair twist.

"But I was," Jocelyn said. "And I was so wrong. There, done," Jocelyn said. She set the brush down and stepped back. "I am going to get a letter to JG as soon as I possibly can and beg his forgiveness for leaving as I did."

Alice turned to her. "He'll understand," she replied tenderly.

"I know. He's such a good person."

"Yes, he is," Alice agreed.

"Alice, I'm going back. I'll see everyone at home and pack properly. But I am going back. Our parents will not like it, but I am an adult."

"How will I do without you?" Alice asked as her eyes filled.

"First things first. You need to eat."

Less than an hour later, as rain poured, Alice and Jocelyn sat facing one another at a wooden table in the saloon where first class passengers dined. Others sat playing cards or dice, but with the noise of the drumming rain and the interaction of the others, they had a decent measure of privacy. Staterooms bordered the dining hall, so there were louvered doors all the way around.

Alice had eaten and explained what had happened the night of the Roxon ball. Jocelyn failed to understand her suspicion of Miss St. Clair, so Alice reminded her what she'd overheard at the Foster Soiree.

"Alice, did it not seem suspicious that Miss Fletcher, who I was warned about at the very first ball, I believe it was Jonathan who said she was a mean-spirited viper and best avoided, which they all agreed with. That doesn't matter. The point is, this conversation you *accidentally* overheard just so happens to occur right outside the retiring room you had gone into?"

Alice frowned. "It wasn't just that."

"Then what?"

"Nigel was behaving strangely. That night, after I heard what I did, he claimed he was leaving when we did, but I saw him go back inside as we pulled away."

"So?"

Alice huffed. "What do you mean 'so'?"

"Perhaps he had to relieve himself. Or tell a friend he was leaving. There are a dozen good reasons he might have gone back in."

"You are just playing Devil's advocate," Alice accused.

"I'm not playing anything. What I am is the concerned sister who doesn't understand the terrible things you got into your head about the man who loves you and the man you love."

Alice leaned forward. "I saw them toasting one another. Nigel and Miss St. Clair. Right after his father told him the news, he took champagne to *her*."

Jocelyn held up a hand. "Let me make certain I have this straight and please correct me if I wrong." She paused. "After seeing Nigel and his father speaking, obviously Lord Merton telling him the big news, and after Nigel has been handed two glasses of champagne, you lose sight of him."

Alice nodded.

"Then a bit later—"

"Moments," Alice corrected. "Seconds."

"How many seconds?"

"I don't know. Twenty, thirty, ten, I don't know."

"All right. So, let's say twenty seconds later, you see him again and he's speaking with Miss St. Clair."

"Yes. He was *celebrating* with her."

"So you heard them?"

"No. Of course, I didn't."

"Why did you think they were celebrating?"

"They each had a glass of champagne. This is directly after he's gotten the news. What else would they be doing?"

"I am trying to picture it. She has a glass of champagne and he has a glass of champagne."

"Yes."

"Are you certain he isn't still holding two? What if she already had one and it was a chance encounter?"

Alice was stymied. Then she shook her head. "He was not holding two. He'd given one to her."

"You're certain?"

Alice hesitated. "Yes," she replied.

"So why did he show up with a glass of champagne for you not even …what? Five minutes later? Or was it longer?"

"I don't know how long it was," Alice snapped. Warmth had flushed her face and she was feeling prickly with an acute uneasiness.

"All right. Let's relive the last conversation the two of you had. I'll be Nigel."

Alice grimaced. "No."

"I need to understand. Please." She paused as Alice considered. "I'm walking up with a glass of champagne for you."

"I don't remember what was said," Alice hedged.

"You have an uncanny memory. You will get close enough."

"Fine. Let me just do it, then." Alice closed her eyes and huffed. She put her elbows on the table, holding her hands up. She did have an extraordinary memory and she needed to get beyond the doubt and pain she was feeling. "I suppose we need to talk," she said, waving the fingers of one hand. Her expression grew hurt, although her eyes remained closed. "Champagne," she scoffed drolly, wagging the fingers of the other hand. "Why not?" She paused, replaying it in her mind. "Is there something you want to tell me?" waved the fingers of the first hand. "Isn't there something you want to tell me?" the second hand snapped angrily.

She paused and cocked her head as she remembered. "Yes, I do. My father won a large sum of money." Alice swallowed. "I heard," the second hand said. "So there is no more debt. No more need for me."

"Go on," Jocelyn urged.

Alice opened her eyes. "He said …there's someone else," she uttered tonelessly.

"He said it or he asked it?"

"He said it," Alice said hesitantly.

"Are you certain?"

"I thought I was," Alice said barely over a whisper.

Jocelyn nodded. "Go on."

"So I said—"

"Try to remember exactly."

"I said yes. And you are sorry and I am sorry."

"Oh, Ali! Don't you see?"

"See what?"

"With your amazing writer's mind, imagine for a moment that he does not having feelings for Miss St. Clair and never did. I have no idea what the conversation was between them, but what if it was totally innocent? Imagine you are him and on the opposite side of that conversation." She paused, letting that sink in. "It sounds as though you wanted to leave him."

Alice shook her head in denial. "No."

Jocelyn nodded slowly. "If he did not *say* there is someone else, if he asked it—"

"No. Stop. Just let me think." Alice covered her face with her hands to relive the conversation again.

It was not the last time she would do it.

Chapter Thirty-Five

There were fourteen blocks between Clara and Ross's home on Hancock Street and theirs on Mt. Vernon Street, and Alice walked them at an unhurried pace. It was not because she was enjoying the stroll as much as she was killing time. Since arriving home five days ago, that's what she'd done. Kill time. It was an appalling concept.

For five horrendously long weeks, she had been imprisoned by melancholy that sapped her strength. Her parents and sister had hoped she would improve once they were back home but she had not. She did not want to visit friends or have them visit her because she didn't want to talk about their time in London. She could not bear to.

She'd lost her ability to concentrate, so she was not working on the book. She needed to write to Nigel, and she had tried to numerous times. It was ironic that Jocelyn wrote page after page to JG while she, the supposed writer, agonized over a single sentence. When she managed a paragraph, she hated every word of it. She had no idea how much paper she'd wasted attempting a letter, but it was enough for a worthy short novel.

If only she knew exactly what had happened the night of the last ball. She should have gathered all the facts before she'd left London, but she had not asked the necessary questions. Instead, she had assumed. What if she had been wrong? If so, she had been horribly unfair to Nigel, perhaps even cruel. It was possible that if she had been mistaken in her assumptions, he would want nothing more to do with her. When she finally found the right words and wrote the letter, he might tear it up without even reading it. Or directly afterwards.

What if he had not developed feelings for Miss St. Clair until after she left? What if the two of them were together right now because she had misjudged the situation? For nearly six weeks, she had suffered with the thought. She had gone back and forth wondering whether she would prefer having been wrong or having been wronged. Both were abysmal choices.

She turned onto their street hoping she had missed all the morning callers. Word had gotten out that they were home, so social visits had commenced. She simply slipped away before they began. She was hiding; that was the sad truth. There was no carriage out front, which was a relief, but she entered a side door of their home so she could find an avenue of escape if any visitors lurked, having been dropped off.

She did not hear any voices. Still, she proceeded carefully, peeking in rooms as she passed. The drawing room, the music room they rarely used, the parlour. Alice passed by, then stopped abruptly and backtracked, having spotted Jocelyn in the parlour, absorbed in a letter she was reading. "Jaus?"

Jocelyn looked up with tears welled in eyes. She rose and hurried toward Alice. "Letters arrived," Jocelyn said. "Lakely wrote me." She handed Alice hers with a shaky hand. "Ada wrote you."

"Why do you look like that? What is it?"

"It's terrible and it's wonderful. Mostly terrible."

"Tell me!"

Jocelyn nodded frantically. "I'll read it to you."

It would be a wonder if she could read it since she was trembling so.

"'Dear Jocelyn. Ada and I so wish we had known what was happening the night of the Roxon Ball. What a cursed night it turned out to be. As to what was happening with Alice at nearly the same time, you will know by now. What I wish to explain is the reason JG was not in attendance that night. His grandfather incapacitated him with a medication that he (Lord Morguston) had from a previous injury.'"

Alice gasped.

Jocelyn looked up at her, and then went back to reading. "'The medication was morphine, named after Morpheus, the Greek god of dreams. In truth, it was the stuff of nightmares for JG who nearly died from the dosage he was given.'"

"Oh, Jaus," Alice breathed.

"'Lord Morguston secretly mixed the powder into JG's wine at dinner so he would be unable to attend the ball. His intention was not to harm JG, but to either to bribe or harass you into ending the relationship that night.'"

Tears had sprung to Alice's eyes, as well. She had never imagined anything so terrible. "Is JG all right?" she asked breathlessly.

Jocelyn nodded. "He is on the mend, according to Lakely. Luckily, Hugh and Jonathan discovered him that night and did not leave him until he was out of danger." She squeezed her eyes shut. 'Please, God, may he be all right."

Alice exhaled shakily. It was difficult to wrap her mind around the act. What sort of desperation had the old man felt? In order to keep Jocelyn and JG apart? "I dislike Lord Morguston deeply but ...how will he be able to live with himself? How will JG forgive him?"

Jocelyn went over and sat again. She exhaled as she leaned back. "I do not know. Read yours."

Alice hesitated a moment but then opened the letter and read silently.

"What does it say?" Jocelyn insisted.

Alice lowered the letter. "You were right," she said quietly. "Again."

Jocelyn got back up and took hold of the letter but continued to watch her sister. "Why don't you look happier then?"

"Because I ruined everything." She turned and started from the room.

"Alice," Jocelyn called.

Alice paused. "I'm all right. I just walked too far," she said in a flat voice. "I'm going to lie down."

Jocelyn watched her worriedly, but then bent her head to scour the letter.

Alice's statement to Jocelyn had been an understatement. She felt wretched in every conceivable way. Weak, sick, foolish, regretful. Curling up on the bottom stair like a cat and sleeping for a week sounded far more desirable than dragging herself up to her room. Did she even possess the strength to climb the stairs? She saw the staircase with a sort of tunnel vision.

"Alice," her mother said.

"I'm not well, Mama," Alice murmured as her hand gripped the banister. She would make it to her room because she had to, and that was that.

"There's someone here to see you," her mother said.

No, no, no. Not a visitor. Worse yet, her mother was standing at the front door, which meant a visitor was also standing there watching her. She was caught. She had walked right by them without even seeing them. She should have gone to rest in the drawing room, but it was too late now. The only way out was to slump in a faint to get out of the visit. Truthfully, it was not far from how she felt, but she had never fainted in her entire life. No, she would face the dreaded caller. It was past the hours someone should have called, but she would visit briefly and then explain she did not feel well.

She turned to her mother standing only a few yards away from her and holding a bouquet of yellow roses in her hand. Alice looked quizzically to the visitor and saw Nigel standing there with a huge bouquet of colorful flowers. *Nigel.* Looking so handsome. With flowers. It could only mean one thing. She was hallucinating.

"Alice," her mother cried worriedly. "Dearest, what is—"

"Is Nigel here?" Alice breathed while staring right at him. She felt something cold and tickly on her face and her upper lip.

"Yes," Nigel said, stepping forward with a look of grave concern. He set the flowers aside and came to her. He placed warm, strong hands on her arms. "I am right here, my love."

My love? He still loved her? After everything? Shaking like a leaf, she leaned into him and he wrapped his arms around her. "I'm sorry," she whispered.

"I'm sorry, too," he whispered back.

He was sorry, too? She didn't know what he was talking about, but she could not move.

"Nigel," Jocelyn called joyfully. "You're here! It's so wonderful to see you!"

"The parlour is—" Mrs. Weatherly said, gesturing toward it.

Nigel nodded and began leading Alice away who clung tightly to him. She did not ever want to stop clinging to him.

"They need some lemonade," Jocelyn said to her mother. "She does."

"I think she may need something stronger than that," her mother replied. She turned to their maid who was discreetly waiting. "Bring lemonade please. And wine. And tea. And whatever else we have. Bring it all."

The maid hurried off.

"Are you all right?" Jocelyn asked her mother.

"The look on her face," Eliza said as tears filled her eyes. She pulled a hanky from her pocket and dabbed at her eyes and nose. A moment later, she stuck a finger at Jocelyn. "You, my child, are going to come tell me every single detail that has been withheld."

Jocelyn smiled agreeably. "Yes, Mama."

~~~

Nigel sat Alice on a sofa and knelt in front of her to ascertain her state of health. It had been frightening to see her walk into the foyer looking like the ghost of herself. She hadn't even noticed him standing there. He pressed his handkerchief into her hands, and she dried her face.

"What on earth are you doing here?" she asked with all the breath she could muster.

"My youngest sister slapped me back to my senses and so here I am … having followed the woman I love."

The words were crushingly sweet. "I am so sorry," she uttered shakily.

"So am I." He took her hands in his. "Alice, do you love me?"

She smiled through her tears. "So much it is killing me."

He smiled. "I can't have that," he replied with a shake of his head. "I need you."

"I need you," she echoed.

"Will you be my wife?"

She nodded. "If you will still have me."

"If I will still have you? My darling, it is you. It has been you since the day we met and you didn't know a thing about me. You couldn't even recall my name when you accosted your father."

"I did not accost my father," she laughingly objected. She was trembling all over and breathing was far too difficult. "Not exactly."

"We will tell that story and laugh about it one day," he said.

"There are a few stories we will laugh at."

"Yes, indeed."

"Nigel, I don't know a thing about being a baroness."

He stroked her cheek. "I only care that you become my spouse, dearest friend and lover, forsaking all others. And I can promise the same."

She nodded. "I want that." He reached into his pocket for a small but bulky dark velvet pouch and handed it to her. She looked at him and then opened it and pulled out a ring box. In the box was a betrothal ring, a pale emerald and a pale sapphire surrounded by diamonds. She began to cry. "It's so beautiful."

He took it from her and slipped it on her finger. "This could not belong to anyone else. Nor could my heart."

She leaned in and kissed him and then she cupped his face. "You came all this way."

"Of course, I did. I love you." He gripped her wrist feeling remorseful. "I was an idiot for not grabbing you up and telling you everything I felt, but …I was a coward, really. I thought you were leaving me."

"I am so sorry. I was just so certain that—"

"What?"

"That you'd agreed to marry me for duty's sake, but that your heart was with Miss St. Clair."

"No," he said firmly with a shake of his head. "And no. Well, yes," he relinquished. "To the duty part when it was first proposed. But that was before I met you. But from then on, it was about you. Us." He paused and then rose to sit beside her. "I have to confess something, because I never want anything but complete honesty between us from now on."

She nodded.

"I thought you'd developed an attachment to Dab."

She drew back in confusion. "Dab?"

He nodded. "I am ashamed of it, but I saw a few conversations between the two of you that seemed too … what's the word? Deep? Passionate?"

She shook her head in bafflement. "We didn't have many conversations. He once came into a ball late and I was there. That's the only time I can recall us standing alone. He explained he was late arriving because he'd gotten word that his father was ill."

Nigel cocked his head in surprise. Dab hadn't mentioned it.

"That was the deepest conversation we ever had. I think he has a very complicated relationship with his father."

"He does. With all his family. He really doesn't discuss them."

"He didn't that night either. He said he had gotten word his father was ill. I was waiting for him to continue and he said he appreciated that I had not declared right away that he ought to rush off to him. He said nine out ten people would have declared as much. So, I explained my writer's mind tries to see every side of a story."

Nigel nodded slowly. "Suspicion and insecurity poisoned my thinking. You didn't deserve it and neither did he."

"Oh, Nigel, I did the same thing." Her voice was strained, her throat constricted. "How did we get so tangled up?"

"It's simple really. We were idiots."

She laughed and nodded. "Yes, we were."

He took her hand in his and caressed it. "As for myself, I think at the root of every misunderstanding was a fear of rejection. Along with a healthy measure of protection for my own vanity."

She sighed tiredly. "Let's promise never to do it again."

"Never," he agreed. He brought her hand to his lips and kissed it and then leaned in for a real kiss, one she met him halfway to share. Then they were standing, the kiss deepening, each clutching the other with hunger and need. Had it not been for the clearing of a throat from the doorway, they might have spiraled completely out of control. It was the maid who brought in a tray and quickly left.

Nigel chuckled and straightened his jacket. "How is your sister? And the new baby?"

"They are both well. You'll be able to meet everyone now."

"Yes. And I would like for us to go ahead and marry here."

"Really?"

"Yes. It will make the voyage back home far more enjoyable."

She blushed wildly but she could not stop smiling.

Dearest Jocelyn,

It is the fourth day of July, and I am able to sit up today and write. That may not sound like a great victory, but it feels it. I have learned what occurred in my absence from the conscious world and it causes me great anguish to think of what you went through. I am so sorry for it. I wish I could have been there to protect you.

It may come as a surprise, but Grandad is deeply remorseful for his actions. He is not well. I discovered that he has fallen several times and not told me. His hip is fragile and his spirits are low. I have forgiven him for his actions in regard to me, and he assures me he will grant his blessing to whomever I choose to marry. He asked to write and ask your forgiveness, but I feel he needs to do that in person. I will forgive him his transgression toward you only after you do.

You will be able to tell by this shaky writing that I am not quite steady yet. Because of that and because Nigel is so anxious to leave to get to Alice, I will keep this short and trust him to convey what transpired. He has promised to first assure you that I am getting stronger and will continue doing so. I will be fine.

I pray that we still have a chance for a life together. Will you return to me? If not, I will follow you to Boston. As I told you before, I can give up anything except for you.

I am yours forever,

JG

Chapter Thirty-Six

lice latched the travel bag she would carry with her. "How soon will you come?" she asked Jocelyn who was seated at the vanity watching her final preparation.

"A month or so," Jocelyn replied. "This is difficult for Mama and Papa."

"I know."

"You will give my letters to JG as soon as you can?"

"You know I will. I only hope the weight of the package doesn't slow the ship down too greatly."

Jocelyn laughed.

Alice glanced around her room. It was strange to be leaving, but home was with her husband now. Nigel had stayed nearly three weeks to get to know her family, but it was time for them to return. He had responsibilities and they had a life to build. As she left the room, arm in arm with her sister, she was fighting a wave of emotion.

"Are you sure you don't want us to see you to the harbor?" Jocelyn fretted.

"Yes, I am sure. I will cry if you do and I'd rather not begin the voyage with an aching heart. It will be difficult enough as it is."

"Concentrate on the joy of it. You have married the man that you love, and you will have such a happy life."

Alice smiled.

"Will you go to Merton Hall right away?"

"We'll recover a few days at Larkspur House and then go, but only for a month or so. We'll be back in the city for the holidays."

"I'll be there, by then. It's a strange thought …and it isn't."
They reached the staircase and faltered. "Shall we say goodbye
here?" Jocelyn asked.

Alice blew out a breath before turning to her sister and
nodding.

"No tears, Lady Alice."

"I cannot promise."

Jocelyn looked thoughtful. "Do you know, you are the only
American Baroness I know?"

"I'm not a baroness yet."

"But you will be."

"And you will be a duchess. Will I have to bow to you?"

"Yes," Jocelyn exclaimed to which they both laughed. They
hugged tightly. "I love you, Ali."

"I love you," Alice returned.

They pulled apart, nodded once for courage, and started down
the stairs.

Acknowledgment:

In 1820, the Massachusetts Historical Society, founded in 1791, did not yet have possession of the letters between John and Abagail Adams. That was artistic license.

Jane Shoup is an award-winning author of different genres, but her mainstay is historical with romance. *An American Baroness* is her first foray into Regency romance. She lives in Greensboro, North Carolina with her husband, Scott, and their rescue pup, Gabby, and near her daughters and their families, including four fabulous grandchildren.

Visit her website at www.janeshoup.com

Coming Soon! The Next Book in the Sons of Barons series:

Nearly a Marquess

Twin brothers Joel and Jonathan Stewart have always enjoyed an enviable connection with one another. Joel, the elder by eight minutes, inherited the baronage, and then is unexpectedly awarded a marquisate leaving him conflicted and Jonathan struggling to come to terms with his own worth and place in society.

At twenty-four, Jane Lloyd is a widow and the mother of a young son. As Lady Jane Kingman, the eldest daughter of an earl, she could have married a peer of the realm, but she followed her heart and chose a commoner, a soldier, who perished in the war. All these years later, she attempts to reenter society only to discover she has been forgotten. She feels utterly shut out.

When Joel and Jane meet, there is an immediate attraction and an easy friendship, but nothing is simple in the ton when many would betray a friend or a sibling to get ahead. In *Nearly a Marquess,* loyalty and love are put to the test.

Enjoy the following excerpt.

Chapter One

Jane was a sorry, soggy mess. She was still in bed, curled on her side, the pillow beneath her head uncomfortably wet. The handkerchiefs wadded in her hands were soaked through and there were no more dry ones within reach. She had gone through them all. "Get up, damn you," she whispered crossly.

It took a herculean effort, but she rose and washed her face. Good Lord, her head ached! Repeated splashes of water helped with the redness and puffiness of her face and eyes but didn't fully erase the evidence of her self-pity. She had just turned twenty-four, but did she look ten years older? Feeling lethargic, she donned a robe and left her room for the nursery, not even bothering to tie the belt.

Her younger sister's bedroom door was open and, unfortunately, her mother, sister and the dressmaker were all inside. Jane attempted to slip by unnoticed.

"Jane," her mother exclaimed, having noticed her. "It is past ten."

Jane heaved a sigh before going back. "Thank you, Mamma That saves me the trouble of looking at a clock."

Jane's sister, Alexandria, stood on a study stool as the hem of a new gown was pinned watching herself in the full-length mirror. Why not since it was her favorite sight in the entire world? She would probably strain her neck trying to maintain a view of herself as she was made to turn. The dressmaker was kneeling with straight pins held between her lips, while Jane's mother, Lady Carrick, sat on the chair facing her youngest daughter.

"You know I do not care for sarcasm," her mother admonished. "As you can see, Mrs. Hightower is here."

"Yes, I can see that," Jane said evenly. "Good morning, Mrs. Hightower," she added before her mother could comment again.

Mrs. Hightower bobbed her head, a tight smile on her closed lips.

"You should be measured for something new," her mother said. "The Christmas Cotillion is coming up."

Alexandria made a sour face. "She won't want to go to that, Mamma. Will you, Jane?"

The assumption grated on Jane's nerves. "Oh, I don't know," she replied, despite the fact she could not possibly have cared less about the event. It should have been named The Season's Unofficial Launch or the Marriage Mart Sneak-Preview. "I might."

"Seems a little silly," Alexandria said offhandedly. "After all, you had your chance."

Jane stiffened and Lady Carrick cleared her throat, a subtle warning that *that* was enough. "We were discussing appropriate matches for your sister," she said to Jane.

"I made a list of my top choices," Alexandria said. "And Papa compiled a list of the wisest and best given their standing and wealth and all of that. Did you do that?"

"No," Jane replied flatly.

"Turn," Mrs. Hightower said in a muffled voice, as one will with lips lined with straight pins. Alexandria turned on the stool.

"You will recall your sister married at seventeen," Lady Carrick said tightly. "She met Hammond in her first season and never looked back. We did not have an opportunity to make a list."

"I was eighteen when we married," Jane corrected. "If you recall."

"Of course, I recall," her mother stated testily.

"Really?" Jane challenged.

"Yes, Jane. Really. Go and get dressed."

"Don't be cross," Alexandria said to her mother. She looked at her sister with mock sympathy. "You must wish you could go back and choose differently."

Jane worked to remain expressionless. She did not want to give her sister the satisfaction of seeing that the comment had gotten under her skin. "No. Never. I do not regret one moment I spent with Hamm. I would never choose differently."

"Of course, you wouldn't," her mother said. "Really, Alexandria, that was not very kind of you."

Alexandria huffed. "It was a *question*. I was simply being honest. Come look at my list, Jane. Tell me what you think."

I think I would rather eat those straight pins.

"Who should I choose?"

"I feel certain that you'll choose who you want and ... hopefully get who you deserve. I do hope so." She turned to go, leaving Alexandria wondering if she had just been insulted or not, but she then turned back. "Mamma, you say you remember when I got married."

Lady Carrick looked vexed. "Yes. I was present, was I not?"

"So then you recall that it was six years ago today." Jane waited for the tell-tale gasp and signs of distress and then walked on, feeling strangely better.

"Don't feel badly," Alexandria said to her mother. "Jane made her choices."

"I'd forgotten it was today," her mother whispered.

"He is gone! What does it matter? Is it still an anniversary if one of them is dead?"

"Turn," Mrs. Hightower uttered as best she could. If Lady Carrick was not mistaken, the lady's face had tightened with dislike, which needled her, although, admittedly, it was easy to get irritated at Alexandria's petulance and to feel badly for Jane's misfortunes. Lady Carrick rose and went to the window to look out on Brook Street. It was a bleak, cold day. A dismal sight. She would be so glad when winter was over. She was ready for spring and the Season.

Alexandria would glow like a glorious star. She felt certain an excellent match would be made for her youngest this year. And, this time, with their guidance, the right man would be chosen. Jane had never consulted them and then she had refused their guidance or counsel. It was not as though they had not cared enough to try. But Lady Carrick did wish she had remembered the anniversary. She detested being caught out.

Jane went to the nursery, which doubled as a schoolroom for her four-year-old son, Arthur. She cracked opened the door silently as not to interrupt the lesson being given by the new governess, Miss Philippa Starr. Miss Starr was in her mid-fifties with steel-gray hair and thirty to forty excess pounds packed around her five-foot three frame. Miss Starr had been hired by Lady Carrick while Jane and Arthur were visiting the Lloyds, Arthur's paternal grandparents. Jane had chaffed at the interference, but reluctantly agreed to give Miss Starr a fair chance since she had impeccable credentials.

It was not easy, because she disliked the governess. She disliked the way Miss Starr clasped her hands in front of her. There was too much tension in them, in her whole body, as a matter of fact. Jane suspected Miss Starr disliked her lot in life but was forced to paste a pleasant enough expression on her face and get to it anyway. Jane did not care if the woman loved or loathed her life, as long as her son did not suffer because of it. Jane wanted Arthur to find learning fun and engaging.

"No, D," Miss Starr was saying, while pointing to a D elegantly written on the chalkboard. "Dee as in Da-dog," she stated, enunciating crisply. "Da-duck."

Arthur listened with a frown of anxiety.

"Now what is the letter?"

"D," Arthur repeated dutifully.

"As in?"

"Da-dog."

Miss Starr squinted, trying to determine if the child was mocking her. Excellent credentials or not, Jane suspected Miss Philippa Starr was basically an old meanie.

"Or da-darling," Jane said as she opened the door all the way, surprising both teacher and pupil. Arthur's face showed pure joy and it gave an instant boost to her spirits. "Or dill pickle," she said playfully as she went to him. "Ding-dong. Do pass me the da-dinosaur pie."

"There is no such thing is as dinosaur pie," Arthur laughed.

Jane bent down to him and feigned a look of alarm. "There had better be. I ordered it for your d-dinner."

"Did not."

"Very good. Did starts with a D. What else does?"

Arthur thought about while whispering da-da-da. "Do?"

"Yes! Do not punch me in the nose. And the dew falls at night, doesn't it?" Jane looked at Miss Starr with a cordial smile. "Today is rather special, Miss Starr, so I'll be taking Arthur on an outing."

"When?"

"As soon as I'm dressed."

"Where, Mamma?" Arthur asked. "Where are we going?"

"It's a secret," she whispered. The truth was, there was no plan. She had only just decided to rescue Arthur as she said it.

"Mrs. Lloyd, it is most irregular—"

Jane stood and looked at Miss Starr pointedly. Since she was five eight, Miss Starr was forced to look up at her.

"That is to say, we need to adhere to a schedule as much as possible," the older lady stated.

"I do not disagree, but today is special." She smiled down at her son. "I will be back shortly and we will go on our adventure." She looked at Miss Starr again. "Giving you a free day, which I hope you will enjoy."

"Had I planned on one," Miss Starr began stiffly.

"You're right, of course. I hope you will enjoy the day just the same." And, with that, she turned and left the room, leaving the door standing open.

Once back in her room, she rang to ask that the carriage be brought round for her use. There was no call for vanity, so it took her ten minutes to ready herself for the day.

"Where are we going?" Arthur asked again when they were in motion. He was bundled in his coat, hat and mittens, his eyes dancing with excitement.

"To be honest, I have no idea. I decided that we needed a holiday the moment I said it." She shrugged. "We shall have to make it up as we go. Shall we begin with having our lunch out?"

He nodded exuberantly.

"And then a walk in the park? Now, if you would rather not, I can take you straight back to Miss Starr."

His forehead puckered and he shook his head with a serious frown. "Miss Starr is not very nice."

Jane considered how to respond. "I think she takes her responsibilities very seriously. And sometimes when a person seems not very nice, it is because they are not very happy."

He pondered the statements and then gave her a quizzical frown. "Is it really a special day?"

"Yes, it is. Today, November thirtieth, is an anniversary. Do you know what an anniversary is?"

He shook his head.

"It is a day we celebrate something special that happened on the same day in an earlier year. Like a birthday, except for a different reason." She paused to let that sink in. "Today is the day your papa and I were married. It was six years ago."

"Oh."

"We loved each other very much and so we had you."

"I wish Papa hadn't died," Arthur said solemnly.

"So do I, darling. But he died a hero fighting for his country. Never forget that. And he lives on in my heart and in the hearts of all his family and friends who loved him. There were many of those."

"Grammy and Gramps."

She smiled. "Yes. He was their little boy."

"And Aunt Tess and Uncle Morgan."

"That's right."

"And Grandfather and Grandmother?" he asked doubtfully.

Her parents had probably never given Hamm a moment's thought in the past few years. Perhaps if Arthur resembled him, it might have been different, but he looked like her. "Yes," she replied anyway.

"And Aunt Alexandria?"

Jane nodded, although fibbing made her neck muscles stiff. "*Mm-hmm.*" At least, it was a lie for a good reason. She hugged Arthur. "We shall have such fun today. And find all sorts of D words. I love you, my darling."

"Darling is a D word," he said.

"Yes, it is. That was …da-devilishly clever of you."

Chapter Two

It was just past noon when Jonathan Stewart walked through the front door of his family's terraced home on Grosvenor Square, having spent the morning in a boxing lesson. He stopped in front of the hall mirror to appreciate the swelling of his right eye. It was a badge of honor, as far he was concerned. He walked on, glancing in the dining room and morning room before finding his twin brother in the library. Joel sat at a mahogany table puzzling over documents. A book of maps lay open on the table. "Hello," Jonathan said.

The brothers were identical in their six-foot three-inch height, dark brown hair color, light blue eye color and facial features. Jonathan wore his hair a bit longer and had a faint scar on his chin, while Joel sported a mustache, but those were the few differences in appearance, besides Jonathan's recently acquired shiner.

Joel glanced up at his brother and winced. "What happened?"

"I went a few rounds with Gentleman Jackson himself," Jonathan replied with a proud gleam. "He's still got it."

"He's still not got it, all right. And it looks like he gave you some of it."

"Yes, he did. What's your excuse for looking so glum? Someone send a surprise left hook your way?" he asked, jabbing for effect.

"As a matter of fact, yes. Gerald Gibbon, also known as Lord Larrowford. And his left hook is quite a feat, given that he died in fifteen."

Jonathan came closer. "I'm not following."

"He was a distant cousin on father's side."

"Wait a minute," Jonathan mused. "Larrowford. It's ringing a bell."

"Are you sure it's not your ears ringing from the punch? Anyway, the man died with no children or siblings."

"In fifteen," Jonathan repeated. "Five years ago."

"Five and a half. Yes."

"The war?"

"No. He was an older man who died at home of natural causes. Apparently, Father learned of his demise and petitioned the crown for the title."

"When?"

"I don't know. The letter doesn't say."

Jonathan pulled back a chair next to his brother and sat. "Go on," he said as he began perusing the papers on the table.

"Apparently, the petition got lost in the cracks, what with the war ending and the king's failing health, slash madness, slash death. But it was recently found and processed. Meaning it passed through the House of Lords and then to the Committee for Privileges and …it was granted."

Jonathan looked up at him sharply. "Granted."

Joel slid the letter of acknowledgment closer.

Jonathan reached for it. "What's the title?"

"Marquess," Joel replied meaningfully.

Jonathan's gaze shot up at him. "My God! You'll be a bloody marquess?"

"So I've just learned."

"Where?"

"It's in Gloucestershire." Joel paused, looking troubled. "Why didn't Father tell us?"

"I don't know. But you'll be a marquess." Jonathan huffed. "But for eight minutes, it might have been me. It's so unfair you got to come out first."

"I believe you've mentioned it," Joel said dryly. "But seriously, I don't know why you wouldn't get the barony, in that case."

"Because it doesn't work that way. The bloody firstborn gets everything. The sad little twin that followed eight minutes later is lucky to get table scraps." He leaned back. "Lord Larrowford," he said, trying it on for size. "What's the property?"

"The house is called Manoria. It's near the village of Larrowford."

"Manoria," Jonathan repeated slowly. He saw the official form had been signed by the king, no less. "I remember us visiting when we were nine or ten."

"We were more like twelve."

Jonathan shook his head. "We were not that old."

"I think we were. It wasn't long afterwards before we went to school. We saw some factory in Gloucester and then we went to Manoria …Hall? Is it Manoria Hall?"

Jonathan shrugged. "I don't recall. Does it not say?" He reached for another document.

"No. It just says Manoria."

"There are seventeen hundred acres with it," Jonathan exclaimed.

"I saw that," Joel returned calmly.

Jonathan looked up at him. "You don't seem pleased."

"I'm surprised. I am just profoundly surprised."

"Understandably. You can also be happy about it. I won't hate you any more than I already do."

Joel smirked. "Good to know."

"Did you eat lunch?"

"No, but I'm not hungry."

"Well, food would do you good. You're looking a bit peaky. I ate at Cribb's with some of the fellows."

"To show off your eye?"

"And regale my fans with details of the bout."

"Fans," Joel repeated. "*Mm-hmm.*" He pushed his chair back and rose. "I do need to eat and then delve into Father's records."

"I'll start on the records," Jonathan offered. "Looking for anything related to Larrowford or Gibbons."

"Gibbon," Joel corrected. He left the room looking a tad unsteady. The news he'd received had truly rocked him.

It took the better part of an hour before Jonathan found the file. It was labeled Gibbon/Larrowford. "Found it." He opened it and pulled out a copy of the application their father had made. There were also letters written to him and copies of letters he had written in regard to the manner. There was a map and page after page of detailed notes. "The Bristol Channel flows just west of it," he read.

Joel pushed in to see, so Jonathan handed it over. The marquisate had been created in 1763 at the end of the Seven Years' War to honor Sir Tobias Gibbon who had been instrumental in some way. It then passed to his only brother upon his death and now it would go to him. No, it *had* gone to him. He was now the marquess of Larrowford even if it didn't feel like it.

"The petition was dated the first of August of sixteen," Joel read. He looked up. "Four and half years ago." A full year before the accident that claimed their father's life, although that remained unsaid. Joel and Jonathan had been touring through Italy at the time their father had made the petition, but they'd returned in October. "He must have wanted it to be a surprise if it came through."

"I suppose," Jonathan murmured. "So how exactly does this work, I wonder. Can you just show up at Manoria and say, 'Hello. I'm the new lord of the manor. Can you direct me to the wine cellar?'"

Joel laughed. "That would be your first request."

"Yes, it would. But seriously—"

Joel shrugged. "I have no idea. It's the first time I've been made a marquess."

"The solicitor," Jonathan said. "Fowler will know the ins and outs of it." He leaned back in his chair and sighed toward the coffered ceiling. "But for eight bloody minutes," he complained.

"It's true," Joel commiserated. "You could strangle me in less time."

"That's a thought," Jonathan said agreeably.

They both resisted and then cracked a grin at the exact same moment.